IN THE CHAMBERS OF THE SEA

IN THE CHAMBERS OF THE SEA

Susan Rendell

killick press
an imprint of Creative Publishers

St. John's, Newfoundland and Labrador
2003

©2003, Susan Rendell

Le Conseil des Arts | The Canada Council
du Canada | for the Arts

We acknowledge the support of The Canada Council for the Arts for our
publishing program.

We acknowledge the financial support of the Government of Canada through the Book
Publishing Industry Development Program (BPIDP) for our
publishing program.

Newfoundland and Labrador
Arts Council

The author would like to acknowledge financial support from the
Newfoundland and Labrador Arts Council.

∞ Printed on acid-free paper

Cover art by Ronan Kennedy

Published by
KILLICK PRESS
an imprint of CREATIVE BOOK PUBLISHING
a division of Creative Printers and Publishers Limited
a Print Atlantic associated company
P.O. Box 8660, St. John's, Newfoundland and Labrador A1B 3T7

First Edition
Typeset in 12 point Garamond

Printed in Canada by:
PRINT ATLANTIC

National Library of Canada Cataloguing in Publication

Rendell, Susan, 1953-
    In the chambers of the sea / Susan Rendell.

ISBN 1-894294-66-1

I. Title.

PS8585.E662I5 2003   C813'.6   C2003-905883-2

for Jane, sister and patron
my daughter, Jessica

and One other

Outside of a dog, a book is a man's best friend.
Inside of a dog, it's too dark to read.

— Groucho Marx

CONTENTS

The Way to Get Home

*For he shall deliver the needy when he crieth: the poor also,
and him that hath no helper.*

— Psalms 72:12

Today Jessie brought me a toothbrush she got at a church. I almost asked her why she didn't keep it for herself, but it skipped my mind. Later I remembered she has no teeth. When you first meet someone who has no teeth it is the most prominent thing about them, like baldness or a wheelchair. But after your friendship has gestated, you fill in the missing bits, teeth, hair. Legs that work.

Jessie doesn't have teeth because Welfare will only give her a pair if she signs her name Marie Skanes and she won't. Because she is not Marie Skanes, she is Jessica Horwood, wife of the Anglican Archbishop, Dennis Horwood. Marie Skanes is a mad woman from Bell Island. She follows Jessie around, sleeps next to her in the room at the boarding house, tells people she is Jessie: Marie is trying to drive her crazy for some unfathomable reason. But Jessie is smarter than Marie. And stronger. *They all try to drive me crazy but they'll never do it. They'll never drive Jessie crazy because I have a good friend who looks after me.* She points upwards, her knobby arthritic forefinger parodying Adam's on the Sistine Chapel ceiling as she stretches it towards the Son.

Jessie's hair is sparse and thin, hanging from her head in inch-long yellow-white tendrils like alfalfa sprouts. She always covers her head with a baseball cap, her head that is like an old frayed baseball discarded by some teenaged boys who have worn it out reducing their testosterone levels under a macho August sun. Even when she is wearing her garden party outfit, a lavender dress with a white acrylic shawl and purple pumps, Jessie has a cap on her head: the shape stays the same, only the logos vary—Pepsi, Blackhorse, Errol's Groc. and Conf. Jessie gets invited to the Lieutenant Governor's garden party every year because Prince Philip is her uncle. Jessie's mother was Prince Philip's sister, the Lady Marion, who once played the harp in an opera house in Montreal, her fine white fingers making the sharp strings shiver out "Greensleeves."

Alas, my love, you do me wrong
To cast me off discourteously;
When I have loved you for so long,
Delighting in your company.

A man who came here from Quebec told Jessie that, and she cried because the Lady Marion had died giving birth to her, her only child. When Jessie was ten she asked her father if he was sorry she wasn't a boy. He hit her and told her to go to her room. *Because he loved us more than anything, me and my mother; he never remarried, he wasn't that kind of man. And he put death into my mother along with my life, and he felt so bad. Men, they have so much to feel bad about, I wouldn't want to be one.* After Jessie's father died, they locked her in a room in the palace, not to punish her but because she wouldn't behave; she kept crying and screaming that he wasn't dead. *And that is not the way a member of the Royal Family is supposed to act.* Jessie puts an *h* on *act*; it sounds French. Or the way someone from Bell Island might produce the word if they chopped it, 'hacked" it off through rock-hard gums.

Jessie says she has her father's eyes. When she was young she also had his coal black hair, good French hair. Jessie's father was a French diplomat who was assassinated during the Korean War. Jessie was twelve when he died; she had just gotten her first pair of penny loafers the day before they told her. *Shoes the colour of my hair, and two new pennies shining up at me. And then he was dead and they didn't shine no more.*

One night a man walked up to Jessie in a bar and said, "Jessie, that was the worst assassination I ever saw, your father." Jessie tells me this story once a week; it means that her existence is large and true, bigger than the lives of the teenagers who taunt her—"fifty cents, Trixie"—and the grown men who pelt her with raw potatoes. Greater than that of the woman who threw a quarter on the ground and told Jessie she could have it if she would pick it up. Jessie stepped over it. But afterwards, she turned around to look, knowing what she would see: the woman in her blond wool coat crouched on the icy sidewalk, plucking at the metal sliver with leather-tipped fingers. And Jessie laughed her silent laugh, audible only to dogs. *And to sad small children, and the moon when it is thin and grieving for the sun.*

Jessie's eyes can see farther than anyone else's. She can see beyond the hills that hunch around the harbour to the coves on the other side. The light in Jessie's eyes beams in from somewhere so far away and old that the suns of Bootes are juveniles in comparison, this light that shows her seagulls suspended over distant promontories, and even the Stairway to Heaven rising over the Narrows, a silver band floating in a sea of brilliant colours: so lovely, she says, like the little cross of stars that dangles outside her window sometimes. And the moon following her, and sometimes even the sun. *The sun follows me because it is the Son, you know, the Son of God, my Lamb.*

Jessie says a prayer for the moon when it shines in her window, a prayer of thanksgiving because it has brought her home safe. She told this to a nun once and the nun said that the moon is the Virgin's lamp, and that she, Jessie, was special, beloved of the Mother. A chalice is kept for Jessie at the Basilica. *Although it is the cup of the Lamb it is more like a basin than a cup. And it is pure gold, not brass like the regular one. I go up first, alone, before the rest of them, and drink from my special cup; I don't share the same cup like the others.*

I do not tell Jessie that she is singled out because they are afraid of her, afraid of her old bald gums and her madwoman's spittle. She wouldn't believe me. She would put me in the same category as the quarter woman or the Bishop's false wife. And I would never see her again in my house, shining the kitchen sink, polishing the little life I have left.

The only thing that ever casts Jessie down is her husband's treachery. The Bishop has spurned her: some hussy has taken Jessie's place in the Bishop's house, a harlot who calls herself his wife. This woman has given him drugs that make him forget his true wife; he won't even let Jessie into the Cathedral anymore. And she loves the Cathedral; it reminds her of the forests of her English childhood, cool and dark and mysterious, the light coming down slanted from the little sun of the rose window high up behind the altar, falling between the dark mahogany columns, lighting up the clearing in front of the case that holds a marble sculpture of the dead Christ. Jessie used to prostrate herself in front of this glass mausoleum, lying there for hours sometimes. But they won't let her in now; they tell her she is upsetting the parishioners, but she knows this is a lie: it is all the doing of the Bishop's woman, who is afraid of Jessie, afraid and jealous because of her husband's love for his true wife. Jessie's eyes well up when she tells me about her lost husband, but the tears never descend. I don't think they ever have, because there are no lines in her face for them to run along, although she must be somewhere on the thin dry road between fifty and sixty. *I used to be beautiful and my husband loved me; now I am ugly. But this is the way God wants me to be. He has not forsaken me, it is just a different part of the story he is making up, he needs me to look this way now. And I love my ugly face because He does.*

The other thing that makes Jessie's eyes creep back into the hollows beneath her eyebrows is when children call her a witch and run away from her. Or when parents tuck their offspring behind them as she walks down the street, swinging her crucifix like a yo-yo. Last Easter Sunday when Jessie went to church she tried to talk to a man with a baby in his arms, but he turned away from her, growling a curse over the naked head of his child. Jessie loves children, even the ones who are mean to her. Because they are not always mean: the little boy who mocks her one day may give her a candy the next, or even the gum out of his mouth. Once Jessie picked up a pigeon that had been hit by a car and carried it until it was dead. *It looked up at me and then its eyes closed, like going to sleep.* She laid it in the grass and said a novena for its soul.

The first time Jessie came to me, she was wearing a miniskirt and a blouse cut to there and way too big for her; her breasts kept sliding out of their silky sack like two withered turnips. She told me she was eleven; *I am visiting with my father from St. Pierre, bonjour.* I said *bonsoir* because it was a sweltering July evening. I was sitting on my front steps while the city danced and sang, drunk as ten lords on the humid heat. Sitting slouched like a discarded effigy, listening intent-

ly to the murmuring of the pigeons at my feet, their throats
throbbing with the sound a mother makes when she is
stroking her infant with quiet words to calm its fear.

I need the toothbrush Jessie brought me this morning;
mine is two years old and worn to the bone. Two years ago
I had a new toothbrush; a year ago I had a job, only a small
one, but we looked after each other. As did my lover and I,
who said that nothing in this world would ever part us. Who
asked me to wait by Cassiopeia's Chair for him if I died
before he did. Now I have only two things, essentially: a son
and a small stretch of life to walk, or crawl or slither on my
belly down until I come to. . .

Until I die.

One fat cyst of a year left, perhaps even two, if I'm
lucky.

That's what they said to me—one year, two if you're
lucky. "Where's the luck in that?" I asked the two in white
coats who had just handed me my death as though it were a
sterile instrument. "Where is the rabbit's foot dangling from
this death sentence, where is the sound of bells signalling
three gold bars in a row? All I hear is ring around the rosy,
pocket full of posies, ashes, ashes all fall down," I said, doing
a bitter parody of the old childhood dance while they backed
away from me; politely, of course. "Would you rather die
right now, or watch death parade in front of you every
minute of every hour for seven hundred days? Which one—
which would you choose?" They looked at each other, and at
the floor, and then they said to the wall, "Well it all depends
on your attitude doesn't it? Keep busy, think positive
thoughts." It is useless for the dead to converse with the living, whose ears are stopped up like those of Ulysses' men
against the siren song of death, that fatal lullaby.

My son calls me every week from Scotland, where he pulls the bright mackerel out of the sea for a living. I haven't let him know yet; I am reluctant to put the shadow of death into my son's head by telling him about the shadow that is in his mother's: a grey penumbra on my brain, no bigger than a thumbnail. But big enough to end the world. And to confine me to the valley of the shadow; this is the first death, the introductory chapter. I am afraid of the last chapter, even more afraid that there will not be an end at all, that I will go on like this forever, a dull ash of despair floating in some vast black vermicular eternity—god I hate that word—I hate all words now; how merciful God has been to dumb beasts, that die without knowing they ever lived.

The day I knew for certain that life had no more use for me, my lover and I were in bed, inside a perfect arc of passion. And then the phone rang, squealing through the quiet house; my lovebird in its wicker cage lifted its head from its white breast and opened its beak, but no sound came out. "Let it ring," my lover said to me: he was crouched over my breasts, his penis homing towards my mouth; it had a drop like a tear hanging from its tip. I pushed him away; there was something in the sound of the phone that was more compelling than desire—what could it be? And then Death said hello over the wires.

When I got off the phone, I went and lay back down by my lover's side. "What is it?" he said. "You look like a ghost." And then he shook me because I wouldn't answer. Shook me and shook me, but my body was not inhabited: it was unyielding and heavy in his hands, a dead weight. Eventually he stopped shaking me and got between my legs, driving himself into me with sharp quick jerks as if he was trying to start a stalled car. And then a sound came out of me like the one I made when my son's head was crowning twenty years ago. My lover slapped my face and I started to cry. And I told him what the doctor had said: nothing at all, really, except that he needed to talk to me about the results of some tests I had had the week before. But I knew—I had known for some time. The same way I had known I was pregnant with my son the moment his father removed himself from me and turned away into sleep. The body knows immediately when it has been invaded by life or death, and sometimes the quiescent mind can hear the snapping into place of the new element: a fertilized egg, a rogue cell. A door creaking open deep in the substrata of the self, a glimpse of nascent life awakening. Or death stirring, waiting its hour to be born.

My lover got up and pulled on his jeans. "I need to go for a walk," he said. "Stay in bed, keep warm, I won't be long." He came back the next day with a dozen roses from the supermarket. The kind that are perfect buds which never open, blackening on the stem after a few days. ("O Rose thou art sick./The invisible worm/That flies in the night/In the howling storm/Has found out thy bed/Of crimson joy,/ And his dark secret love/Does thy life destroy.")

I hated God that morning, a God I didn't even believe in. Jessie hated God when He took her son, Raymond; she hated Him for years, soiling herself with prostitute sex and alcohol and drugs to get back at Him. But one night He sent an angel to wrestle with her. *All night I struggled, fighting the angel that had me pinned to the bed, but that angel was as strong as Hulk Hogan. And he loved me so much, just like my father.* Now Jessie loves God's Son the way she used to love her Raymond, who was only two pounds when he was born, ethereal as a cherub. *You never see old angels. They don't age because they have to go to work every morning.* Last week I gave Jessie a picture of the Annunciation a Catholic cousin had sent me when I was pregnant with my son. *That is the Angel Gabriel. Look how happy Mary is, but she's embarrassed too because she's not married. And she's sad because she has to marry that old man. But you never know with God, you just have to do what you're told.*

A month after I was sentenced, I saw my lover and a young red-haired girl walking along the harbour apron. We had been apart for two days—he told me he had to go to Halifax for a week on business. "Rest," he said, "keep safe until I come back—how can I miss you if I don't go away?" I saw him only once again, as a part of me, my life. Five days later he came to my house for his sunglasses—and a Judas kiss. He lives with the girl now, in a house by the polluted river that slides through the heart of the city like a soiled snake, blindly seeking the ocean in which to slough its foul skin.

When I told Jessie about my lover, she said that the girl must have drugged him like Bishop Horwood's false wife did to him or else he would never have betrayed me, never abandoned his true love. Yes, I told her, I do believe he was drugged. She asked me if I thought it was Haldol, which some doctor had put her on once; it had made her so crazy, she said, that she used to sit in her boarding house room rocking back and forth and praying to her Lamb that she wouldn't kill herself. No, I said, I don't think it was Haldol, I think it was Spanish fly. Or Ecstasy. Jessie laughed and laughed at that one, her big alien's eyes as wide as windows, her toothless gums gleaming like pink roses wet with the dew.

Before Jessie came, when the snow was throwing itself down in fistfuls for the wind to toss around, I used to think about driving out to Salmon Cove with a picnic basket full of pills and wine. There is a place on the top of the cliffs near where the eagles have their nest, a dark bed in the bracken, broad enough for two. My lover and I used to go there on summer days the colour and intensity of Jessie's eyes and pick each other clean. Afterwards, we would walk to the edge of the cliff and watch the two eagles, male and female, fierce hieroglyphs of fidelity wheeling against the mandala of the sun.

On those winter days, I would look out my crusted front window at no one coming up the steps, and imagine the bed I would make in the wine-stained snow, how I would lie down and fold my hands across my breast like a marble effigy on a tomb. And let the clicking sleet knit itself up around me, like a baby's bunting bag. Bye bye baby bunting, Daddy's gone a-hunting. To find a living woman's skin to wrap his joy and hunger in.

I had managed to forget about death for a little while on the evening Jessie came, her hands and breasts crisscrossed with silvery white scars from the fire that consumed Raymond when he was five months old. The fire the Bad Man set. One of Jessie's hands is more afflicted than the other; *sometimes I go wild with the pain in it, it is like it is still on fire.* The only thing that helps is when the priest anoints it with holy water and the divine atoms in the drops exorcise the memory of the flames that burned her baby to death while she held him.

Jessie won't tell me who the Bad Man was or why he set the fire, or what went before or after. When I bring up the subject she will say she is a Syrian Jew, which according to the Bible means she is more precious than rubies. Or she will describe to me what the ten tribes wear on their heads, how the colour and shape of each person's headgear corresponds to his rank. Or she will tell me about being a Korean war orphan, and having the mark on her foot that all war babies have. All the orphaned babies of every war have this stigmata on one foot; it is the shape of a crescent moon and red as blood. Jessie never shows me her cicatrix and I never ask to see it. I am careful when she is barefoot in my house, cleaning the floors or sitting at the kitchen table with her legs crossed, a child's sandal dangling off her crimson-tipped toes; I never look down.

The evening Jessie came to me I had taken a handful of pills of all colours, like Sweetarts: pills they gave me to control the seizures, sleeping pills, Aspirin and old odds and ends of discarded medications I had found at the bottom of my bathroom cupboard. I imagined that the pills were lover's candies, but instead of saying "You're Mine" in pink letters they were mute and black-bordered. I was sitting on my front steps, waiting for the pigeons that live in the eaves of the building across the street to descend. I had put bread on the sidewalk in front of my house, the ends of three loaves I had been living off for two days, rye and flax and raisin. And little winged packets of birds were dropping at my feet when Jessie appeared in the middle of them like some freaky St. Francis.

I thought the pills had conjured her up until she sat on the lowest step and leaned her head against my shin. *Bonjour*, she said; I said *bonsoir*. And then she began to tell me about her father and her dead son, about her Lamb and the newly lit moon chasing her all over the city until she came and sat down by me because God told her to. *I think I must go there, I don't know why, God says go here, go there, so I go.*

I sat up then, and listened to her like Sheherazade's husband; but after a time I began to feel faint, and I excused myself and went inside the house. The front hall was strobing, pulsating with the colours of the pills I had taken; it took me a long time to find the phone. When I called the hospital they seemed happy to hear from me, excited even. "We're coming for you, don't move," they said. "You're going to be fine." I would be fine: it had all been a mistake then, a stupid practical joke, a puerile prank by some big dumb goof of a god who had had his fun and was letting me go. I lay down on the floor and wept while life bounced around, licking me all over. Several hours later I woke up in a hospital room with death lying next to me as if we'd never been apart.

When I came back to my house the next day, Jessie was there again. Or still. *What you did last night—that is not the way to get home.* In her hands was a purple sash, from the altar at the Basilica. When we went inside, she said *Put it around Jehovah,* mistaking the bust of Zeus on the top of my bookcase for her god. And I took it from her and tied it in a bow around his neck. And then she cleaned my kitchen and made me tea in a Christmas mug. *Look, there is a French Santa on it: see, he has a long robe and a tall hat. One time I got a talking doll for Christmas; "I love you," she said, you had to pull out a string on her neck to make her say it.* The tea Jessie made was stronger than I usually have it, but it was hot and sweet and my body took it like an embrace, even the residue at the bottom. And then she made me come and look at the kitchen sink, which she had scrubbed with Javex. *We say Javel in St. Pierre; look, look how it shines! Like silver, like the moon when there are no clouds over her face.* Jessie and I peered into the sink together; two shimmering women as beautiful as the souls of stars looked back at us. And we laughed. *Better than in the mirror.*

Jessie died herself once, but she didn't go home because it wasn't time. She was hit by a car in front of her boarding house, hit in the head; people gathered to see the great mystery of death, and someone called the police. The bumper of the car that hit her was dented: bits of her hair pasted on with blood decorated the chrome cavity. *It was all black, everything was black, but it was not cold black, it was warm like hiding under the covers when you are small. And then an angel pulled me up out of the blackness and I was alive again. The woman who hit me with her car was crying, 'Jessie, we were sure you were dead.' 'No, not me, I told her,' I have a friend, a very good friend who looks after me. I am in good hands, don't worry about me.'*

The police called an ambulance but Jessie waved it away and asked for fish and chips. The woman who had killed Jessie gave a little boy a twenty-dollar bill and he ran to Johnny's Diner and got Jessie two of the biggest orders they had. And she and the boy sat down on the side of the road and ate them, with everyone gathered around, amazed as anything. *There wasn't a mark on me the next day, not a scratch. When the police came to Mrs. Lynch's in the morning, they are looking at me* (she does an impression of a perplexed cop, taking off her baseball cap/police hat and scratching her head), *they can't believe it. Everyone says it is a miracle, a miracle.*

What is a miracle? That some live when they shouldn't, or that others must die when life is beside and behind and before them and they feel as safe as houses inside its radiant circumference? Are these both miracles, or only one of them? Or is it all a miracle, every sublime horrible idiotic unquantifiable leap life takes? On the mornings Jessie is with me, saying *look, look at the cat rolling in the grass!* and I look— really look—at the blissful conjunction of cat and grass and Jessie's toothless joy, it seems to me that everything in the universe is perfectly aligned and singing like a nightingale— it's all good, very very good a voice far away and yet inside me says, and I believe it. And then Jessie goes away, and I think that maybe everything is an illusion—perhaps even the hand with death and sorrow scribbled on it that Jessie gives me to hold on to when I cry—that there is no rhyme or reason to any of it, no point; no great shining Point, waiting at the end to scatter the small shadows that are our deaths. But then she comes back—*look, look! see how many flowers are on that tree; so small, such a small tree, but so many flowers. Like little stars, baby ones.*

One night last week Jessie and I talked about heaven. *I can see the Golden Gates, and past them where it is quiet and there are colours you can't see here. And you never grow old, no one ever grows old there, you grow young.* And then she told me about the thing that is going to happen to all the countries, the bad thing. There was a meeting about it, she said, with the military and the men of god, priests and ministers and rabbis; even her husband the Archbishop was there. She says she may be leaving for East Germany next week. *But don't worry. You will have eternal life because you have been good to me, and I am a Syrian Jew, more precious than rubies, and also a war alien baby.*

When she left, Jessie told me to lock the door because you never know who might try to get in. I smiled; she doesn't know that she is the thing most doors and minds are dead-bolted against. And then she hugged me and said *I love you; don't forget me if I can't come back.* I watched her out of the window as she walked away, and then I looked up into the sky, at the moon bouncing along behind her like a child's ball.

Ozymandias in His Pyjamas

When Stan pulls up in front of his father's house, the lights are wrong. It is just past twilight and the round globe over the front door is a bowl of darkness; the panes in the window of the door look like rectangles of black ice. There is no light anywhere: the house stares blindly at Stan as he sits in his car, trying to decipher the meaning of the blackout. His father's dark blue Dynasty, the automotive equivalent of the Union Jack that flies over Buckingham Palace when the Royal Family is in residence, is in the driveway, so his father must be home. Stan's father never goes anywhere unless he does the driving.

The windows in the top of the front door of Stan's father's house are like narrowed eyes turned sideways, or medieval fenestration. Sometimes when Stan walks up the front steps of his father's house, he thinks arrows are going to fly out of them. They wouldn't be Indian arrows either, with supple brown shafts that still had the green blood of the tree in them, and the bright feathers of a wild bird to wing them on their lethal way. If arrows ever came out of his father's door, they would be thick black iron arrows, crossbow arrows. The kind of arrows that were cutting-edge military technology in the Middle Ages.

Stan's father had been a rear gunner on minesweepers in World War II. He had enlisted during the first year of the War, when he was eighteen. Stan's father hardly ever talks about the War, but Stan's mother told him something once. She said that Stan's father had panicked the first time enemy aircraft flew overhead, and "dropped all his eggs." When he heard the feral whine of death about to pounce, Stan's father had shot blindly over and over into the sky until an officer grabbed him. The day had been overcast, but Stan's father had let the German planes know there was a convoy underneath them. And so the bombs fell out of their metal wombs, and two ships went down under the cold skin of the North Atlantic. The men who hadn't been blown to bits screamed for help in the water that was on fire from leaked oil. But it was against the rules to stop and pick them up.

They had sent Stan's father to the brig, but not for long. He was only a raw recruit, after all. Stan thinks of the phrase "raw recruit" and the image of a carrot wearing a navy cap and jacket floats into his mind. Later, Stan's father had been decorated for something to do with Dieppe; he has told Stan a little about it. "The sea was flat calm," Stan's father said, "as flat as this table," and he had hit the kitchen table he and Stan were sitting at for emphasis. "And the moon was as bright as those goddamn lights in Wal-Mart. We didn't know where we were going or why, but then we never did until the last minute. And I got back to England, but a lot of my buddies didn't." Someday Stan intends to ask his father to tell him the middle part of the story, but so far he's never had the nerve.

Once when Stan was looking for some three-inch nails in his parents' garage, he found an old notebook in a drawer. It was green and dusty and small enough to fit in a breast pocket. When Stan opened it, on the first page in his father's writing was "WWII, September 1941—June 1942." Stan's heart leapt like a startled cat and his palms broke out in a sweat. He sat down on a lawn chair and looked at the book for a

few minutes, and tried to blow the dust off the cover. Some
of the dust stayed put and Stan wiped it off with the hem of
his T-shirt, wishing he had one of those brushes archaeologists used. And then Stan pulled back the cover and looked
at his father's handwriting again; the letters were sharp and
black and unconnected, like fragments of glazed pottery.
Stan felt as if he was standing with Cortez gazing down
upon an unknown sea, or in Africa with Leakey looking at
the fossilized footprint of a three-million-year-old human
being. Here in this nondescript notebook was the map to the
lost continent of Edward Elliot Hopkins, the Rosetta Stone
of his father.

But the contents of the notebook had turned out to be
nothing but page after page of dates, place-names and
weather conditions. "December 21, 1942. Off Gib. Sunny—
temperature 63 degrees." As far back as Stan can remember,
his father has noted the day's weather on the calendar before
going to bed. The calendar hangs beside his father's fridge
next to a framed copy of Kipling's "If."

Another War story Stan's father told him was the one
about being courted, if that wasn't putting too fine a point on
it, by another sailor. One summer's day in the middle of the
Mediterranean when the War had slowed down a little, another rear gunner had walked up to Stan's father and asked him
if he wanted a manicure. And although Stan's father wasn't
entirely sure what a manicure was, he said "No way, b'y."
Later some of his father's mates told him that the guy was a
poof; later still, they told him what a poof was. Apparently
Salmon Cove, Stan's father's natal village, had been poof-free.
In fact, it had been relatively devoid of abnormalities of any
kind. Stan's father told him that he had never seen any
deformed people when he was growing up, except for one

girl who limped a little because she had had polio. All those people who would have grown up to be drains on society died in infancy, Stan's father said, because that was the way Nature intended it. Stan looks at his father's house with the moon above it like the tip of a fingernail, and he thinks of Jacob—*Oh brave new world, that has such people in it!*

When Stan was twenty, his buddy Steve got them both a summer job with a government-funded project called Train-a-Champ, which hired students to look after retarded kids. That was back in the days when you could still say retarded, and blind and deaf. At least in casual company. Stan has a hard time keeping up with what anything is supposed to be called anymore. Even his department at work has gone through three name changes in as many months, spinning like a weathervane in the mad winds of jargon.

Stan hopes things will settle down soon, but he doubts it. Hype is the latest craze, after all, worse than the Jitterbug or zoot suits. Stan is not exactly sure what a zoot suit is, and he has no intention of finding out any time soon. He intends to let it tantalize him until the day he won't be able to stand it anymore and will have to look it up on the Web. Stan likes the Web; at three o'clock in the morning you can find out what a zoot suit is in less time than it takes to boil a kettle. "Open Sesame" Stan always says to his computer, after he has typed in his request and before he hits the 'go' button.

Stan works for the same company his father worked for for thirty-five years, Provincial Hydro. Stan is a senior civil design engineer. Although he is in middle management, Stan works in a space the size of a coracle, one of dozens moored side by side and ringed by upper management offices that block out the sun. Sometimes when Stan gets a break from figuring out how many cubic metres of concrete are needed for the support pad of a new transmission tower, he redesigns the Trojan Horse to fit more Greeks in, or fewer, depending on how he feels about Troy or Greece on any particular day. Mostly, Stan is for the Trojans because he doesn't like the fact that Agamemnon sacrificed his daughter to the gods before the Greeks went to war so that they would have a better chance of winning. It certainly wasn't something Toe Blake would ever have considered doing, even if it was overtime in the Stanley Cup finals and Rocket Richard was in the penalty box. Stan thinks maybe some of the new hockey coaches would embrace the idea since it might possibly lead to increased productivity, and it would certainly be cost-effective. But human sacrifice wasn't a culturally sanctioned practice in this century and country, at least not in that blatant a form.

The other thing Stan does when there's a bit of down-time is redesign the slave ships that brought the Africans to the New World. He and Steve did a course together on slavery in the Americas, and there had been a drawing in the textbook of row upon row of long thin black men stacked below the decks of a slave ship, their arms and legs in chains; they had looked like shackled eels. On Stan's ships, the ones he draws with his body hunched over the top of the quad paper because the cubicles are designed so that everyone can see what everyone else is doing, the slaves are up on the main deck. They are lying in hammocks or sitting in canvas chairs, and they are holding big drinks with little paper parasols and fruit in them. And they are smiling to beat the band. Stan draws their teeth way out of proportion to their faces, hoping that in the unlikely event that anyone ever sees one of his drawings, they won't think Stan is racist. He just likes the way it looks, all those big white teeth shining in the sun like the sails of some triumphant armada.

Stan was glad to get the summer job at Train-a-Champ because it paid pretty well and it beat pumping gas. And he and Steve would be together for the whole summer. Steve and Stan went way back, all the way back to recess on the first day of Grade 3. "Hi," Stan had said, "Montreal or Toronto?" "Montreal," said the new kid, and Stan had wanted to throw his arms around Steve, which had made him feel weird for a minute. You could only do that to another guy if he scored a goal during a hockey game. But most of the guys in Stan's class were for the Leafs, and it was good to have a Habs fan to hang out with.

The first day at Train-a-Champ Stan thought he would have to quit, it had been that disturbing. All these retarded kids came in a bus to the local civic centre where Steve and Stan and ten other people were waiting. Because Stan was the new guy, he got Jacob, who was fourteen chronologically but about three in his head and heart. Jacob was small and thin as a rail, and he made a noise like a frightened puppy when Stan went over to him. Later that morning Stan discovered that Jacob wore diapers underneath his baggy jeans. Stan had never even changed a baby's diapers: changing the diapers of a fourteen-year-old male was the most surrealistic experience Stan had ever had except for the time he and Steve had tried mescaline. Stan told himself he'd give it a week and then find some way out that wouldn't make Steve lose respect for him. But a week went by, and then another; after the first couple of diaper changes Stan felt as if he'd been doing it his whole life, and he had wondered if new mothers felt the same way.

Jacob lived in a foster home, and the foster parents were responsible for sending Jacob's lunch to Train-a-Champ with him. Every day when Stan opened Jacob's Winnie the Pooh lunch box, there was bread and butter and Tang in it. And every time Stan changed Jacob's diapers, the sickly sweet smell of unwashed flesh wafted up into the chrome air of the civic centre bathroom. So Stan went to the co-ordinator, Mr. Walsh, to tell him about these things, the lunch that wasn't a lunch and the stench from a body that was rarely, if ever, immersed in water. Mr. Walsh would call the authorities, whoever they were, and Jacob would get a new home.

But Mr. Walsh, who had been a social worker for twenty-five years, had said, "Look, Stan, the authorities know all about Jacob and the family he lives with. They even know things you don't know: for instance, when Jacob gets home from Train-a-Champ, his foster parents lock him in a room and leave him there until the bus comes the next morning. Because they're only in it for the money and if there was another way to get the good government money that comes with Jacob, he'd never get across their doorsill again." Jacob was lucky to have a roof over his head, Mr. Walsh told Stan. His mother was an alcoholic, a schizophrenic, and a prostitute, and she had had three kids so far, all more or less like Jacob, only he was the worst. And it didn't look like she was going to stop having babies any time soon either, and there was no way anyone could make her stop. And the government only had so much money to spend on kids like Jacob. Most of the money had to go to the children who had some chance of growing up to be contributing members of society.

So Stan started giving Jacob sponge baths in the bathroom at the centre, athough Jacob would always try to eat the bar of Ivory, and sometimes he would whimper because the washcloth seemed to hurt his skin even though Stan had gone to Sears and bought the softest one he could find. "What you're doing is against the rules," Mr. Walsh told Stan.

"It's not against the Golden Rule," Stan said, and Mr. Walsh had smiled and said, "Just don't get caught." And Stan started bringing extra lunch with him, tuna sandwiches and BLTs, celery sticks plastered with Cheeze Whiz. And orange juice, which Jacob guzzled like an old rummie.

Stan and Jacob spent a lot of time out behind the civic centre that summer. The back of the centre had escaped being tarted up like the front, which had golf-course grass and rhododendrons, and bushes in wire pens that looked like breasts in push-up bras. The bushes hadn't really looked like breasts, Stan decides in retrospect, but when he was twenty the whole world seemed to be a sort of giant Rorschach test and all the shapes in it had some connection to the female form. In the back of the centre there had been an old field where Stan took Jacob to play catch with a soccer ball. Most of the time, though, Jacob would just go into a laughing fit and let the ball hit him in the chest, and Stan would call time out. And then they would go lie down in the grass together, and Jacob would nestle into Stan's chest, yawning and drooling into his shirt. "We may be lying in the gutter, Jacob, but at least we're looking up at the stars," Stan would say to the top of Jacob's musty curls. Stan had really liked lying in the grass with Jacob, and the bugs, and the neighbourhood dogs who would come over to check them out and end up lying around too. Not many people got paid to lie in the grass on hot summer days with someone they were fond of.

Three weeks before Stan was supposed to leave his job at Train-a-Champ and go back to university, he decided he was going to take the term off and stay with Jacob. He phoned his parents; his mother had answered. When he told her about Jacob, she said, "It's your life, Stan. You do what you think is best and let the chips fall. But your father is going to hit the roof." The next day Stan's father flew into the city where Stan was attending university and booked himself into the Holiday Inn. And then he called Stan and Steve's apartment and told Stan to get the hell over there right now. It was a Friday, and Stan ended up spending the weekend at the Holiday Inn, swimming in the pool every morning and getting drunk on airplane bottles of Jack Daniels every night while his father ground away at him like a John Deere tractor. By Sunday evening, Stan had agreed to go back to university. Stan thinks that if his father hadn't gone in for engineering, he could have been one of those guys who gets hired to kidnap people's children from cults and re-brainwash them. A few hundred years ago, he would definitely have qualified for a position with the Inquisition. Torquemada Hopkins.

On his last day with Jacob, Stan gave him a pair of choco-late brown flannel pyjamas to match his eyes. And a pair of Batman underwear because "Batman" had been Stan's nick-name for Jacob. After they had gotten used to each other, Stan had taken Jacob to the bathroom every day and put him on the toilet. And one day when Jacob had been sitting on the can for fifteen minutes, with one of his hands in Stan's and the other gripping a wad of toilet paper that was sodden with snot and sweat, the sound of urine hitting the water in the bowl rang out like the peal of miniature church bells. "Hey, my boy, you're a bathroom man now," Stan had said to Jacob, and Jacob had let out a whoop and yelled "batman, batman!" Stan wonders if Jacob kept going to the bathroom after he left, or had Jacob been too scared to go without him? Or had he just forgotten the whole concept of sitting on a toilet without Stan there as a sort of human mnemonic device?

When it was time for Stan to do engineering, his father had wanted him to go to his old alma mater in the province next to theirs, but Steve was going to a university out west and Stan decided to go with him. Steve had taken an arts degree, majoring in English, and Stan did some of his electives with Steve: the course on slavery, one on mythology, a history of Central America, and even a couple of literature courses. Stan had discovered that poems and stories could be decoded like blueprints, which helped him get over his fear of them. Steve's favourite poet was Dylan Thomas, but Stan couldn't go there; he always lost his feet before the end of the second line. Once, though, Steve had read "Fern Hill" out loud to him, and although it sounded at first as if the words had been put together by someone who didn't know what they were doing, in the end the poem had reminded Stan of a night at the local pub when a girl had sung a song in Gaelic. Although Stan hadn't had a clue what the song was about, he had felt like asking the girl to marry him when she finished.

Stan liked the old English poets best, even when the poems went on for pages. They were like well-designed buildings, or ships; you could climb aboard knowing you were safe from being sunk by some crazy metaphor or waves of stanzas with a load of existential debris on their crests. And the small poems were like house cats. Even when they were aloof or snarly, they still had familiar shapes. You could have contemporary poetry, it was too confusing. And a lot of it was sad and solitary, like masturbation. Stan got the impression that modern poets didn't care if anyone else was there or not.

Stan's father had told Stan that he'd better knock off the arts courses or he'd end up being an architect, which was almost as bad as being a poof. "All architects are poofs at heart," Stan's father had said to him. "They think they're better than engineers, but who does all the work? Them and their goddamn Silver Ring ceremony, the elitist bastards," said Stan's father, working his Iron Ring around his finger. "Who ever heard of a silver bridge? Besides, Stan, God is an engineer. If He was an architect, we wouldn't be here. We'd just be some half-assed idea in His Mind."

Stan's paternal grandfather had been a blacksmith. He had made Stan's father work in the forge every Saturday when the other kids were up in the woods or down by the harbour. "Your father was afraid of the horses," Stan's mother told him, "and, of course, he hates working with his hands." Stan thinks of the things he has seen his father do with his hands: shave, eat, use a pen, shake another hand, make a phone call, knot his tie, mow the lawn. One day Stan saw his father use his hands to hold his head while he cried, but he couldn't tell his mother that.

Once Stan had felt the ghost of his father's hand on his shoulder for a whole day. It was after he had been graduated, and his father had gone with him to The Ritual Calling of an Engineer, a ceremony Rudyard Kipling had made up. Only engineers were allowed to go; it was a secret and sacred initiation, a Masonic-type thing. When they put the Iron Ring on Stan's baby finger, Stan's father had placed his hand on his son's shoulder. For some reason, his father's touch made Stan want to lie down on the floor and go to sleep; he suddenly felt as if he had been up for a hundred years or had just run a thousand miles without stopping.

Stan's father has been a widower for two years. Before she died, Stan's mother had asked him if he thought she had ruined Stan's father's life. "Because when I met him, Stan," she said, "he was sitting in his room in the boarding house, reading a book, and he looked so peaceful." Stan had said, "No, Mom, you didn't ruin his life, you gave him a life." And he was only half lying to her because she was dying; part of him thought it might be true. She had given Stan his life, anyway.

"I thought your mother was too old to have children when I married her," Stan's father had said to him a couple of months ago. Stan's mother had only been thirty-five when they got married and Stan had wondered if his father had been off sick on that critical day in Grade 8 when the health teacher explained about the birds and the bees. But then there hadn't been a health teacher in the one-room school house in Salmon Cove; there had been one teacher for every subject and every grade. Still, Stan's grandmother had given birth to his father when she was forty-three. But everyone Stan knows has one or more black holes in their consciousness into which reality gets sucked every now and then. Stan's father hadn't wanted children, so the idea of Stan never got to the drawing board. But it had been curled up in his mother's heart ever since she was a young girl, and so Stan was born eleven months after the wedding.

On the day Stan's father had mentioned that he hadn't expected Stan to exist, they had been having lunch together on his father's patio. His father had been telling Stan about the first time he ever saw Stan's mother. "She came into my boarding house to see the landlady about a room for her cousin who was coming to the city to work, and they were talking outside my door. The door was open, and I looked out and saw the most beautiful woman in the world. She was standing there like a goddess, wearing a grey dress with pearl buttons." "Battleship grey," Stan said, "or dove grey?" He had wanted to see his mother too, looking like Aphrodite or Athena instead of the wrinkled, overstuffed woman he had been used to most of his life. "*Grey,* Stan," his father had said. "You know, grey like the *colour* grey."

Since his mother died, Stan and his father have lunch together most days. Stan usually picks up a couple of burgers or some fried chicken, and his father always says, "I don't know what you're wasting your money on fake food for." And then he asks Stan to get the ketchup out of the fridge.

Once Stan asked his father what his paternal grandmother had been like. "She was a small woman, Stan, but she was a hard worker, a great worker, she never stopped," was all his father said. Stan's paternal grandmother had died before Stan was born and there wasn't even a picture of her kicking around. She has always been a Swiss clock figure to Stan, a little old woman in a black dress and a head scarf who pops into Stan's mind every now and then, sweeping furiously with a miniature birch broom. Stan's maternal grandmother had been straight out of Disney—blue hair, chocolate chip cookies, the works. She had lived on a farm with geese and cows and pear trees and a brook that ran under the window of the room Stan slept in when he and his mother went to visit her. Sometimes Stan thinks his maternal grandmother hadn't really existed, that he made her up, and the farm too, and the trees and the animals and the soft-voiced men and women that were his mother's people, so lush and foreign were his memories, like some story in a children's book. The farm had been as far away from here as you could get, although it wasn't that far when you looked at it on a map. Once it had been in another country altogether. A little while after the War, his mother's country and his father's country had been joined in the political equivalent of a shot-gun wedding.

One night when Stan's father was drunk, he told Stan that when he got back from the War his mother had taken him in her arms and said, "My son, every time the moon was full over the harbour, I thought about where you was under

it." And then she had cried. Stan had thought he saw tears in
his father's eyes when he told Stan this, but it had probably
only been a trick of the light. Or a trick of the rum. Stan's
father has been drinking a lot since Stan's mother died, but
Stan has never seen him pass out or even walk lop-sided.
And no matter how much he drinks, his words always stay in
the right order and they are as crisp as crackers. And he never
goes on a crying jag or laughs until he almost loses his breath
either. Stan's father never shows his teeth when he smiles,
although they are good teeth. The Royal Navy had been generous when it came to dental work.

Stan has seen his father cry once. He and Stan were sitting at the kitchen table in his parents' house one scalding
July afternoon three years ago. Stan's mother had been in the
hospital for two weeks; his father had told Stan that his
mother was having her pleural cavity flushed and not to
worry. So Stan didn't, because he didn't know what there was
to worry about. For starters, Stan wasn't sure what a pleural
cavity was—it sounded as though his mother should be at
the dentist's instead of in the hospital. But the pleural cavity
thing had turned out to be a half-truth. Stan's mother had
breast cancer, and it had metastasized. And so his father had
had to tell Stan that his mother was dying, his face twisting
up until it looked like the Greek tragedy mask that had hung
on Steve's bedroom wall back in their university apartment.
And then he had cried, making a queer noise like rusty gears.
And then he had apologized for crying, saying "Forgive me
Stan, I shouldn't cry about it." Stan had said, "What should
you cry about, Father? God didn't put tear ducts into the
design for no reason, you know. One of their functions is to
flush out the heart." When Stan said this, he was surprised,
because he hadn't thought of it before. Stan's father didn't

say anything. Later, he and Stan went out to the backyard and put a couple of steaks on the barbecue. They talked about global trade for an hour, and then Stan went home. His mother died a year later.

Last Saturday afternoon Stan and his father painted his father's shed. After his father had drunk three or four bottles of beer, he said, "You know Stan, the thing I really liked about your mother when we were going out together was that she was always happy to go anywhere with me, she never complained." Later, after he had had another three bottles of beer and four drinks of rum, Stan's father had said to him that all women were parasites, what else could you call them, they just used men to get houses and children and clothes. Stan had wanted to say, "Mom had the grey dress with the pearl buttons before she ever met you," but he knew it would sound stupid so he didn't. He had badly wanted to come up with something, though, that would fix his father's neurological system, stop it from sparking so crazily because too much juice was running through it. He knew his father didn't mean half the things he said when he was drunk. But which half?

When Stan was a boy, his father and mother had fought like the English and the French. Lying awake listening, Stan sometimes heard the word *divorce*, and it scared him, like the word *death*; both words were too big, he couldn't get a bead on them, couldn't figure out their proportions or their capacity or their power. *Death* wasn't that bad. It mostly stayed in the Bible and only came out in church on Sundays with a lot of other serious and grim words. But *divorce* got too close on the nights Stan's mother and father shouted at each other; it came right in his house and he never knew if it was going to be gone in the morning. It was like the German Shepherd down the block that ran the length of its chain every time

Stan passed by, missing him by that much. By the time Stan
was twelve, his father was the only one still yelling, like some
crazy shadow boxer. *You and your tribe, you always thought you
were better than me; yeah, yeah, go ahead and divorce me, who'd have
you now, not any of your fancy old boyfriends.*

Once Stan had asked his mother why his father got so
mad at her. She said, "Because I taught him to say *this* and
that instead of *dis* and *dat*, and how to hold a fork correctly.
And he never forgave me." Stan's father yelled at Stan a lot
too. Each session ended with "You're no good, you never
were any good, and you never *will* be any good."

For a long time Stan had believed that his father had seen
into the depths of Stan's sorry soul and was driven to bewail
his son's fate like a male version of Cassandra on the walls of
Troy. But a few years ago Stan read the autobiography of a
writer who had grown up in the outport next to his father's.
On page forty-three of the book were these words: "You're
no good, you never were any good, and you never will be any
good." The writer's father used to say them to his wife and
children when he came home tired from fishing all day, and
tired of being poor and ignorant and less of a man than the
merchant who owned him lock, stock, and barrel.
Apparently it was the tribal chant of a race of men that had
spent generations in colonial custody, a collective bellow of
frustration. Stan wishes they had just shut up and kicked the
dog, not too hard or anything. Sticks and stones can break
your bones, but words can only screw up your head for life.

Stan gets out of the car and closes the door, closes it
softly, gently, as though it is three o'clock in the morning and
he doesn't want to wake some neighbour's child, some little
boy fast asleep in white pyjamas with black cowboys and
Indians on them, a boy who has listened to his parents tear

at each other for hours and is now safe asleep, his mind in some happy dimension where winged horses fly over the Little Dipper and hippopotami splash around in the ponds of English country gardens. He begins to climb the steps. No arrows fly out of the windows in the door. In fact, the garrison feels deserted. The steps, though, they seem to go on and on like the ones in the pictures of Aztec pyramids. Steps that go up and up and up until you got to the top where the Aztecs used to practice human sacrifice. Every day they would plunge an obsidian knife into the live body of a young man and cut out the beating heart. They did this to keep the sun from getting thirsty and to move the universe along its proper course. The Aztecs had been even stranger than the ancient Greeks. But at least they had given the world chocolate. Stan thinks that if he had to choose between democracy and Mars bars, democracy might not make it. Especially considering the shape it was in these days.

Stan finally reaches the top of the steps and tries the door. It is locked, which means nothing. Stan's father always locks the door, even when he is out mowing the lawn. The door is oak and dotted with brass studs; it has a latch, not a knob. The key to this door should be old and black and the length of Stan's hand but it is only an ordinary aluminum key. You wouldn't be able to get copies made of the other kind, Stan thinks. Not at Canadian Tire, anyway. Perhaps the old man at the ironworks downtown could make one though. Stan notices that his mind doesn't seem to want him to go any further than the door. It is trying to lead him down the garden path, or at least away from the path that goes past the door and into the porch and down the hall to his father's bedroom. And then Stan suddenly acquires vampire senses: the sheen of the brass studs on the door hurt his eyes; the scent from the flowers of the laburnum by the hedge is overwhelming, nauseating; the faint sizzle of a dying street lamp down the road hits his ears like the sound of a thousand steaks on a giant's barbeque. Far beneath him, his heart has turned traitor; it will not keep a steady beat. Stan wishes he had a bagpipe player with him, even though he doesn't have any Scots in his DNA as far as he knows.

Something brushes against Stan's right leg and Stan knows what it is without having to look down. It's Homer, his father's cat. Homer shouldn't be out at nine-thirty. Three times a week, Stan's father comes to supper at Stan's place, arriving at six on the nose. He and Stan eat at six-thirty, talk politics until eight-thirty, and then they watch *Jeopardy* until nine-thirty. Both Stan and his father are pretty good at guessing the answers to the *Jeopardy* questions, which is something they have in common. Sometimes Stan thinks it is the only thing, besides their short tempers. Stan is the only person alive, though, who knows he once had a short temper. He has been lengthening it since he was a child, pulling it out like taffy, and now it is long and flaccid and harmless instead of hard and tight and brutal like his father's.

As soon as *Jeopardy* is over, Stan's father looks at his watch and says, "Well, it's time to go home now and shut 'er down for the night and feed the boy." Homer is "the boy." A year ago, he was a gaunt stray who took up residence under Stan's father's shed. Stan was surprised when his father let the cat in to live with him. Stan's mother and father had been out walking one evening before they were engaged, and his mother had stopped to pat a cat that was sitting on someone's front steps. "I'm not having any goddamn cats in my house," his father had said, and then Stan's mother knew for certain that he was going to ask her to marry him.

Homer is a fat and arrogant princeling of the castle now. If Stan's mother were alive, she would say that Homer has nouveau riche manners. Stan is amazed at what his father lets Homer get away with. Homer scratches the furniture and rugs with impunity; he is allowed to get up on the table in the middle of dinner and snatch whatever he can from Stan's father's plate; he defecates regularly in the urns in the living room where Stan's mother's jade plants grow, even though he has two litter boxes, one upstairs and one down. Homer can even claw Stan's father if he's in a surly mood, which is generally the case, and Stan's father just gives him a poke and says, "You're some boy." There are only two rules by which the cat must abide: he is not allowed out after eight p.m. and he is not allowed to set foot in Stan's father's bedroom. And so Homer spends his evenings in surveillance of both doors. He has no interest at all in the cracks and crevices through which field mice sometimes gain entry to the house.

Once, during the time Stan's mother was lying in bed waiting for death to come by, she told Stan's father that she fed the mice, giving them their own corner in back of one of the kitchen cupboards, which she heaped with flour and rice. So that they wouldn't get into the family's stuff, she explained. Stan had been there at the time: the corners of his lips leap back towards his ears at the memory of his father's face when his mother told him about the mice. For once, Stan's father had had nothing to say. The idea of the whole thing was so foreign to him that he had been unable to absorb it. The words had hit Stan's father in the face like a soccer ball; he had put his hands up in the air in front of him as though he could deflect them onto the bureau or throw them back at his wife, so thin from the labour of dying she looked like a gruesome Gumby. Stan's father had played soccer in England during the War, and he still has the legs. Legs like Ozymandias. *I met a traveler from an antique land/Who said: Two vast and trunkless legs of stone/Stand in the desert.*

Stan's father is a legend at the hydro company. When the island was first being shaken out of four centuries of feudal inertia, Ed Hopkins had been in charge of making electricity flow into the hundreds of coastal villages crouched between the knuckles of its stony headlands. He had deflected the course of great rivers and scored the ancient migratory paths of caribou with roads; legions of trees had fallen before Stan's father's chainsaw-wielding hosts. But in the end, light and warmth had penetrated the darkest and most isolated corners of his country. Your father, the men told Stan when he worked as a teenager one summer in the woods camps, is a good man, a smart man, a fair man. Stan had been glad to get this new father from the men of the camps. He had superimposed him over the other one and fiddled with the design until Edward Hopkins looked like neither a god nor a monster, but just a man. Sort of.

Homer starts to wind around Stan's legs like a solo conga dancer. When he is distressed, Homer's voice takes on a high-pitched whine that Stan wishes was beyond the range of human hearing. He is using this tone now, and Stan says, "Hang on a minute, buddy, you'll be face down in your food bowl shortly." Stan decides he likes Homer best when he is in surveillance mode. Homer looks intelligent and mysterious then, especially when he is sitting in front of the entrance to the sanctum sanctorum, the door to Stan's father's bedroom. Stan sometimes wonders why Homer wastes his time trying to get into his father's room. Did Homer think that if he managed to break in some night, Stan's father would pull back the duvet and say, "Hey there, are you having nightmares— come and crawl in with me, boy"? That he would get to spend the rest of the night curled against Stan's father's shoulder, dreaming of big fat mice falling out of kitchen cupboards. Stan has checked the back of the cupboard where his mother used to lay out dinner for the mice. There is still a heap of flour and rice there, so he figures his father must have called the exterminators.

"Well, Homer," says Stan, "here goes." He puts his hands in the pocket of his jeans. The key is there on the ring with the rest of his keys: his house key, his car key, the key to the office, the key to his girlfriend's apartment, and three other keys that are vagrants but which Stan can't bring himself to throw out, just in case. Stan takes out the keys and puts the one to his father's house where it belongs. It resents going in and Stan has to wiggle it around a bit. Eventually it gives up, and all Stan has to do is press down on the latch. But instead he takes the key out and sits down on the steps. Homer walks over and climbs into Stan's lap. It had rained earlier in the evening, and Homer's coat is damp. Stan picks some cobwebs off the cat's back, and the wing of a white moth, which adheres to his index finger like a second epidermis. Stan looks at the wing and thinks, *Moth wing! Moth wing! burning bright!/ On my finger in the night/ What immortal hand or eye/ Could frame thy fragile symmetry?* William Blake had been a Romantic, but not the kind his girlfriend wants him to be. It was odd how much difference a capital letter could make. Stan thinks there should be more of them, but there seem to be fewer all the time.

Homer has never been in Stan's lap before. "And the lion shall lie down with the lamb," Stan says to him. Homer blinks and starts to knead the bottom of Stan's sweater. "I am not your mother," Stan says, but he lets the cat push his claws into the thick cotton and pull them out again; Stan figures it is probably the feline equivalent of nail biting. He looks down over the lawn at his blue German compact and considers getting up and walking down the thousands of steps between him and the car and getting into it and driving home. But the car is too far away, it is in another country now, it is not even the same car he came in; also, he is not the same Stan who drove it here. Even Homer seems to be undergoing a metamorphosis; he is not as distinct as he was five minutes ago. But that could just be because there is not much light left, only a thin line along the horizon. The moon is high over Stan's father's house, the new moon with the old moon in her arms. And there is a ring around both of them, which means it will rain again tomorrow.

Stan scratches Homer underneath his chin and thinks about the Greek guy who had to go into the labyrinth at Crete and face the Minotaur. He wonders if the guy hung around out in front for a while, or did he just saunter right on in like Robert De Niro? But that guy had had a partner, a woman, who gave him a ball of string tied to something outside the monster's lair so he wouldn't get lost navigating the interior. Stan wishes Steve would suddenly materialize like Captain Kirk, teleport right in from Nova Scotia where he teaches English in a rural school.

Most of Steve's students are black, and poor. "They really like Othello," Steve had told Stan the last time they talked. "He is definitely de Man. I get them to make up raps about him, you know, 'Othello, you shouldn't be messin' with that Desdemona, she bad news, man, you better get a new momma.' And so on. Works for us."

But Steve isn't coming, no one is. Stan feels a sudden rush of pity for Jesus in the Garden of Gethsemane. Had He wanted to make a run for it, hop the nearest donkey back to Galilee?

"Take this cup," Stan says to the box cedar by the steps. And then he snorts. Greek mythology is one thing, but if his mind thinks it can just up and sprout a messianic complex it had better think again. For what was he, after all, but a grown man afraid to enter a dark house. Stan looks down at his index finger, at the moth wing. What a piece of work it was, finer than onion skin and soft as the inside of his girlfriend's thigh, yet strong enough to carry an insect through an entire life in the air. No engineer could have thought up the concept of moth wing, not in a million years.

"You're wrong, Father," Stan says out loud, too loud for the quiet street; too loud for Homer, who stops trying to unravel Stan's sweater and tenses his body for flight or fight. And anger rises up in Stan from some deep hole he thought he had screwed a lid on years and years ago; he lets it fill him until he feels swollen and hard and deadly. Like he de Man. And he decides that he is going to go into the house, where his father is fine and not in a coma or anything, just passed out drunk in bed or on the couch in the den in front of the TV, and he is going to shake his father until he comes to and then he is going to tell him that God is not an engineer, He is an architect. And a homo to boot. Actually, he is going to tell his father that God is a black *lesbian* architect. He may even tell his father that he is no good, never *was* any good, and never *will* be any good.

Stan rises from the step as if something has pulled him up by the back of his sweater. His getting up is so abrupt that Homer falls out of his lap and doesn't land on his feet, thereby destroying a perfectly good myth, one even the cat had believed in. Stan thrusts the key into the lock like a knife and hits the latch with his fist. The door jumps back, and Stan and Homer step over the threshold together. Stan strides through the porch without turning on the light and turns left. Homer takes a right, not needing light or radar or anything to know where his food bowl is.

Stan's father is lying face-down on the hall floor. Stan looks down at him: he is obviously dead and has been for some time. He is wearing navy blue linen pyjamas with gold piping around the collar and cuffs, which gives him a quasi-military air. Stan wonders for a moment if his father wore pyjamas like that during the War. And then a roaring begins in his ears. Through it, Stan can hear his father telling him the story of Pat, his father's brother, who knocked on a neighbour's door one morning and fell through it dead as a nit just as the neighbour's wife was saying, "Come in come in come in."

"Pat, Pat on the mat," a voice in Stan's head says, and then it starts to chant "dead Ed, dead Ed, dead Ed" until Stan says "shutup, shutup, shutup" to make it stop.

Stan's legs feel as insubstantial as mercury; he leans against the hall wall to steady himself, but the wall doesn't seem to be quite vertical. Stan's head is next to a shaded fixture his father leaves on at night in case he has to go to the bathroom. The fixture is on, which means his father has been dead since last night. Or early this morning. The light from the fixture circumscribes Stan's father's body on the white shag carpet; half a face is floating in the yellow pool. It looks more like a fragment of a mask than a face, like a piece of one of those Aztec masks that sacrificial victims were forced to wear. It is so deep a crimson it is almost black. And the eye hole is empty.

Stan feels a rush in his head, a wave of disorientation that constricts him; down down down goes Incredible Shrinking Stan until he is a small creature crawling along on its hands and knees, which are tingling from contact with a carpet that is not this one. It is a soft, narrow carpet the colour of tangerines, but Stan is in the same hall. The sun from the window by his parents' bedroom is warm on the back of his neck, and he is looking down at his hands on the fuzzy orange surface. They are so tiny—how can they possibly bear him along?—so tiny, and innocent of rings. The path Stan is crawling along, the path the sun is making for him, goes all the way to the knees of a man at the far end of the hall. Up above them, the man's voice is saying, "Come to Daddy, Stan, that's right, come to Daddy." And when Stan gets to the knees he looks up, and the man looking down at him is his father. But he is so young, and he is smiling—his teeth are big and white like marshmallows. And then two enormous hands grab Stan around his middle and he is flying up up up—and he is laughing and the man is laughing— even the sun is laughing.

And then Stan is big again, and he is somewhere darker than the Labyrinth of Crete. He looks for light and finds it at his feet, a sphere of light that begins at the tips of his sneakers. An old man's body is lying in the middle of it.

A shadow slithers into the light. It is Homer, who has just had a disappointing experience in the kitchen. The cat moves like a crab towards Stan's father's body, his fur erect, his tail like a bottlebrush. Stan watches as Homer sniffs his father's cheek and then his nose. Homer and Stan's father seem to be a long way off, as though Stan is looking at them through the wrong end of a telescope. "Doornail, Homer," Stan whispers to the cat. Or maybe he means *dormouse*; Stan closes his eyes and the icon that comes up when he defrags the hard drive on his computer sails across the inside of his lids, all the little coloured bits flying apart and then back together again. But his mind doesn't seem to be able to restructure itself properly; maybe it's the white noise, his father's house is full of white noise, just like at the office, only louder. "*If you can keep your head. . .you'll be a Man, my son!*" Stan announces sternly to the wall opposite him.

Homer looks up at the sound of Stan's voice, and then down the hall. The door to Stan's father's room is ajar, a little more than the width of a man. The cat backs slowly away from the body of Stan's father, and then he suddenly whirls around and strikes out for the bedroom. It seems to Stan that the cat is moving in slow motion with a lighted torch in his paw; the title track to *Chariots of Fire* starts up in Stan's head. In his haste, however, Homer miscalculates; he hits the door and his momentum causes it to rebound off the cedar chest behind it. The sound reaches Stan in waves; he can feel the air expand against his body: the noise is like a small tree being snapped in half. Then there is a new sound, the indignant squeal of elderly bedsprings: Homer has landed on his field of dreams. In Stan's mind's eye, the cat is standing on his father's bed with his forelegs extended above his head; somehow, even though he lacks opposable thumbs, Homer is giving the victory sign with both paws.

Stan starts to giggle and can't seem to stop; he may never stop, he doesn't *want* to stop, and then he is sliding down the wall; the light fixture passes him by like a small boat going in the opposite direction, all lit up in the night. When Stan reaches the bottom, he falls forward; the feel of the rough shag makes him sad, and he can't remember what was so funny a moment ago. He crawls on his hands and knees to his father's body and lays his head on his father's back, and puts his left arm around the rigid thighs.

Stan's right hand reaches up and touches the nape of his father's neck. His index finger still has the wing of the white moth attached to it. Cold, so cold, his father's neck, his back, the thighs too—so cold and hard, like iron. The linen cloth of the pyjamas, the moth's wing, Stan's finger, are all too thin, too weak to warm his father, and the shame of it goes right down into Stan's groin. In his heart there is a feeling he cannot identify; it is like despair, but lighter, and sharper than ten thousand obsidian knives. It hurts more than any pain Stan has ever borne or imagined bearing, and he knows that if it stays at such a pitch he will die from it. But it is all right, because Stan finds he can move away from it, move right out of his body, in fact, and he does. From somewhere else, he watches his hand leave his father's neck and slide down over the shoulder until it comes to rest beside his father's hand. Stan's father's arm is bent at the elbow, making a right angle to his forehead as if he had died saluting Death. Stan and his father's baby fingers are touching; the Iron Rings look like a pair of miniature handcuffs, a couple of dirty little shackles.

Stan pulls his hand away from his father's and takes off his Ring. He flicks it with his thumb and forefinger as hard as he can: its trajectory along the carpet is soundless, and there is not enough light to see where it has gone, but it is probably somewhere in the depths of the blue shag in the sunken living room at the end of the hall. And then Stan takes his father's hand in his. It is unyielding, but the hand and all the fingers appear to be smaller, as though they have shrunk since his father was alive. Stan pries the Ring from his father's finger slowly and patiently, as though he is removing a scab from living flesh. The Ring finally falls off the fingertip and into Stan's palm; he looks at it. It is not exactly like his Ring after all; the wrought iron is soft and thin; he could probably snap it in half with his bare hands if he felt like it. "With this Ring, I thee dead," Stan says to his father, and then he sends it down the long white strand of the hall carpet; there is a clink as it hits his own Ring. Stan has a vision of the two Rings lying there side by side for centuries, buried deep in the thick pile of the living room rug. Someday, archaeologists will stumble upon them and wonder what strange and primitive ritual they represented. "Ha ha, what a joke," Stan says to his father, "they'll never figure it out, not in a million years." Roman candle spirals of laughter suddenly start shooting up from the hole inside Stan, and he rolls over and curls into a ball and lets them shake him like a rat terrier.

A man is crying, he is sobbing to break his heart. He is saying, "Daddy Daddy Daddy, oh, Daddy, no, please don't be dead." Stan knows it's not him. He hasn't cried since he was fifteen, and he has never called his father anything but Father. "Shh," Stan says to the man who is crying, "don't you cry. You'll wake up the boy in the blue pyjamas. And he is in a good place now, a safe place; he is in an old house by the sea, he is in his mother's arms. And look!—the smiling moon is coming down over her silver bridge—look! she is bending down to embrace the poor young sailor and his sad old mother. And the forgiving moon, in her joy and her delight, is lifting him up up up. And now they are like Michelangelo's Pieta, full over the harbour."

When I Was a Dog

Our perfect companions never have fewer than four feet.

— Colette

These are the last words he ever said to me: "I think we need to be apart for awhile, but someday I'll come back and we will live in a house by the sea." "Oh. Well," I replied, with a catch in my throat, "Um. . .what about lunch on alternate Fridays?" But his phone, which had been beeping because he rarely remembered to put it back on the holder to recharge—"I'll 'beep' come 'beep' back"—suddenly died. And so I went downstairs and had a cup of tea and a raisin bun, and waited for the sorrow to come, the long high tide of regret and longing that would wash over me like a wave of immortal love breaking on the cruel rocks of "See ya." The existential agony of an inhabitant of Dumpsville, population one.

But I waited in vain: another cup of tea and two more buns went by without a tear or even an adder-tongued lick of anguish in my breast. You're probably in shock, I told myself, and so I went back upstairs, to my CD player, and I put on *Irish Heartbeat* to make the blood of grief flow, as was fit and proper. "No life have I, no liberty/For love is lord of all," Van Morrison sang in the ragged, slightly hysterical voice of one who has been left too long on the rack of love, and the fiddle agreed with him completely, but I couldn't. Little poppy bits of relief were dancing around in my heart like carbon bubbles; indeed, my very DNA seemed to be uncorkscrewing and re-corkscrewing in joyous abandon. So I put on Great Big Sea and did a mad jig up and down the hall. And then I went to bed with my cat, Omar.

"I have been dumped, Omar," I said, and sighed as though I meant it. "I told you so," he replied, his green eyes blazing in the dark with love and contempt. And then he turned around twice and settled down for the night, with his back to me.

He, the Eternal He of My She, had said to me more than once that I would rather have the cat in bed with me than him. When we sparred, I did indeed long for the peace of cat love—Omar's love, to be precise; Omar who is black but comely, and whose teeth are like a flock of sheep that are even shorn.

"Why do you tell him he has teeth like a sheep's?" my human beloved asked me once. "I mean, most people just say "pretty kitty" or something like that."

"I didn't say that he has teeth like a sheep's," I replied, "I said his teeth were *like* sheep. It's from the Bible. From a passage he is fond of because it reminds him of our past life together in the Middle East."

"I see," he said, but I don't think he did.

The first time My Sunny Valentine ever told me that he loved me, it came from his dog. "Rufus loves you, you know," he said, staring into my eyes desperately, begging me to understand that he meant *he* loved me, but fiercely willing me not to make him have to substitute "I" for "Rufus." I looked at him solemnly, with the full force of my equal regard for him, and confessed, "I love Rufus too." The relief in his eyes was almost a sound. And then we had wicked sex right there in front of poor Rufus, who got quite upset and eventually had to be shut up in the cellar. For the truth was, Rufus did not love me at all. He detested me, as much as a Lab can detest anyone, for it is not in their nature. And so poor Rufus was invaded by alien forces, jealously and hatred and sorrow and fear, and, in the end, they took him howling to his doom.

Rufus was old when I met his master, and it was very unfair of the latter to have loved me when he had loved only Rufus for so long, even though my Prince of Pucks had once been married and was, indeed, the father of two grown children. Whom he loved as well, but they were girls, and they scared him a little, and confused him to no end. He had been particularly traumatized during their early adolescence, when they were wont to shriek at him and maul him by turns, and descend upon him once a month demanding that he go to the drugstore and buy tampons. Which, because his wife had gone missing some years back, he was forced to do, or else face the wrath of two preperiod daughters, whom he referred to at such times as the Guerrilla Barbies. He would rather, he told me, end up at Shopper's Drug Mart with his arms full of Kotex in front of a smirking biker at the checkout, which was inevitable, than be subjected to the terrorist tactics of his rosy cheeked and newly bosomed girls, tactics which included, o horror of horrors, crying; wasn't that against the Geneva Convention he asked me plaintively? Unfortunately not, I told him, but perhaps one day when the world is a kinder place, someone will think to include it.

And the girls couldn't play hockey or softball with him, which Rufus could do and did, and they wouldn't go swimming with him or wait by the door until he got back from being out with his mates, or curl up on the couch with him while he watched soccer. All the things I ended up doing after Rufus was deposed. And, of course, I could do the other thing—the great, sublime, mysterious thing—which to Rufus was just another sport, and he never understood why he wasn't allowed to play.

The Sun of My Existence told me that he and his wife had parted company because she had been insane. Only pity for her condition had kept him in the marriage, he said; eventually, she had gone entirely around the bend and had deserted him and their two offspring. Much later, I discovered that our definitions of the word *insanity* were not in accord. I had pictured his former spouse as a sort of sister to the mad wife that Rochester kept in his attic in *Jane Eyre*; a poor, gibbering, violent wild-eyed beauty damaged beyond repair, victim of bad genes and faulty rearing. His wife *had* been violent: for instance, she had once thrown an iron at him when she discovered him in *flagrante delicto* with the next door neighbour's sister-in-law. And her violent proclivities did appear to have been inherited. His mother-in-law, a small woman, had once gotten up on a footstool and slapped him across the face when news of another indiscretion he had committed reached her by way of the local hairdressing network.

"Well," I said, "you were unfaithful; what did you expect?"

"But I loved my wife," he replied, staring at me as though I were standing there cheering for the blue team instead of his beloved red team, "and what I did with those women meant nothing to me."

"Do you suppose," I queried, "that it might have meant something to your wife? Or to the women?" He looked at me as if I had just told him that Tiger Woods was a lacrosse player.

Before I met my Lord of the Links, I hadn't caught a ball since I was a child, and I had never sat shivering in a rink looking down upon a mass of men propelling themselves furiously towards a spherical piece of white netting like sperm heading for an ovum, or dragged a bag with iron sticks in it over peculiar-looking grass. Or waited anxiously long into the night, in a house that was not my own, until a drunk and untidy man came in through the door, at which point I would run to him and rub my face against his jacket and sniff his cheek for the scent of other women. But all these things and more I did, after a time. Not too long a time after we met, either. He told me once how stubborn Rufus had been as a puppy, how much time and patience it had taken to bring him to heel, but although I heard what he said with my ears, my limbic system must have been asleep at the time; at least, no brain-gut reaction occurred.

"You must love me unconditionally," he said, "for I have to do what I want to do when I want to do it."

"Nice work if you can get it," I said to him the first time he told me this, but some scant months later it had become the first verse of the Apostle's creed of my new religion. Other verses included "Thou shalt not cheer for the blue team, for my wrath on that day will be greater than in the days when thou wouldst not wear fancy lingerie," and "Thou shalt listen with respect to the voice of Don Cherry, even though it soundeth to you like nails on a blackboard." Nine-inch nails.

I do not know how it happened that I so easily became a dog. My upbringing had been middle-class and Protestant, liberal and loving. The only leash I had ever worn was that of my own conscience, and it was long and light, its main purpose being to keep me from hurting others. He, on the other hand, had grown up working-class and Roman

Catholic, barely tolerated as an individual and tightly bound with the briars of RC dogma and lace-curtain Irish social dictums. And therefore his main aim in life was to flout both Church and community, but never openly, or even in his own mind, because then HE WOULD GO TO HELL, wouldn't he? Or at least be banished to a Protestant purgatory—probably a place something like the suburb I grew up in: trips to the library on Saturdays and no Jigg's dinner on Sundays.

And so he was a first-hand slip-slider, manipulator and liar, although these talents were wasted on me. To his amazement, he could tell the truth and do just about anything he wanted to do without being beaten within an inch of his life. "Could you write a letter to the Pope about self-actualization?" he asked me once. "No," I said. "But one day I might take it upon myself to torment your mother with such a missive." His mother lived in Ireland. Some nights he would wake up in a cold sweat, positive he had heard her shouting at him across The Pond about the stains on his sheets.

And I must confess: when I met him, I had decided it was time to devote myself to a man with all my heart and soul. I now have no recollection of what prompted that decision; there is a faint memory of eating bad Chinese the day before I decided to become a Real Woman. And of course, an archetype in jackboots was waiting in the wings for just such an anti-epiphany. Well, actually, he was wearing athletic sneakers. That's all he ever wore, besides skates and golf shoes.

It was fun at first, the most fun I'd had since I was a child. I got to play a lot of games out of doors. I didn't have to make any decisions. I was petted when I was pretty and good and quiet, and punished when I argued or wore the same sweater for three days in a row or beat him at crib. Life was simple again. The treacherous genes of millennia of helpmeets sprang readily into action and quickly made mincemeat of my personal history as a free-spirited blue-stocking. One would suppose that I had spent my entire life walking back and forth to the well with a jug on my head.

We only made love at my house twice; after that, he told me he couldn't come there again because he was allergic to cats. "But you said that your family had a cat for twenty years," I protested.

"The allergy is new," he replied, "and when allergies surface in middle age, they are not to be trifled with.

"I don't suppose," he continued, cocking his head to one side like Rufus when his master produced the leash, "you would consider getting another home for your cat, would you?"

"Give Omar away?" I said, shocked to the very marrow of my marrow. "Give up my darling whose locks are like unto those of a young goat's on Gilead? Besides, he is too old now to get along with anyone but me."

"I suspect he always was," said my Knight in Nikes. That was the first cryptic remark I had ever heard him make. I was so proud.

The first time I brought home the Grail of My Heart's Longing, Omar tried to escort him to the door before he had even taken his coat off. When his efforts failed, Omar sat down by the door and watched our antics on the stairs. For, quite often, we were never able to make it to a suitable surface upon which to perform the ancient ritual; we were for-ever tearing articles of clothing off each other willy nilly as long as there was a locked door behind us.

"I don't feel right about the cat sitting there staring at us," said the Archangel of My Affections at one point, com-ing up for oxygen from a *Guinness Book of World Records* kiss.

"Well, we can put him in the cellar if you like," I said. "After all, he's got a couple of projects on the go down there, so he won't mind."

"Projects? What kind of projects?" he queried, deftly removing a small splinter from his left buttock. (I had had to take the carpet off the stairs owing to Omar's habit of creeping up them on little cat feet after he had been down in said cellar, which has a dirt floor, dirt with bits of bituminous coal mixed in. Also, the second step from the top is his favourite place to deposit fur balls.)

"Oh, you know, he's got a sort of archaeological dig happening," I replied. "There's a dead sparrow buried down there, and even though I put a rock over it, he does keep burrowing around the edges. And then there's Serena, who used to live here, and he was very fond of her, and sometimes I find him sitting on top of her grave in sort of a meditative position. I think perhaps he is trying to commune. . ."

"Serena was?" he inquired, pulling up his trousers and looking down at Omar, and then rather wistfully at the door.

"My au pair," I said, annoyed at having been thrown off the satin cloud of ardour and onto a set of decrepit old stairs.

"Oh," he said, "I was hoping she was a dead dog or something."

"Cat, actually," I confessed.

"Well, cats don't really make the best au pairs, do they," he said kindly, patting my head rapidly two or three times. "Much too independent to take care of others' needs properly. Why don't you go put Omar down with his friend, and I'll just pop upstairs and have a little lie-down."

WHEN I WAS A DOG

"Speaking of au pairs," I said, "I have *au* pair of fishnet stockings left over from last Halloween, and an apron my old granny gave me for Christmas once."

"Well," he said, "well," and I could tell from the way he was having trouble fastening his trousers that I had hit upon something.

Omar growled the entire way to the cellar. "You are a such a fool," he said, biting my arm as we rounded the corner into the kitchen.

"You don't understand," I replied, pinching his ear in retaliation.

"Oh yes, yes I do, you tart," he said, struggling mightily to get out of my arms as I reached for the knob of the cellar door.

"For that," I said, "you can stay down there until the cows come home."

"One of them already has," he hissed as I closed the door on his tail. Not too hard: leaving his tail sticking out of the door is a favourite trick of Omar's; like most cats, he hates making up his mind in a hurry. Some people think that women are like cats and men are like dogs, and current research on the human brain seems to support this. Apparently, when a man is confronted with a situation that requires a decision, one lone neuron comes on in his brain and he must obey its dictates. Such as "stay" or "go." But women's brains light up like little cerebral Christmas trees, and they may choose from a variety of responses; I believe this is called "thinking."

The next time we tried spending an evening at my place, Omar was the soul of *bonhomie* and *savoir faire*. "I think he likes me," said my Lord and Master as Omar purred and wound himself like a cottonmouth around my human darling's legs.

"And why wouldn't he?" I replied, serving one a cup of tea and a raisin bun and the other a saucer of tinned milk with a few cornflakes floating here and there in it. I had to give Omar his milk on the floor instead of in his usual place at the head of the table, but he gallantly ignored the slight.

"After all," I continued, "you both love me, so why wouldn't you like each other?" As soon as I realized that I had uttered *love* aloud, as though it were just another harmless word and not sort of a verbal hand grenade where men are concerned, I did the only thing I could, which was drop to my knees and proceed to unzip his corduroys.

"But I haven't finished my bun," he protested, although without much conviction.

"Darling," I said, "the bun won't go stale that fast. As a matter of fact, judging from the last pack I bought at Zoobie's, it has a shelf life of approximately eight months. Genetically altered, you see."

"I didn't know they made genetically altered raisin buns," he remarked, lifting me onto the table and spreading my hair around the sugar bowl and the milk jug as though he were arranging a still life.

"Oh, yes," I said, "oh yes, yes yes!" Out of the corner of my eye, I watched Omar leave the room, his tail as erect as. . . well, erect.

"The inside of my sneaker seems to be wet," said my Jack of Hearts much later, as he was preparing to leave, all soft-eyed and swollen-lipped and tousle-haired. He took his foot out of the sneaker and looked up at the ceiling to see if there was a leak. But I knew he wasn't going to find one.

Omar was sitting at the top of the stairs with a big smirk on his face.

"Damn you!" I said, *sotto voce*, glaring at him. "If I was Medusa, you'd be a garden ornament now."

"But you're not, are you," replied Omar, "although by the look of your hair, snarled as it is from the latest bit of toss-and-tumble, one might be excused for thinking, in this dim light . . ."

My love was standing by the front door, fondling his wet sock and sniffing his fingers. "I think," he said, "I think that the cat . . ."

But he couldn't go on. "I'll get you a clean sock," I said, "and you can throw the sneaker in the wash when you get home. With some vinegar."

"Vinegar," he repeated, looking intently into the depths of his soggy sneaker as though he were scrying. Scrying was a popular form of divination in Elizabethan times; one stared into a bowl of water until shapes took form. The Queen's scryer, John Dee, was particularly adept at foretelling the future by this method. I don't know if it is possible to scry using a sneaker full of cat urine, though. Perhaps if you were John Dee you might manage it.

"Omar only did that because he lo. . .likes you," I said. "That's what cats do when they are fond of a person," I continued, touching my nose to make sure it wasn't expanding.

"And what would he do if he didn't like me, do you suppose?" asked my irate Adonis, tapping the banister rather forcefully with his soiled footwear. "Chew off my gonads, perhaps? Burn down my house? Slaughter my offspring?" I was unaware that male voices could rise so high after puberty: how sad that they made all those little boys into castrati for the papal choir; obviously, it hadn't been a bit necessary.

"No," I said, "he would sneak over to the rink and jump on your back just as you were about to make the overtime winning goal in the year-end tournament against your arch rivals, the Shay Heights Muzlims."

"Oh my god," he said, turning pale and sitting down abruptly on the bottom step.

"Just kidding," I murmured, and I went to my bedroom for a fresh sock.

"It's quite dark out," I told him when he started to protest as I slipped the sock over the most neatly turned male ankle I have ever seen in my life. "No one will notice that it's lime green or that there's lace around the top. Just don't get into an accident."

"I think I might leave the car here for the night," he said. "I feel like a walk, anyway."

"I wouldn't have thought your legs were up to it," I said archly.

"They aren't, really," he said, "which is why coaches tell us to stay away from women before a game. And during. And after." He gave me a perfunctory kiss on the cheek and disappeared through the door.

I watched him out of the living room window as he walked down the lane; every now and again he would look around furtively and then reach down and tug on the trouser leg that had my sock beneath it. If he had not been the Mate of My Soul, Very Mate of Very Mate, I must confess that I would have perhaps laughed aloud at the sight. But anger and pity were beginning to rumble in my heart. I turned to Omar, who had come downstairs and was curled in a ball on the sofa. "A little music, I think," I said to him, "to soothe the savage breast."

Omar leapt up quickly. "You wouldn't," he said, "not for something that. . .that *trivial*."

"Wouldn't what," I said, "play 'Flow Gently, Sweet Afton' on my harmonica? Oh yes I would, I would indeed." I could feel snakes growing out of my head at the very thought of it. Some people think that dogs are the only domestic animals that are highly sensitive to sound, but anyone who owns both a harmonica and a cat knows that is a fallacy.

"Would you put me in the cellar first?" asked Omar, in an uncharacteristically humble voice.

"No," I said. "I was thinking that we might go to the sunroom, and I will shut the door, and we will both serenade the moon through the windows. For I know you will join in—you always do."

"You are a pitiless bitch," Omar snarled as his head and shoulders disappeared under the sofa.

"Yes; yes I am," I remarked, hauling him out by the hindquarters.

But after a year of being a very good dog, I began to chew at the leash, just a nibble or two at first; after, however, my beloved's third indiscretion with a very *déclassé* barmaid at the local pub, and the fourth loan of several hundred dollars which went down the toilet at said pub, never to return again in any form of green, I refused to play ball any more, metaphorically and literally. I began to wear panties from MallMart that looked like prison issue undergarments. I wrote a book of poetry, which became a modest local success. I took to missing hockey games in order to have tea with young sociology professors in Oxfam poster cafes.

He sulked, he whined—his belt became so notched with beer-slinging slatterns that it was unwearable. And then one

day I informed him that you could put the word *fore* before
the word *play*, making it not just another golfing term but
something he might want to look up in *The Joy of Sex*. Or at
least in *The Condensed Oxford*. Not long after that came The
Phone Call.

Poor old Rufus, he met a very bad end not long after his
master disposed of me. The mad woman who runs a local
animal shelter broke into my Departed Darling's house and
made off with Rufus; a neighbour had rung her and complained that he was an abuse case. The fact was, Rufus was
elderly and despondent, and the combination had rendered
him remarkably like an ambulatory version of a bad taxi-
dermy job on some sort of half-decayed wolverine-like
thing. The mad woman is very fond of guerrilla tactics, however; one day I heard her boast that she had just snatched a
kitten from a student and had barely managed to escape with
her life, the student having thrown a balled-up bit of paper
at her in retaliation.

"I was incensed," she said, making a characteristic grab
for the designer scarf that hides her wattles. "I mean, the
next time it might be a gun." I hope someone does pull a gun
on her someday; I'm sure that she'd overpower them easily,
immobilizing them with her basilisk glare and then whipping
off The Scarf and garroting them on the spot.

Anyway, she wouldn't give Rufus back to his master for
two days, and poor Rufus was so traumatized when he did
get home that he had to be put to sleep. *Rescued* and then *put
to sleep*: what odd creatures humans are, to bend words to our
will like Humpty Dumpty in *Alice*. ("'The question is,' said
Alice, 'whether you can make words mean so many different
things.' 'The question is,' said Humpty Dumpty, 'which is to
be master—that's all.'") What actually happened to Rufus

was that he was thrown in the clink for looking unsightly while he was out having a pee, and then he was done to death by lethal injection. After being horribly betrayed by the man he had served for his entire life like, well, like a dog. Thank god for opposable thumbs and a well-developed cerebrum, even if I do keen and weep from time to time over the uses to which human beings put these things. But Rufus is in a plastic container now, and I am not.

Last week when I was out for a stroll, I thought I saw my former Galahad a block or so away; I even imagined that he called out my name; and indeed, these things may have been so, but I didn't wait around to see. I broke into a run the moment his spectre showed itself, and as I hadn't run or even walked anywhere much for several months my legs almost gave way, at which point I darted into the nearest alleyway and forced them to propel me over a medium-sized wall. There was a little park on the other side, with trees, and I went and stood behind one that was wider than I until I was quite sure the coast was clear. Omar would have been exceptionally proud of me. In fact, he was, when I told him about it later.

"I knew you'd come to your senses eventually," he said, stretching out one arm across the table and placing his hand, or paw, if you like, on my arm, something he does only when he is particularly pleased with me.

"Well," I said, "it was just instinct."

"Just instinct!" said Omar, drawing up his top lip so that his long incisors were exposed, making him look like a feline vampire, "and what else is there, after all?"

"Oh, you know," I replied, "memory and desire, faith and hope. Elizabeth Barrett Browning. If I had stopped to think, I would have probably run towards him."

"And eventually," said Omar, "you too would have ended up looking like a half-decayed wolverine or that mad woman from the animal shelter. And, in the end, there would have been the plastic container."

"There will be, anyway," I said, "in the end."

"Oh no," said Omar, "if you stay with me, we will be immortal together, as we have always been. . .remember Persia. . .those arabesque nights in the perfumed gardens of the seraglio, o most treasured of all my odalisques?" And he started to purr.

"Omar," I said, "you are such a liar. But that one deserves at least a drop of tinned milk."

"With perhaps a few cornflakes in it?" he asked, idly licking the fat ebony pads of his hands as though the cornflakes were of little consequence. But I knew better.

"Perhaps," I said carelessly, and we grinned at each other across the table.

In the Chambers of the Sea

In our sleep, pain which cannot forget falls drop by drop upon the heart until, in our despair, against our will, comes wisdom through the awful grace of god.

— Aeschylus

The air on the ward is hot and dry, and tastes like sand. Not that I have ever tasted sand, at least not since I was a child in a soft, sandy country, far from here.

In the cruel days of August, when the city became an asphalt oven, my mother and my sister and I would go off to the pretty little beaches, the domestic beaches of my childhood country. We would lie on the backs of their tame dunes and scuff along in the deep bone-white sand that was farthest from the sea, bending now and then to retrieve the half-buried remnants of dead sea babies: solemn little periwinkle cases, tiny bumps of limpet shells, stiff pieces of pink starfish. And bits of mother-of-pearl from the big mussel shells, which my sister and I pretended were solidified mermaid pee.

My favourites were the sand dollars. Every sand dollar, from the largest to the smallest, had a perfect flower etched on it, and I used to imagine that God's Wife spent the long summer days making them in her shop in Heaven. At night She came down and tucked them one by one into the soft brown sand just under the lip of the sea, for me to find. (Like stars, sand dollars make it easy for a child to believe in God: look, there is a pattern, and another, and another. He must Be!)

I took dozens of sand dollars home every summer. But after a few days they would start to rot, and by the end of the week they would have been consigned by my mother to the big aluminum garbage can. This made me bitter, as bitter as a child is able to be; I felt betrayed. I didn't know then that the sand dollars had been alive when I picked them from the sea, and that the flowers of the sea will not, cannot, take root in a suburban backyard.

The air in the hospital burns our eyes and flakes our skin. No one wears their contact lenses any more, and bottles of skin cream are handed around like whiskey at an Irish wake. The air is so dry because they nailed all the windows shut two weeks after I got here, when a young man jumped to his death from one of the other floors. He landed on a ledge outside my room, about a yard or so up from it. It was early in the morning, just before daybreak. Two nurses ran into my room and nearly ripped the blinds down from the window. "Sweet Jesus," said one to the other. "Can you see it?" And then they turned around. I was sitting up, groggy with sleeping-pill sleep, but already aching for a cigarette. "You'll have to get up, my duck," said the red-haired one. "We'll open up the smoking room for you." I asked what was going on, but they wouldn't tell me. I didn't really care anyway; the smoking room was to be opened, and I could sit and look out its east-facing window and watch the sun come up, if it was going to.

While I smoked I leafed through old copies of *Reader's Digest* and waited to be allowed back into my room. ("It Pays to Increase Your Word Power"; in the beginning was the Word and the Word was with God and the Word was God. But what was the Word: Was it *Love*? *Om*? Was it *Good-bye*?)

Early that afternoon they summoned us to a grief therapy session. It was conducted by some nurses and a specialist in grief, a large woman in a suit; her hair was also wearing a suit, and her eyes were buttoned up tight. She introduced herself and then told us that a man, a young man, had "suicided." He had jumped from the seventh floor, she said, and had landed, dying on impact, on the ledge projecting from the west side of our ward ("Western wind, when will thou blow,/The small rain down can rain?/ Christ, if my love were in my arms/And I in my bed again!"). The grief lady talked about the need for us to come to terms with the Terrible Thing. I recited Leigh Hunt's poem "Rondeau" over and over in my head while she talked. "Jenny kissed me when we met," Jenny kissed me, Jenny kissed me.

The grief lady said we should share our thoughts and feelings, and "vent if you need to." We patients are always being encouraged to "vent"; indeed, we are ordered to vent, at least biweekly. This process of venting is as intricate as a minuet: it must be done in front of a group, it must be done one person at a time, it must never contain anger or sarcasm or be directed at another person in the group, and, ideally, it should involve copious amounts of tears. To vent, to cry, to take a sea against an armful of troubles; to vent, perchance to heal; beat, beat, beat against thy cold grey breast, o patient; vomit up the sorrow that nourishes the worm of depression, flush it away with tears, idle tears. Weep, weep, weep; it seems odd to me that the air in here is as dry as it is.

When it was my turn, I said that at least the boy was at peace now, and that perhaps we should think of that and be glad for him. The doctor was waiting for me when I got back to my room. The nurses had told on me: Death was the Enemy here, and I was a traitor. "You should not say such things," said the doctor angrily. "What about his family, and all the people who must suffer now because he has done this thing? And how do you know that he is at peace?" "How do you know he is not," I said. "What *do* you know, actually and really?"

The doctor reminds me of Toad of Toad Hall in *The Wind in the Willows*, only he is not as much fun. He doesn't like me. In the beginning, when he flicked out his thick tongue for my responses to his probing, I kept putting words on it that he couldn't digest. These days, I don't give him anything at all. He has told my husband that I won't listen to him, that I am stubborn. Now that I am eating three times a day, Dr. Toad mostly leaves me to his medical clerk, although he would be happier if I would cry in public, just once. Or even in private, as long as it was reported and noted on my chart.

Once, Dr. Toad's clerk asked me what my pain is like. I told her that I would rather go through childbirth every day than have this pain. But the pain is not in your body, it is in your mind, she said; no, I said, you are wrong, it is in every cell of my body, it bites at every nerve ending, it is immortal and omnipresent and omniscient and omnipotent. That was last month, though, before the pills kicked in. I can live in my body now, if I want to. It's a nice, safe, dead shell.

We heard later that the boy who jumped would have died within a day or two anyway. He was too young and impatient to wait, I guess, so he made the great leap into the arms of the Dark Angel. I imagined It carrying him out of his defeated body, up, up through the autumn fog, past the gulls that look like the silvery ghosts of birds and cry like ghosts, too; they sound so plaintive and eerie and anguished, although I can't hear them any more since they nailed the windows shut. But where did Death take him, I wonder. Somewhere? Anywhere? Nowhere?

There is a girl in here who sounds like a gull sometimes; she is fifteen, and she is here because she took a lot of LSD all at once. Last night I heard her keening in her room, like a gull with a broken wing. It made my stomach churn, but it is no good going in to her, because she doesn't know you are there when she is like that. One afternoon in the smoking room I saw her get up and claw at the air. She went up on her toes like a dancer *en pointe*—was jerked up, almost—and her head fell back, and she made a terrible noise in her throat. One of the other patients went for the nurse, and two of them came and led her away. She is never left alone, not even when she uses the bathroom. Her name is Deirdre, and she is elegantly slim and strong like a dancer, and shy and rude by turns, like most fifteen-year-olds. Unlike most fifteen-year-olds, she wants to die.

They tell me that I am here because I said to my husband, quite calmly, that I intended to commit suicide. I don't remember saying that, but he wouldn't make it up. He has never made anything up in his life.

Before my husband could get me to the hospital he had to coax me out from under our dining room table. Apparently I had been sitting under it for an entire night and day, propped up against one of the four great carved mahogany legs, rocking myself and moaning. I hadn't eaten for five days, my husband said, although I don't remember. I don't remember, I just don't remember; I remember the things I should not remember, and I leave unremembered the things I should remember. And there is no health in me.

I read Deirdre's palm the other night. It was difficult, because no one is allowed to touch her except her mother. Deirdre's mother reminds me of our old arthritic Lab, Mickey. Like him, she is short and dark and round and worn at the edges, and moves stiffly. Her anxious dog's eyes watch her daughter the same way Mickey used to watch my husband and me when we went where he could no longer follow, such as into the North Atlantic at Salmon Cove. ("It's okay, Mickey," we would yell above the noise of the breakers, but he never believed us.) Deirdre's mother is waiting for her daughter to return from the sea of madness, waiting for the waves to throw up her real daughter, all bright and shining like Aphrodite on her shell in Botticelli's painting. But the nurses whisper and shake their heads when Deirdre passes, a bad augury.

The other night Deirdre's mother got Deirdre to hold her right hand out so I could divine her future; it moved slightly back and forth in the dim, aquatic light of the smoking room like a frond of the ferny seaweed you find in tide pools, and it was hard to make out the lines. She is so young, after all; even the major lines—the heart, the head, the line of life—are faint at her age, and Deirdre has fine skin. I never read my daughter's palm. I thought it would be too soon; her hands were only the size of sand dollars.

Deirdre's head line indicates that she may stay mad. But at least Deirdre's mother will always be able to touch her daughter's soft brown hair and hold her long, thin hand, and breathe in her essence. I do not pity her.

My closest friends in here are Mary and Lenora. Love is everything to Lenora; she must have it washing over her like a wave constantly; it is air to her, the gills of her heart are drying up for lack of it. I feel as though I am in the presence of a beached dolphin when I am with Lenora. I run my fingers over her back like rain until they ache, and then I let her lie in my arms and I try to brush some life into the brittle strands of her bleached-out hair. No one ever comes to see Lenora except her son, and he looks like he just stepped out of the shower when he leaves; she soaks him with her tears.

Mary is tiny and wiry and somewhere around seventy, I think. I won't ask her how old she is because she takes great pains never to be seen without lipstick on, although it looks queer in her old oyster-shell face. She is the only person I remember clearly during my first week here, except for my husband and one of the night nurses. Mary sat with me a lot, without talking or expecting me to talk. Most people don't know how to do that.

Before he left me that first night, my husband took off the T-shirt he had on under his sweater, and put it on me as a life jacket against the torrent of pain that was drawing me under. I went to sleep with his smell in my nostrils, a sweet, strong, acrid smell, a smell more intimate than my own smell. I love my husband, even though we are chalk and cheese. Because we are chalk and cheese.

Mary lost her husband last year. For forty years, she and Frank never spent a day apart, she told me. They were a lot alike, she said, and from the way she talks about him I can tell that they swam through life together perfectly synchronized until he died. Her children are still close by, but all of them work, including the girls, and they live in small houses; none of them have enough time, or room, for their mother. But they are all good children, Mary says, and think the world of her, especially Francine, the youngest. That's just the way it is nowadays, Mary says; they've got to think of their youngsters first, after all.

When Frank died, Mary moved into a senior citizens' complex. Although she had her own apartment, they wouldn't let her have a dog, or even a cat, and if her children or grandchildren came to visit they had to leave by midnight: there was a strict rule against overnight visitors. One day Mary fell and broke her shoulder. When she got back from the hospital she found it hard to cook and clean, and she ended up in the hospital again, this time on the psychiatric ward. "I don't know what I'm doing here," Mary said to me. "They says I told Francine I was going to do away with myself, but I can't remember saying it. Anyway, if I did, she should have had the sense to keep it to herself."

The nurse who put me to bed the first night I was here was a man. I had never had a male nurse before, but then I'd only been in the hospital twice in my life, at sixteen to have my tonsils out and at thirty-one to have a baby out. I read a lot of Sylvia Plath when I was pregnant with my daughter, because you can read her when you are happy. When they put sweet, bloody blue and red Jenny on my stomach right after she was born, I thought of the opening line of "Morning Song," of my child beginning her journey through time like a watch starting to tick, a watch that love had wound up. Now I only consider the last line of that poem, the breathing of a sleeping child like the sound of the sea. And I hear another sea, one that roars like a hungry Cyclops. A sea that has silenced my daughter's nighttime breathing forever, a sea that swallowed that small dreamer's flawless face and turned it into a half-digested piece of itself. Sylvia Plath committed suicide when her babies were half Jenny's age, a sea of sorrow taking her down so fast that even their tiny arms around her legs couldn't hold her. I used to feel sad for her, but now I envy her—at least her suicide preserved the natural order: that parents should die before their children. Die, dying, death, dead—what is the use of life, anyway, life with its dirty little secret, standing there in a respectable suit leering at little girls while their mother's backs are turned.

When I first looked into Jenny's eyes, I was startled, then awed; I saw an ancient one looking out at me, the oldest thing I have ever seen. Later, after she had been washed off and swaddled, her eyes had the unfocused gaze associated with infants. My sister is a doctor, so I asked her about it. "Yeah," she said, "I know what you mean. They look right at you, and their eyes are like that creature's in *Star Wars*—Yoda, right?"

The male nurse was very kind; he was short and stout and had a guppy's mouth and friendly eyes. He asked me a lot of questions, but I only remember one of them, which was whether I was having my period. I didn't answer right away. "I have to ask," he said, apologetically. "We've had cases where the nurses checked a female patient at night and they noticed some blood on the sheets, and they assumed it was menstrual blood, when in actual fact the patient had cut their wrists." No, I said, I wasn't on my period, but all of a sudden I felt like screaming at him. Screaming what's wrong with you, surely to God you must know the difference between the blood of the womb and the blood of the heart, between strong, thick, sullen menstrual blood with its sea smell and fresh, thin, bright arterial blood spraying from a shocked heart. But I didn't say anything; what did it matter?

Two years ago, my mother died of breast cancer at seventy-seven. Last year, my seven-year-old daughter drowned. Seven, seven, seven, seventy times seven, unto the seventh generation. Sometimes I think God is math and math is God.

My husband teaches math and physics at a high school. I learned about Fibonacci's numbers from him, and about atoms and quarks. *Quark* really rhymes with *lark*, or *snark*, although most people give it the sound of *quartz*. (We used to call our daughter the Boojum, from Lewis Carroll's poem "The Hunting of the Snark.") Besides *The Norton Anthology*, I am reading Stephen Hawking's *A Brief History of Time*. The physicists now say that the smallest element in the universe is the superstring. If you could blow up an atom to be the size of the universe, one superstring would be the size of a tree. Superstrings loop around the eleven dimensions of the universe, holding it together like a cat's cradle. I wonder, Who is holding the cat's cradle? Someone? Everyone? No One?

They don't care what I read in here, because, besides Stephen Hawking, I read only poetry and fiction. Poetry can't hurt you because it is not true. They like to see me read; to them, it means that I am getting better. I couldn't read at all when I first came in, or for months before: the words hurt like knives, they were all so sharp, even, especially, *love, child, sea.*

My daughter Jenny died on a hot day in August. Jenny never liked August; every August within her child's memory (three of them, in fact) one of the family cats had been killed. I never saw this as synchronistic myself, only coincidental. We had always had too many cats, up to five at one time. The vet said to keep them indoors; I could not keep them indoors, especially the older ones. What would their lives have been? August is the first harvest month. My daughter was harvested in August by the Grim Reaper.

We were at our summer place in Salmon Cove when Jenny drowned. Salmon Cove gets its name from the salmon river that runs through its middle. Jenny used to swim in the part of the river that is by the beach; the water there is only up to her shoulders. Was up to her shoulders. Her little brown shoulders; her little brown face with its blue eyes like two flames. What I want to know is how do you like your blue-eyed girl, Mister Death.

In August, the water in the river is almost like bath water. Jenny was a good swimmer, a natural swimmer, a baby porpoise. Even so, we never let her out of our sight when we were by the water. But she got up early that morning, and went off by herself with old Mickey while her father and I were still sleeping. She had never done that before. And she must have gone to wade in the sea, and she waded out too far, and the undertow got her. The Under Toad. What I want to know is how did you like your blue-eyed girl, Mister Under Toad.

We waited and waited for Jenny to come back. The physicists are right about time; it is relative. I have been here for two months, but it has not been anywhere near as long as the two weeks we waited for Jenny. One of the women here, Cass, told me about a vision she had in which she saw, among other things (for instance, the Face of the Saviour), what a human life is. Cass says it is like an atom in God's body, and each of our lives is less than a second long in God's time. (Cass scares me; but then, poor Cass scares herself.)

They finally found Jenny's body out by the Terrified Rocks. The Terrified Rocks are about ten yards off the beach at Salmon Cove. There are three of them, three megaliths with coarse grass growing on top in which the terns make their nests; they look like Easter Island statues with toupees. Jenny must have been taken way out at first, and then somehow she found her way back to the Cove, like the salmon that swim up its river in the spring. My husband didn't want me to go with him to identify the body, but I went anyway. I had to know. I thought she would be blue and bloated, but this is not the case with bodies that have been in the sea. If she had drowned in fresh water, the pathologist said, she would have swollen up, but salt water has an affinity with our own fluids; there is an osmotic effect. My daughter had suffered a sea change, but her eyes were not coral: she had no eyes. For a long time after, I thought of them lying like twin sapphires on the bottom of the ocean. Later, I learned about the sea lice. (Sometimes, I wish the Under Toad had kept her.)

Last night I fell asleep in the moonlight. The blinds in my room open even if the windows do not, and the moonlight was right on my pillow at bedtime. The moon was close to full last night; I think they call that a gibbous moon. *Gibbous* is such an ugly word; it has always sounded to me like *gibbet*, and I think of white dead bodies hanging in the moonlight with heads like rotten melons. Or how Jenny might have looked if she had drowned in the river instead of the sea.

I dreamt that Jenny and I were riding bicycles on the dirt road that used to run by my grandmother's house in the country I grew up in. My mother was waving to us from the veranda; she was in her early forties, dark and pretty, around the age she had been when I was Jenny's age. My mother married late because all the healthy young men were away at war when she was young. Jenny and I were going to the little store over the hill from my grandmother's to buy ice cream, but when we got there we decided to get candy hearts for my mother instead. Mine was large and mauve and made of gelatin; Jenny's was smaller, harder, and bright crimson.

When we got back to the place where my grandmother's house should have been, there was a steep hill with a huge bronze lion at the top there instead. "Let's go see," said Jenny, and she and I climbed the hill and sat on the lion's paws. I looked back down; we were high, high up and it had become night all of a sudden, and I was afraid. I have always been terrified of heights, and somewhat afraid of the dark. "What if we fall?" I said to Jenny, and I lay down on my stomach along the length of the cold legs of the great lion, shivering. "We can't," she said, laughing. "Let's go sit on his back." So we climbed up over the lion's face, up over its curly brazen mane and onto its back. We sat down together, and I held on to Jenny from behind, and I buried my face in her child's neck, fragrant as sweet grass.

When I looked up again, I saw the biggest church I had ever seen, bigger than the biggest football stadium; its spire touched the moon. It reminded me of our Anglican Cathedral, although it was not Neo-Gothic, or any recognizable type of church architecture (it could have been all of them combined, or none of them.) The church was made of some kind of iridescent stone, like labradorite. The sight of it filled me with dread and longing. There was a light around its vast doorframe, and I knew that if I were to go in, there would be some sort of celebration going on. And then I heard the sound of galloping hooves, and I looked up. A herd of wild horses was coming towards Jenny and me; they were small but shaggy and fierce-looking; there were hundreds of them, yet they moved as one. Jenny pulled away from me, and got up and ran towards them. They were only yards from us by then, and I saw that they were quite mad—they were rearing up like huge breakers about to dash against rocks; their eyes were rolling, showing the whites, and huge flecks of sweat, like sea foam, flew from their streaming flanks. I screamed at her: "Jenny, come back—they'll kill you!" "No they won't," she said, turning around and looking at me with Yoda's eyes. "They can only hurt you if you *think* they can." And then the lion turned his big bronze head around, and he was laughing, and I started to laugh, too, and the lion switched his tail gently against my daughter's legs, propelling her into the midst of the horses, and I heard her shriek with pleasure, and then she was gone. And I woke up.

Moonlight was in my eyes and it was all glowing and liquid like moonlight dancing on the sea; it was the whale's path, the swan's road, and in its silver wash phosphorescent sparkles shimmered all blue and gold; it was alive and full of itself. Somehow it seemed to me that I had always known that that was how moonlight really was, not pale and thin and sad, not just the sunlight's ghost, but thick and rich and molten, a live and joyful thing in itself. And I lay there and let it wash over my face—it felt so good, I felt it go right through my skin, right down into my heart—and I heard voices in the distance, the voices of men and women and children, voices rising and falling in a light, happy cadence, and I thought that perhaps my husband had been unable to sleep, and had gone into the den to watch television. And then a bright light shone suddenly in my eyes; it was the night nurse's flashlight, and she was asking me why I was awake, and if I needed something to help me sleep. I looked away from her concerned face, and up: the moon was a speck in the top left-hand corner of the window, high and far and tiny; it had gone from my pillow hours ago.

And then a line came to me from the Bible, I think, or maybe a hymn, or perhaps the Anglican liturgy: "And the sea shall give up its dead." And suddenly I knew. The sea had already given up its dead; rather, it had never had them in the first place, only for the briefest of moments before each sparkling soul shot Heavenward. The sea had held my daughter in its salty womb for less than one millionth of a second in God's time, and then she had been born into All That Is and Ever Has Been. The mottled and eaten thing that they had said was my daughter *never was* my daughter. I started to cry then; satisfied, the nurse went to get me a pill. But I didn't take it.

This morning the sun has managed to poke a couple of skinny yellow digits through the slats of the blinds; it is stroking the pewter frame of Jenny's school picture. Mary was by earlier. She is going home next week, home to Francine's house. Apparently Francine found a bit of space somewhere for her little mother to curl up in. Mary will have to keep taking antidepressants, though, and she's not too thrilled about that, being someone who would rather suffer a headache than take a pill. But that's the way it has to be, says Mary.

On Radio One, Sass Jordan is singing about time and rivers and how all you want to do is hold her, but what you try to grab evades your touch, her voice twining around the sun's fingers like rings of lapis lazuli. In her Grade 2 picture, Jenny is smiling.

I have a feeling I may be going home soon.

Justine

Now when I go to my bed of slumber
The thoughts of my true love roll in my mind
But when I turn around to embrace my darling
It is not gold, but brass I find.

— "As I Roved Out" (traditional)

In her thirty-seventh year, Justine looked over her life and saw that everything she loved or had ever loved was missing from the landscape, or lay in ruins upon it. In front of her, the plain of life rolled on flat and naked to the rim of the world; dark mountains stood like half-parentheses along the edge. Beyond those mountains were her dead parents, and the children she had never borne. And her oldest friend, Rachel, who had died of an obscure Eastern disease when she had gone to India to seek the meaning of existence. Justine hoped Rachel had found the embrace of some god she could understand before her little life flew away in the cumin-scented air; Hare Krishna, Rachel, Hare Rama, did your heart look for me at all in the end?

On the moonscape of Justine's life was also the last man she had loved; an angel with a flaming sword barred Justine's way to him. The angel was a cherub, a baby boy. Her lover's son. Two months after he left Justine, her lover had married the woman who was carrying his child. Justine had seen her once when they had been having drinks in the bar where the woman waited tables. She was a small, nondescript creature who carried herself like one who knew she wasn't worth much, a little goblin woman who had looked at Justine's lover with greedy eyes: "Let me in—let me in!" Justine had sat as far back in her chair as she could, shaking her long brown hair over her face, trying to shield the woman—*beware, beware! weave a circle round me thrice, for I have fed on honeydew and drunk the milk of paradise*—for Justine could not bear to see another destitute when she was overflowing with love, thick with its myrrh, gleaming like Danaë after Zeus fell upon her in a shower of gold.

Later, after she had heard about the child and her lover's marriage, Justine remembered something he had once said to his mother when she had been present. "It is best," he had said, "to go with a woman who has low self-esteem. You can make them do what you want, and they'll never leave you." The sister of Justine's former lover has told Justine that his wife is over the moon with happiness. And drunk on the elixir of possession. "If he stops to talk to anyone on the street," his sister said, "she wraps herself around him like a python." "Does he love her?" Justine had asked. The sister had shrugged. "He loves the baby. He takes it with him every-where, strapped to his body, he never uses the carriage. And he is happy to have a free roof over his head." The woman's parents had bought the couple a house, a cradle for their first grandson, a strong stone crib webbed with ivy, laced up tight against changelings, and the ghosts of departed lovers.

When Justine thinks about what her lover said that day in his mother's living room, she is amazed that neither woman had reacted with angry words. But they had only laughed at him as if he was a small child saying an outrageous thing, an impotent little boy kneeling by his mother's hearth trying to coax a dead fire into blooming while the two women sat drinking coffee and gossiping behind his back.

After he left her, Justine had lain still in her life for a long time. When she finally arose and shook off the shroud of memory and desire, she thought she might lie back down and wait for death, she was so frozen and impenetrable underneath it, like a stone on a winter beach. But she knew she was too young, and that death was not likely to come for her, death who preferred carrion more often than not, and Justine was not that yet. Even though she sometimes woke up at three in the morning and thought she could smell her heart rotting in its cave of bone.

Justine's last lover had been the only one who hadn't plundered her openly. Most of her lovers had dug deep into her and taken what they admired—to fill up the holes in themselves with, complaining when they turned up some quality that was of no value to them. They came to Justine as penitents, saying you are so lush, Justine, so rich, so full of love, may we rest awhile? And Justine would unlock her gates and let them in to lie down upon her cool pastures and drink from her still waters. But ultimately, swollen with Justine's largesse, mostly given but sometimes pilfered, they would try to steal the bright ember that burned at her heart's core. And then beautiful Justine, sweet Justine, generous Justine would rise up with the face of an enraged harpy, and she would lift the beggar-thief in her claws and drop him so far from her memory that he could never get back.

"I don't know why they do that," Justine said to her friend Grace once. "It's like killing the golden goose, isn't it?"

"More like killing the silly goose," Grace had replied. Grace had been divorced for over twenty years, but she was still grateful. So grateful, in fact, that she had gone to her ex-husband's funeral in Toronto five years ago, even though she couldn't really afford it. When she got back, she said to

Justine, "I threw a rose into the grave, just to keep my sons happy—after all, they had only been reconciled with their father for such a short while—but I was wishing it had been a hand grenade all the same."

Justine had given the keys of her kingdom to her last lover so that he might come and go as he pleased, for he had moved lightly and asked for nothing, other than to be kept. He was a writer, but his art could not sustain him, and he had no other way of earning a living that would keep him and his dignity both. But his love had been such balm to Justine that she was grateful to be able to give him food and clothing and the shelter of her loft. Her work flourished, and her health; she became impervious to colds and other seasonal maladies; indeed, she had felt that she could walk the streets of a plague-stricken city with impunity, that the legions of deadly microbes in command of the air would part for her like the Red Sea.

Yet she had never felt quite sure of him. There had been something in his depths that had made her uneasy; a vortex, a counter-tide to the easy flow of his love, an agitation of the heart she could neither mark nor measure. Sometimes when he came to her studio after she had been there all day and half into the night, Justine saw a thing in his face when she opened the door to let in his long soft light, a thing that distorted his features, an imp grimacing at her from behind his tranquil eyes. But the thing fled so swiftly when she turned her face full into his that she could never be sure it had not been engendered in a dark place of her own.

The thing had also been there whenever she came home after a night out with her friends, or when her work had been praised in the newspapers. But he was so good, so gentle and loving and kind, that she would not let herself think about this other face. To look upon the face of love at all is to court disaster, and Justine had no desire to end up like Psyche, undone and alone in Hades, for the sake of a vague disquietude.

Grace took a more prosaic view of the situation. "Justine, not only should you look a gift horse in the mouth, but you should also lift its tail and take a bloody good look at its arse. This one sounds as if they left the balls off."

Once Justine had said to him, "Please don't take this the wrong way, but being with you is as good as being alone. It's like being alone magnified and glorified and quadrupled." Her lover had smiled and said that he took it as a great compliment; after all, she was so perfect that she didn't need anyone else to complete her, and he was glad that she didn't find him intrusive.

"You are so much better than I am," he said. "I don't know why you want me."

"Because you are prana," she had replied, "prana and manna, life's great warm blossoming breath and spirit made flesh, to comfort and succor me in the wilderness of being."

Not long after this conversation, he left her. It had been an ordinary afternoon; they were having a picnic on the rocky beach where he had asked her to make love on the eve of the solstice the previous year. "We will go into the ocean," he had said, "and lock ourselves together under the face of the moon, so that the goddess will see us and be glad, and allow us to be that way for all time." Justine had said no, she was afraid of drowning; the current in that place was notorious for its capriciousness, a girl and her lover *had* drowned there once: there had been a photograph of the two of them lying by the same sea, naked and dead, a still life of two stilled lives. It hadn't made the newspapers, but because of its aesthetic value it had circulated through Justine's social microcosm. The picture had been Pre-Raphaelite in its sub-

ject and composition, the girl's hair spread out on the black
rocks around her head as though it were floating on a midnight sea, her white perfect face the face of a dead mermaid
or a face in a negative, the eyes open wide, staring up at the
treacherous moon. The boy lay on top of the girl, his head
nestled into her shoulder, his eyes closed, dreaming. He has
killed her, Justine thought when she saw the picture, killed
her with the weight of his body and his love.

"You don't need me," Justine's lover had said suddenly as
they stood side by side watching the birds called kittiwakes
spin around one another over the net of the sea. "You don't
need anyone." And then he had picked up an empty wine bottle and thrown it into the water. Wait, Justine, had wanted to
say, wait—let me put something in it, let me scratch a rune on
a bit of shell. Because she could not bear to think of the bottle travelling all the way to Ireland, and someone finding it and
throwing it away again because the lovely blue glass held only
emptiness. But she had said nothing; she had stood silently
watching the bottle recede on an indifferent tide, knowing that
in a little while only the vain sun would know where it was, one
more hologram of itself on a vast sea of stars.

And then Justine had looked at her lover standing at the
edge of the water, and when she did everything around him
flew away until there was nothing on the beach or behind it
or in front of it except him, and he was immense, he filled
up the earth and the sky. And Justine had cried out at the
sight and said, "Yes, yes I do. I need you terribly, I need you
to *live*." And when she said this and knew she meant it, she
wanted to say let us go into the ocean and if we live we live,
and if we don't at least we will be together. But something
as stubborn as stone had stopped her mouth. And so he
had said to her, "But you don't need me to survive. And I

need someone who needs me like air. Real air, not the metaphorical kind."

"You mean you want someone who would *die* without you, someone who would lie down and give up if they couldn't be with you?" A kittiwake cried out when she said this, its cracked voice cleaving her words, splintery and unsound as ancient driftwood.

"Someone who would at least want to die if I went away."

And when Justine looked at her lover for the last time, he had seemed to her like the plant that grew on the peat marshes outside the city, penile-shaped and veined like a heart, filled with treacherous waters in which the fragile insects of the bogs went to their deaths, flickering briefly in the impassive liquid and then going out forever.

———

Justine was a potter. She made ceramic fountains and adorned them with water spirits, mermaids and selkies and dryads and all manner of nymphs from the rivers and oceans of mythology: Justine's Undines, they were called. Justine put ceramic fish and aquatic mammals beside her water devas, so that they would have the illusion of the comfort of flesh, and in each fountain a concealed diffuser caused a mist to rise up and garment the backs of dolphins and the shoulders of Justine's water daughters like living silk.

But Justine was no longer able to make her fountains. The last one sat empty in the corner of the studio; no spirits came to play in the waters of her imagination; there were no waters.

"I know a psychologist you should see," Maria, the potter who shared Justine's studio, said to her one afternoon as

Justine sat watching the clay spin between Maria's thick fingers, envying the ease with which Maria's mind and her hands and the sleek clay schemed; a form was rising up out of their combined energies, a whirling dervish dancing itself into a vase.

"I went to him after Esther, and he saved my life." Esther was Maria's daughter, who had died of leukemia just after her twenty-first birthday. "Like the sun going out at midday," Maria said. "I will never understand it, life packing up and leaving like that when it just got here. But go see Brendan, Justine, he is a good man, a very spiritual person."

Brendan's office had a statue of a Tibetan buddha in one corner; on the walls were paintings done by the same artist. They were technically proficient, and yet they were crude; there was a corruption in them, they were somehow pornographic, even the still life; it seemed to Justine that beneath the shimmering surface of its apple a worm coiled around itself, waiting. A troubled boy has done those Justine thought. But when Brendan came into the room and found her looking at the pictures, he had smiled and said, "Well, what do you think of my small talent?"

"Lie down," said Brendan, and Justine did, on a sea-green couch sprayed with white silk and velveteen cushions. And Brendan sat in his red leather chair and began to talk, telling her how talented and special she was, how she had to open herself up to the world again. "You must," he said, "let the energy of life flow out of you and into the Creation, which will send it back to you purified and renewed." Justine began to weep, and when the tide of her grief ebbed she told Brendan she was sorry, she didn't mean to be so weak: she never cried, not even when death pinched her heart as hard as it could.

"Don't apologize," said Brendan. "It has been scientifically proven that tears take toxins with them when they go. Cry all you like, my dear. You must stop shutting yourself up like an oyster."

"Maybe I'm growing a pearl." The tape deck on the oval table between Justine and Brendan murmured synthetic Celtic music; a wall plug-in hung the air with the scent of artificial vanilla.

"Maybe you are a pearl," Brendan had replied, "a pearl of great price."

"You can't be serious," Justine said, looking into his pale eyes for a speck of deceit or the faint umbra of a lie. But Brendan's eyes had been opaque. And Justine was glad, because he was the healer, the keeper of the knowledge that would make her whole again; she had no wish to peer beyond the veil into the soul of the man he also was.

"I am always serious," said Brendan, his face as inaccessible as that of the buddha in the corner.

"Have you ever lost a patient?" Justine asked him, for the desire to lie down and give up still ran within her like a subterranean stream; it was not as wide and deep as it had been, but she could still hear it, especially at night, and it frightened her.

"Never," said Brendan, "not one of all the hundreds I have treated. I am special, you see, just like you. I was created by the Source of all Being to heal, just as you were made to inspire love and shape clay into beautiful things."

When Justine was leaving, Brendan took her into his arms, and she had wondered if Jesus had ever hugged Mary Magdalene, and she hoped He had, and that it had felt like that.

But on Justine's fourth visit to Brendan, he didn't speak of divine energy or Justine's inner child. Instead, he had looked at her from his crimson chair worked with brass studs, and said, "You know, Justine, you are a very good-looking woman."

"And you are a good-looking man," she had replied politely, but the words were stillborn. A ray of late afternoon sun teased the still life on the wall opposite Justine, making the skin of the apple tremble as though something stirred in its heart.

"My wife and I," Brendan said, "have a working relationship." Justine said nothing; it was good, she supposed, to have a relationship that worked.

"Some of my female clients," said Brendan, "give me presents, you know," and he had picked up an Inuit sculpture from the table that lay between them, a fierce little aboriginal sea goddess with the tail of an arctic char. "Sometimes," said Brendan, stroking the mermaid's soapstone breasts and looking at Justine, "they give me keys to hotel rooms."

"Sometimes," he continued, leaning towards her, the mermaid closed up in one fist so that only a bit of the tail was visible, "they give me chocolate penises."

Justine rose from the couch and went to Brendan's chair. She leaned over him and tossed her head, whipping his face with her long beaded braids. And she had said, spitting the words at him as if they were something foul in her mouth she was anxious to get rid of, "But surely you tell them that you are married, Brendan? And that lying and infidelity are motes in God's eye? That is what you do tell those poor magdalens who come here to be redeemed, isn't it?"

"Of course," Brendan had replied, rubbing the welts on his cheek with a pallid fan of fingers. "Of course I do." And then he had reached up and caressed her shoulder, moving his fingers like someone testing the quality of a peach. "But sometimes, Justine, situations arise when you are special."

———————

"What you really need, Justine," said Grace, "is someone who can give you energy without personalities being involved." Grace was standing on her head against the brick of her living room fireplace with her legs parted, making her look like the letter *y*. On an easel by the bow window there was a painting of an elderly nude, a woman, lying beside an abandoned boat. The boat had decayed through the seasons until its skin had come apart, and it was no more than a weathered grey hull, a whale skeleton, a draughtsman's preliminary sketch. The woman in the painting was the boat's human doppelganger: her ribs echoed its ribs, her sparse pubic hair was like the dried sea moss in the crevices of its bow; her old woman's limbs were as gaunt and crooked as the boat's broken masts. The title of the painting was *Vessels*.

"'Very like a whale,'" Justine had said to Grace about her painted boat; she couldn't think of anything to say about the woman, who distressed her, as she was meant to. "Thank you, Polonius," replied Grace. Justine was always fascinated by the way people's faces looked upside down, especially when their mouths were moving: they reminded her of puppets on Saturday morning children's TV programs.

"I know a woman who can channel energy," Grace said. "She will open your blocked chakras and release all the pain, and then she will set them spinning in their proper fashion." Grace brought her legs together, making herself into a capital *I*, which is what Justine always thought of her as anyway.

When Grace said the words *release* and *pain*, Justine saw a trigger being pulled: the heavy bullets of her despair flew up into the face of the sun, ripping through nothing and falling back down out of the sky hollow and harmless. She sighed. "It sounds wonderful, but will it hurt? And I don't know if I want a stranger to touch me, not even a woman."

"Nadine will not touch you. Her hands will wing in and out of your aura like little doves of peace a few inches above you. And as for hurting, it may, but the pain will be necessary pain. And it will be pure." Grace yawned and turned herself right side up, smooth as a Slinky.

"Pure is good. Pure is the best thing." Justine looked out of Grace's elegant window, its glass half-lidded by a hand-painted shade decorated with apes and peacocks; on the lilac bush in front of the window sat a blue jay, its annular eye reflecting everything, revealing nothing.

———

Nadine lived in a brown Victorian with mustard-coloured gin-gerbread moulding. Above the door a sign said "Sanctuary." There was no bell, so Justine tapped the brazen cat's-head knocker three times. The woman who opened the door reminded Justine of a doorstop her mother had once owned, a wooden mouse in a gingham dress. "Come in," said Nadine, and Justine followed her down a short hall into a dim brown room; in a corner of the room there was a brick fountain with plastic water lilies floating in it. A bee had gotten in through the open window and was clambering over the flowers. In an armchair beside the fountain, a Siamese cat sat watching the bee, its blue eyes darkened by an antediluvian desire.

Along one wall, underneath a poster of three white kittens playing with a ball of toilet tissue, was a table like the ones in doctors' offices, only without stirrups. "Lie down and relax," said Nadine. "This is a safe place, a place of peace." And then Nadine had moved her hands in the air over Justine's body like fluttering birds, just as Grace had said

she would. But they were powerful birds: currents of energy
kneaded Justine like the hands of a Swedish masseuse.

When the session was over, Nadine asked Justine what
she had thought of it.

"It was very soothing, but how long will it last?"

"Not long. It wasn't deep therapy; I was mainly doing a
diagnosis. Your heart chakra is bound tight with violet bands
of sorrow and your brow chakra is obscured by the indigo
clouds of wrong thinking. And your root chakra is covered
with all kinds of old crud."

"Can you fix them?" Justine asked, looking into the little
pool; a dead bee floated beside the faux flowers, making a
shadow on Justine's reflection, a dark dot between her eyebrows. One day Grace had come upstairs to see why Justine
was taking so long in the bathroom and had found her staring into the mirror over the sink. "It's okay, Justine, old
bean," Grace had said, "you're still in there somewhere."

"I can fix your chakras," said Nadine, "but I may have to
touch you; would that be all right?"

"I guess so." The image of Brendan fondling the soapstone goddess rose up and rippled Justine's mind, but she
sent it back down and put a layer of mud over it; *resquiescat
in pace*, she said to herself. And then Nadine had reached out
and taken Justine's hand in hers. And peace had flowed like
a narcotic up Justine's arm, spreading out across the surface
of her body and then sinking beneath the skin and burrowing itself deep into her basal cells.

"I can feel you feeding," Nadine said, "but I don't mind.
I get the same pleasure you get." Justine had smiled at her;
she hadn't been able to speak.

When Justine got home, she slept for four hours on top
of the bed with her clothes on. She dreamt that she was in a

place with white buildings that had triangular greens in between them. An alabaster fountain sang on the central green; a naiad with beaded braids rose up from its waters, attended by otters. Justine's dog, Rajah, was running on one of the greens, Rajah who had died two years ago, old and blind and incontinent and afraid. Justine had lain with him during the night of his death, trying to still his terror, but he didn't seem to know she was there, except perhaps at the end because he had licked her hand. But she had thought it could probably have been anyone's hand, he had just needed to connect with some living thing one last time.

In her dream, though, Rajah was young again, and galloping about like a mad March hare. Justine called out to him and he had looked up and grinned, his tongue hanging out of his mouth like a tired flag. And he had moved over the grass as swiftly as if he were wearing the Seven League Boots of the fairy tale, and when he reached Justine he pounced on her with all the weight of his heart. And then her parents appeared, her mother and father, who had died within a year of each other. They were wearing feathered cloaks, and Justine remembered reading of the excellent monogamy of birds, and she had thought, my parents are wild swans, how lovely, I never knew.

Just before Justine awoke, he had come, the last one, in his brown leather jacket with the ripped right pocket. He put his arms around her, but she had resisted him. "Don't pull away," he said, "you are dying, you need me now." And then he had knelt before her, saying "Take, eat, this is my Body which is given for you." Justine went down on her knees in front of him and they touched palms. And light had come out of their hands, a radiance as soft as the footfalls of a cat.

"It was great," Justine said to Grace the next day. "I fell asleep after I saw Nadine, and I had a dream that was like playing a country and western CD backwards."

"I wasn't aware you could play CDs backwards," Grace said, "but I take it you are speaking metaphorically, as is your wont." Grace was British; she used words like *wont* and *old bean* and *cattle drover*, words Justine was familiar with only from books, and Justine felt like kissing her when she said these words, but Grace was British.

"What I meant about the CD is an old joke. It goes, what happens when you play a country and western CD backwards? The answer is, you get your dog back, your lover back, your truck back, and so on."

"I can't imagine you in a truck." Grace was washing tomatoes under the tap; beneath the stream of water, each fat red sphere ballooned for a moment like a blowfish.

"How can an artist be so literal minded? You know what I mean."

"Paint is a pretty literal medium, Justine. It is wet and sticky and bloody smelly. Anyway, Nadine is releasing your negative energy so that you can restore your inner landscape and make peace with your loss. For there is no loss, really," said Grace the yogi, "it is merely an illusion created by the time-space continuum; nothing is ever lost, particularly love. God cannot afford it. Would you like some tomatoes? They are from the garden in Salmon Cove. I have had to give up on supermarket vegetables; did you know that they are putting the anti-freeze genes of arctic char into tomatoes these days? My god, I said, when I first heard about it, here I am supposed to be a vegetarian, eating a tomato, and I am eating a bloody fish. If a tomato were supposed to be a fish, it would have scales and a tail."

"I know," said Justine. The ghost of Brendan's Inuit mermaid appeared on top of one of Grace's red tomatoes and flicked her tail angrily before she disappeared. "But some things are not what they appear to be."

"Nothing is what it appears to be, actually." Grace handed Justine a paper bag dimpled with the vegetables that some called fruit, the fruit of passion. "That is called *maya*, and even the Buddha had a hard time getting past it."

The next time Justine went to Nadine, Nadine said to her after five minutes, "This is not working." "But it feels nice," said Justine. "Please go on." "I will," said Nadine, "but you must trust me." And then Nadine had held her hands together high above the table as though she had a knife in them, and she brought them down quickly over the place Justine supposed her heart chakra to be. Justine's heart skipped a beat and the muscles in her left arm twitched. One day in a Grade 11 biology lab, the teacher had stuck a pin through the brain of a frog and slit open its chest so that Justine's class could look at the beating heart. The frog's eyes were open and they had seemed to be staring at Justine; she moved over one desk, but the eyes had followed her; she moved again and so did the eyes. And then it came to her that the frog's eyes were like the eyes of Christ in the picture in her grandmother's bedroom, they would follow you no matter where you went unless you got up and ran out the door, and she did, the laughter of the other students loping after her.

"It's no use," said Nadine. "I can't seem to get at you on any deep level."

"I don't want to be got at. I just want peace." Justine
looked at the chair by the fountain; Nadine's cat looked back
at her. A still small voice in Justine's head said, "Go from this
place now," but Justine couldn't think of a polite reason for
leaving. Nadine moved behind Justine and placed her hands
on Justine's hair, and something alien began its slow slither
into the well of Justine's soul; she tried to shout "no, don't,"
but it was like shouting in a dream. And then the thick brown
room fell inwards and covered her all up.

"What did you do, what have you done?" whispered
Justine. She and Nadine were kneeling together beside the
pool; Nadine was rubbing Justine's arms.

"I thought you needed love, so I inserted myself into
your aura," said Nadine. "It's the most intimate thing two
people can experience. I didn't mean to hurt you." Nadine's
voice was sulky, the voice of a rejected lover.

When Justine got home she took off her clothes and got
in the bath, staying there for over an hour because the gleaming faucets at the end of her deep claw-footed tub had held
her hypnotized; there were things in them Justine had no
wish or need to see: dark lacunae in ruined towers; starfish
with broken, bleeding arms; the faces of cruel queens. And
the tipped eyes of the temple cats of Tibet, cobalt pagodas
cutting a jagged line across their pupils.

———————

"Well," said Grace. "I must say I'm rather shocked that
Nadine did that to you. It's against the ethics of her profession, you know. She's not allowed to make the slightest move
into a client's space without permission, much less take a big
bloody psychic leap at you like that. God knows which way

your chakras are rotating now—here, have some ginger jam and toast—that might straighten one or two of them out. Perhaps I ought to take my paintbrush up to her house some night, under cover of darkness, and put another word on that Sanctuary sign. 'Therapist', only I'd leave a space between the *e* and the *r*." Grace grinned at Justine over the lip of a mug that had the Queen's visage on it; a cigarette dangled from the left corner of Elizabeth Regina's lip, and a little cartoon fox sat looking up at Her Majesty with a sad expression on its face. Underneath the fox was a caption that said "This Woman Supports Cruelty to Animals."

"The thing is, Justine, is that all these professionals are only human, after all."

Justine took a bite out of her slice of toast, and then she asked Grace something she had always meant to ask someone sometime. "Why does everyone always say 'only human' when they mean something bad?"

"That is a very good question," said Grace, "and one not even I am able to answer. Look, Justine, I think what you actually could use is a job. Something to get you out of the house. I know a Bosnian immigrant who has a shop downtown, and he is looking for a part-time clerk." Grace made *clerk* rhyme with *dark*, and Justine sent an invisible kiss into Grace's aura, to swirl among all the radiant bits that emanated from Grace even when she was talking about Fuckingham Palace and bloody bourgeois Labour's lost gits who couldn't run a one-stop bus route let alone a bloody country.

"The shop is called The Magic Trunk," said Grace, "and it has all sorts of lovely things in it. You'd feel right at home."

"Home is where the heart is," said Justine. And immediately regretted it.

"If that were actually the case," Grace had replied, "two thirds of the population would be living in a bloody bank vault."

———————

A thin, black-haired man with cheekbones like the prows of galleons is standing behind the counter of the shop called The Magic Trunk. "May I help you, madame?" he says to Justine. Are you a psychiatrist? Justine feels like saying, but she will play it straight because she likes the old dark wood behind the man's head, and the light, or lack of it, that makes her feel as if she is underwater. And whatever it is that has the shop smelling like somewhere Justine has never been but would like to visit sometime. A place where the moon strolled languidly down the corridors of the night, and the sea licked a marble shore.

"Actually, I am here to apply for a job." Before Justine came for the interview, she had taken the beads out of her hair and pulled it into a chignon; she is wearing a long, loose dress from the Oxfam shop and a pair of leather sandals. And she has left her lips and cheeks pale, her face innocent of artifice except that which she might conjure up through the movement of its flesh to the beat of her brain, which seems to be in control of things today. At least enough to manage a simple declaration of her skills for the elucidation of this man who stands so still in the aromatic air, his arms folded across his chest, waiting. Justine smiles at the man and runs her fingers through her hair, dislodging a piece from its prison of pins.

Before she came to The Magic Trunk, Justine had dropped by Grace's flat.

"How do I look?" Justine had twirled around slowly in front of Grace's fireplace, the hem of her dress whispering in the ears of the turquoise tiles ringing the old coal grate. And then she sat down on the arm of the chair that had knees made out of carved pineapples and waited for Grace to tell her that she looked exactly the way a clerk in a shop called The Magic Trunk should look, give or take the dress, the chignon, or the golden brown sandals with fuchsia elephants striding across their straps.

"I have no idea," Grace had replied, putting down a brush that was like the feather of an exotic bird; it was covered in an iridescent green paint Justine would like to give a name to if it didn't already have one. "But I wouldn't mind doing your portrait in that get-up sometime. I'd put a baby in your arms and set you next to a banyan tree, and I would call it *The White Woman's Burden*."

The quiet man behind the counter says, "I see. Have you any experience as a clerk?" His voice is low and dark and his accent menaces Justine; she has heard it many times from the lips of the man in the B movie who has the microfiche in one hand and a heavy black pistol in the other. The man behind the counter gives the word *clerk* two syllables by taking the *k* away from its fellows and making it click its heels.

"I am a potter, and I sell my own work, so I know how to use a register and a credit card machine." Justine is lying about both the register and the credit card machine, but she rationalizes this by telling herself that time is circular, and that soon she will master both these things and, so, in a way, the knowledge is already hers. But her face is hot and she is glad its heightened colour likely can't be detected in this dusky interior. Even by the man with the microfiche.

"And do you like working with the public?"

"I do," says Justine. "They don't stay around long enough to make holes in you." She knows she will never get the job now, but the man only grins; he looks like an animal baring its teeth, but his eyes are mild.

"I am Mirel."

"Justine."

"Come," Mirel says, "I will show you around." Justine follows a pace behind him; her limbs are heavy, particularly her arms, probably from the strain of lying, or being in disguise, or maybe just because she hasn't been wrestling with clay for so long, like a playful lover; she feels as though there might indeed be a baby in her arms, but it is a good baby and she has no trouble carrying it and following in the wake of the man who moves like a fugitive through the cluttered twilight of his shop.

Mirel gestures at row after row of shelves upon which many curious objects sit; silver and inlaid teak, abalone, and brass and painted glass blink at Justine, but she and the man are going too quickly, it is like fleeing through an enchanted wood, nothing has any recognizable form. She wishes he would slow down, she wants to pick something up and allow it to settle into its true shape in her hands. And then she and Mirel come into a clearing; in front of Justine is a wall hung with saris, shimmering along its length like the happy shades of exotic women. The wall has an arched opening dressed with silver and blue tin beads configured like stars and moons.

"What's in there?" says Justine. She thinks of Aladdin's cave; all the treasures of the East that are not on display in the shop must be heaped behind the celestial curtain. Justine has an overwhelming urge to go into the room and kneel down; she will rummage through rubies as big as robin's eggs and goblets sharp with sapphires and emeralds until she finds the bottle with the genie in it. And then she will wish herself away beyond the dark mountains, and hide her face in the twin constellations of Rajah and Rachel while her parents embrace her with outstretched wings, world without end.

"My daughter. She reads the cards in there, the gypsy cards, do you know them? The ones with pictures." Mirel's face opens on the word *daughter*; the prows sink below the waves of his expanded cheeks and little sequins of light bead his eyes.

"The Tarot." Not a genie then, but a witch. Justine starts to move towards the bright beads, but Mirel blocks her way.

"She, Mirella, is blind. A blind seer. Like Tiresias, you know?"

"The Greek guy. But how does she read the cards if she is blind?"

"They have bumps. Would you like her to read for you?"

"I didn't bring any money with me."

"Then it will be a gift. My daughter likes to do the cards for nothing sometimes. She says it is lucky." And then Mirel goes forward and makes a space in the strands of moons and stars wide enough for Justine to go through. As she passes underneath his arm, her head touches the palm of Mirel's hand and Justine has a sudden desire to rub against it like a cat. She blames this on the heavy air of the shop, redolent with harems and houris. But still, she does not like the feel of Mirel receding behind her; she starts to turn around, but a firm hand on the small of her back sends her through the twinkling gateway; on the other side, Justine's destiny waits in cardboard pieces, a puzzle for two blind girls to piece together. But it will be okay; Justine does not really believe in anything anyway, except that somewhere in the Universe, something or someone sentient who loves her always and forever and regardless, is waiting. Plural and familiar, she hopes: the forms of Rachel and Rajah and her parents waver for a moment in her mind's eye and then exit, stage right, followed too quickly by an ache for the sweetness of flesh on living bone, an ache that insists "O! stay and hear, your true love's coming." Hey nonny blarney, Justine tells it, but it throbs on, oblivious to neo-Shakespearean slights.

"Hello, Mirella," says Justine to the girl who turns her head in Justine's direction as she enters the room, which is small but streaming with light from two tall oblong windows. The girl is under twenty, although close to its gates; she has black hair that has stopped just short of her shoulders and broken out into a fringe of red and gold beadwork. Her face is broad, the nose and mouth too small for such an expanse of flesh; her eyes, though, make up for the paucity of her other features, but they are like the eyes of the statue of Mary outside the hospice a block from Justine's house, eyes that see nothing in this world.

Justine sits down on a wooden chair that has wings with gilt pinions painted along its back; across the table from her, Mirella leans back in a rattan swing.

"Your father says you will do my cards. I can't pay right now, but I can bring you the money later." Justine makes an apologetic face, and then remembers that in this room her face is not an instrument of communication.

"No," says the girl. "I do for luck, and for my father." Mirella's voice is the voice of the female spy in the B flick, the girl who will eventually defect because she has fallen in love with the hero. (The hero has a crisp BBC accent; it is obvious from the beginning of the movie that nothing can defeat those consonants, certainly not an enemy whose vowels are as soft as cream cheese.)

"Your father seems like a nice man." The banality of these words appal Justine, who has never been good at small talk. She either makes it too big, upsetting herself and others, or reduces it to a caricature of itself. Someday she will get it right, but not, apparently, today.

But Mirella takes *father* and *nice* out of the limp bouquet Justine has handed her and says, "Oh yes, he very nice, very good man! In Bosnia, he teacher. Here cannot teach, no papers. We have farm, too, many sheeps. My father go with dogs, bring sheeps home from mountains in winter so wolves won't eat." Now Justine and the girl are in Transylvania, rushing through the snowy dark while vampyres leer from behind huge stone cairns and werewolves nip at their cringing heels.

"Your mother, is she here too?" Justine believes this sentence to be about the right size, but Mirella's face suddenly contracts, making her features a perfect fit for the crimped flesh that surrounds them.

"My. . .mother. . .she dead. . .in Bosnia. My *brat*. . .brother. . .also." The girl closes her eyes and bows her head; the biggest tear Justine has ever seen falls out of the oyster of one eye and rolls to her chin, where it hangs suspended, a perfect ovoid of grief. "Oh, I am so sorry," says Justine, and she is, aghast that she has invaded this girl's quiet chamber, strewing blight and misfortune; she reaches out and catches Mirella's tear in a cupped hand before it disappears into the black fringed cloth that covers the table. And then Justine considers getting up and leaving, but when she looks at the beaded curtain it seems to have become a solid mass, impenetrable as steel.

Mirella wipes her eye with a finger tipped with neon blue polish, and then she picks up the deck of oversized cards from the table and shuffles them; on her lips are low words in a foreign tongue; a prayer is being sent to the gypsy gods, whoever they are; Justine hopes they are not tricksters or lunatics or despisers of stupid white women. The girl spreads the cards, face down. "Pick one," she says to Justine. "Is for past." Justine empties her mind and lets her right hand hover over the dragon-backed cards; she drops it when the still small voice says "Now." "Turn," says Mirella, and Justine flips the winged serpent. A fair-haired man is sitting on a crimson throne floating on the ocean. He is staring into the golden chalice he holds in his right hand; his expression is intense and self-absorbed.

"Ah," says Mirella, touching the nubs on the head of the sea serpent lurking behind the water-borne throne, "King of Cups. This man weak. But loving very much, feeling very much. His heart always moving, moving like water under him so he not feel. . . safe. He catch women in cup of love, so not alone, afraid. But he very. . .for self most—sometime women drown. Understand?"

"Only too well." The merman with her lover's face lies flat against the black silk—*look at me*, Justine wills, but he remains lost in his own reflection in the brew of self-love that fills his cup. He will never look at Justine. Or anyone.

"Now I give you future. Not to be afraid, is good, I feel it. Pick, but wait until you *know*."

Justine looks at the cards spread out across the table. She closes her eyes and runs her hands over their laminated backs; she is afraid to stop moving them, she does not want to know the future, she doesn't want a future, she just wants to move away from the heavy globe of herself, move off past the dark mountains where love is still and safe, by some god's willing grace or lazy negligence. And then Justine feels Mirella's fingers touch her temple, so quickly and delicately she thinks she may have imagined it. Justine's hand stops moving. "I pick this one," she says, opening her eyes. She looks at Mirella, whose face is as impassive as Justice, and turns the card over.

A dark-haired man is sitting on an ebony throne. He wears a black tunic hung with golden coins that have no centres. The throne is in a vineyard; it is etched with the heads of rams. In the distance is a castle with coloured pennants flying from its turrets. The man is looking straight at Justine; his face is stern, but there is compassion in it. And something else that Justine can't decipher at first, but then she remembers, because it had been in her father's face. It is character.

"Who is he?"

"King of Coins," says Mirella, running her fingers over the two rams lying at the king's feet. Justine wonders who has painted her nails. Her father, perhaps. Justine likes the thought of Mirel painting Mirella's fingernails; she likes the image of the large hand moving back and forth over the smaller one, the brush in its fingers fluttering like the wings of an anxious bird hovering over its young.

"King of Coins very good man, strong man. Take care of you. Spirit of Earth, good businessman. Stay put, work hard. Make things grow. Even babies, if you want!" Mirella smiles the smile of the blind, which is not for the other but just for themselves; it is the smile of an idiot or a child, or a naked man standing on the edge of a coral reef with a fish twisting on the end of his spear.

When Justine returns to the main part of the shop, Mirel is busy at the cash register. The register is an antique, but apparently still in working order; Justine can hear its old-fashioned bell extolling the bounty that lies in its hold.

"Your daughter told me about your wife and your son. I am sorry." As these words drop ponderously from her mouth, Justine tries to catch them but fails; the movement of Mirel's hands on the tarnished buttons is so fluid and sure, they are the hands of a pianist in some great hall, his slanted face the profile on an ancient frieze—these things have made Justine want to touch him, to enter into the space he occupies: there is something there that is like the sound of the wind when it is still. But instead she has given him a bundle of stiff, possibly dangerous words held out at arm's length; such is the custom of her country. In another country it might be permissible to touch this man, to take his hand in hers and braille her desire along his palm. But in her country words must make the leap across counters and cultures, into the whorled shell of the ear; if the words are good enough, they will eventually find their way into the chamber of the heart that is an exact fit for the way they are shaped. Justine knows that the words she has offered are not fine enough for this; they are words that belong on cheap cards and the tongues of strangers.

"Thank you." Mirel has said these words to many people in many countries, although they have not always had the same form. Grace has told Justine a little about Mirel, how he spent two years moving from country to country in Europe before he was approved for immigration to Canada. Grace did not tell Justine about Mirella or his dead wife and son; perhaps she doesn't know, perhaps no one knows; Justine hopes that her knowing will not cause harm, has not already made a breach in this man's barricade against his loss; if it has, it will not be something he will let her use to pass into his life. It will be an abyss she may never cross.

Mirel turns away from the cash register and looks across the counter at Justine; his brown eyes are full of the grief of the ages and Justine cannot bear it; she moves away from them, letting her own eyes travel the terrain of his face. The thick lines on Mirel's brow and the thin grids beneath his eyes, the faint brush marks on his cheeks are the map of the journey he has made, carrying his child and his pain across the famous countries that Justine knows only from history lessons and novels. Moving and shifting, leaving shreds of memory drifting on the waters of Italian fountains, dropping the words of his language on the roads of Spain, useless words, words worth nothing outside the lines of a small fragment of map. Two years of running from the human wolves who devoured all his hostages to fortune. Except for the one he keeps in the back room of his shop, the damaged but living bough that is all that is left of his careful husbandry. The little blind lamb he has managed to carry to safety.

Justine's eyes fill with tears; the face of the man opposite her dissolves in them and she is glad he has turned his back to her; she hopes that his back is to her; there is only a dark blur where he is standing. She closes her eyes. And suddenly she no longer feels as though Mirel has been interviewing her for a position in his shop; she understands that she and Mirel are two refugees waiting together in a neutral place between two occupied zones. Somewhere, perhaps even in a stark white room high up in this same building, a figure is staring out of a sealed window at a brick wall, deciding what will become of the two who wait below. Let us pass into common territory is Justine's prayer to whatever god cares to hear it. And then a finger wipes the brine from her cheek; it lingers at the corner of her mouth and then stamps her lips firmly. And she is across the border.

Justine opens her eyes. Mirel is reaching into a wicker basket that sits on the counter; his face is still but not empty.

"Here," he says, passing something across the counter to her, "for luck." She takes the small object: it is a brass coin with a square hole in the middle.

"It reminds me," says Justine, "of the coins on Mirella's cards. Except for the missing bit."

"That is why it is lucky. Nothing can be whole that has not been rent. An Irish poet said that. So did a Bosnian one, but no one knows that here."

Justine looks into Mirel's eyes; now there are tiny flames flickering behind the irises, flames from a shrouded source; Justine wants to take the wrapping off; she needs the warmth and light behind it, she must get at it somehow. She breathes deeply and reaches over and touches Mirel's upper arm; it is hard and warm and solid beneath his cotton T-shirt; it is the earth of a fresh country, his biceps are the heads of calves being born into a new world. Mirel doesn't move; he closes his eyes, and somewhere a switch is being turned off or on, something has been released and is coming towards Justine along the veins beneath her hand. And then there is a tinkling sound; it is Mirella moving through the doorway of her sanctuary. Her father takes Justine's hand from his arm, but slowly and gently, as though it is something he would have folded in tissue paper if she had bought it in his shop. And he says, "Can you start on Monday?"

"I can start on Sunday if you like." Justine hates the eagerness in her voice; she looks away casually, at an empty point in space to the left of Mirel. But it is not empty after all. The King of Cups is floating there, gazing into his gilded cup. And Justine is suddenly overcome with the desire to get to her studio: there is a sketch frantic to be let off the tip of her pencil. A merman with a golden chalice in his hand, a triangle-faced sea monster behind him with its mouth splayed open, spiny teeth only millimetres from the bowed head. And an Inuit mermaid watching them from the side of the fountain Justine has begun to create in her newly cascading mind.

"We do not open on Sundays. Even the gods of commerce need a day off. Monday, nine-thirty, okay?" Justine nods. The hair that is loose falls over her eyes, and she is glad, because they are talking too much anyway and she is embarrassed for them.

"Okay."

Mirel walks Justine to the door and opens it for her; behind him, Mirella calls out some words in the Bosnian language, words that must mean good bye. Justine hopes they also mean until we meet again; many foreign words for good-bye have hello tucked somewhere inside them. Justine wishes English had such a word.

Outside The Magic Trunk the sun is high; white cumulus clouds fringe it like the beard of an Old Testament patriarch. When Justine was little, she thought that the sun's rays falling out of the clouds was the light from God's throne. And nothing she has heard or read since she has become an adult has altered this perception: it rises fresh from her child's heart every time she sees the sun shine so. Sometimes Justine imagines her small heart lying like a pink embryo inside the larger one, and she is glad that something has protected it all these years, has kept the toxins from the adult heart from penetrating the membrane that separates them. Such a delicate membrane, thinner than the space between two souls.

Light Years

In memory of Jim Truscott

My name is Jimmy Joe, and I'm from the Cape Shore, if I'm from anywhere at all. The Cape Shore, b'ys, the Cape Shore, that's the place to be. I lived with the McGraths on the Cape Shore until I was eleven. Mrs. McGrath, Mom, she treated me like I was her own flesh and blood. I thought I was a McGrath for the longest time. I even used to sign my name James Joseph McGrath. Sometimes I still do.

Yeah, I'm Jimmy Joe from the Cape Shore, and I'm tough as nails. They'll have to come with a pickaxe to kill me, I'm that tough. You had to be tough in them days. We didn't have any electricity on the Shore back in the fifties; no electricity or running water. B'ys oh b'ys, it was cold them winter mornings, I'll tell you. It was warm in the bed though. We slept three to the bed at the McGraths, me and Brian and Mom's own son, Phonse. Brian was a foster kid too; poor old Brian, he drowned fishing on the Labrador twenty years ago. Left a wife and two youngsters, the baby not even old enough to call him Dad. There's not much chance of drowning fishing these days, is there?

Another thing there wasn't much of down on the Cape Shore was money. The old man worked on the roads once a year, the only time he got money in his hand. But we didn't need much money, because we mostly lived off the land. We was the original hippies, down there on the Cape Shore. I remembers, in the winter, before I went to school in the morning, I had to go and clean out the horse and feed her so's the old man could take her up cutting wood. B'ys oh b'ys, it was cold in old Queen's shed, colder even than outside. And after I finished with Queen, I had to go set rabbit slips. It was some good to get inside the school house after all that, I'll tell you. We had this really nice missus for a teacher; she used to let the dogs come in and sleep by the stove if it was bad out, snowing or freezing rain.

But we had lots to eat on the Cape Shore—fish and moose and rabbit and salt meat, and fresh vegetables out of the garden back of the house. And Mom was some hand at baking—I never tasted nothing in my whole entire life better than her pies—partridgeberry and raspberry and blueberry, and even bakeapple, although I don't know why some people makes such a fuss over bakeapples—they smells like dirty socks to me and don't taste much better. One thing we never seen a lot of on the Cape Shore was fruit, except for berries; no green vegetables neither, unless you counts cabbage and turnip tops. And I never so much as laid eyes on a tomato until I went to Town to live when I was sixteen. I guess that was why we all used to gobble up grass in the spring, just like you see dogs doing sometimes. Bunches of us kids would be out running around and gnawing on handfuls of this sorrel grass. It had red tips, all wrinkly and wavy like wheat. At Christmas, though, we always got apples and oranges in our stockings. And mittens and socks and candy, and sometimes a dime. I loved Christmas. Until I was ten.

That was the year Phonse died. One night in the summer me and him were out jigging conners together and Phonse took a pain in his side. He'd been complaining for a couple of days anyways, but in them days no one paid much attention to youngsters whining; the only attention you were likely to get was a swat from a dishcloth. This was a real hard pain, though; I had to pretty well carry Phonse back to the house. It wasn't far: you could throw a rock from the front steps and hit the water if you were a good enough pitcher.

Anyways, when we got back to the house poor Phonse was carrying on something awful; his face was white as the kitchen sink and all swole up from the pain, and you couldn't hardly see his eyes—they were like two pissholes in the snow. Mom took one look at him and her face turned the same colour as his. "Quick, Pius," she said to the old man, her voice all high and queer like a witch's or something, "go harness the horse and get up to Dr. Morris's." I never saw her so upset before: she was a big, calm woman.

But the old man looked at Phonse laying there on the kitchen floor all white-faced and glassy-eyed and screaming like a pig when its throat's being cut—a terrible sound, like a buzz saw on birch, goes through you something awful— and he said, "No, we got to get the priest." Mom's legs went right out from under her when he said that, and she lay down beside Phonse and screamed along with him. I was some scared, I can tell you. I felt like I was in one of those dreams where you knows you're dreaming but you can't wake up. And then my head got all hot and confused and I couldn't remember where I was, but I managed to get upstairs out of it and crawl into the bed. I couldn't hardly breathe; it was like the old black hag was on my chest try-

ing to choke the life out of me. Brian was still out of doors
somewheres, and I wished he was under the covers with
me, snotty nose and all. I thinks now maybe I loved Brian,
but I never knew it back then.

Love. The first time I ever knew I loved anybody was
the day my daughter was born. She was laying there beside
her mother, and I put down my hand to her and she
grabbed my finger and held on to it like it was the most
important thing in the world. Like I was the most important thing in the world. And I felt something go out of me
like a lightning flash, and it was just like all those drippy
songs said, I loved her so much I would have died for her;
I wanted to die for her or get down on my knees and pray
to her or something, her curled up there like the first baby
that ever was, and she was my baby. But I found out something when she was older: a man might be willing to jump
over the wharf for someone he loves and think nothing of
it, but to stick around and look after them and be straight
all the time is a lot harder thing to do. Heroes got it easy.

The old man was a long time tracking down Father
Daley, two or three hours. And then I heard them come in
through the door, Father Daley talking all loud and bold
like he was in the pulpit and it was Sunday morning. And
then the old man come up over the stairs two at a time, and
he flung open the door to me and Brian and Phonse's
room. "Quick, Jimmy Joe," he said, "you got to get out of
the house. Poor Phonse is dead, my son is dead, oh my
Jesus, he's dead and Father Daley says he's got to bring him
back to life for to hear his last confession and we all got to
go outside." The old man was shaking like a leaf and he
looked about ten years older then when I last seen him. I
felt like I was in the Twilight Zone or something. B'ys oh

b'ys, I wouldn't wish what I felt like that night on my worst enemy, supposin' I had one. But they all loves Jimmy Joe from the Cape Shore, even the Townies, they can't help themselves. And the odd one who don't, well, he'd better keep clear of me, that's all I can say. Cause I'm tough as nails, b'y—you'd need the devil's own pickaxe to make a dent in me.

Me and Mom and the old man went outside and sat at the bottom of the steps, right beside the lilac bush. Sweetest smell in the world, lilac; smells like purple. I don't remember nothing about the rest of that night, only sitting on the steps with Mom and the old man, her and him silent as the grave and me looking up at the stars, trying not to cry. I remembers seeing the Big Dipper hanging over Power's Point. It always was, that time of year, and I was some glad to see it there, where it was supposed to be. When you're looking at the stars, you're looking at the past, you know. Millions of years back into time. That's how long it takes the light to get down here to us. When I was a youngster I used to think the stars were the heavenly host you heard about in church; I thought they was alive and like angels or something. I even thought they could see me, Jimmy Joe McGrath, all the way down in Patrick's Cove, and that they got a kick out of watching me and the b'ys out shagging around in the dark. You thinks some queer things when you're a youngster, don't you? But sometimes I think maybe what you believes back then is closer to the truth than how you looks at things when you're older. Because you're further away now, aren't you, further away in time from from the light of all them stars than when you first started out.

I know a wino who walks out to the seven stars of the
Big Dipper. His name is Mikey, and he must be pushing
eighty but he's still walking the streets as pert as a pigeon.
He's always done up like he's going to a Rememberance Day
service or something—shirt, tie, beret, shiny shoes, the
works. People call him the polite wino because he always
says to whoever he's hitting up, "Excuse me, sir, I'm a bit
short this week. My sick pay's late, and I was wondering if
you could help me out with the price of a cup of coffee."
Mikey reminds me of Wimpy in Popeye; you know, the guy
who says "I'll gladly pay you Tuesday for a hamburger
today."

The last time I was talking to Mikey was when he told me
about walking out to the Big Dipper. "It's as far as you can
go from here," he said, "and you walks out on a sort of silver glow." Mikey says that there is no leader, no God, that a
man's own thoughts is all there is. He told me once he met
the guy that came here as Jesus.

"You know what he said to me, Jimmy Joe?"

"I got no idea, Mikey," I said.

"He said, 'I'm never doing that again.'"

I cracked up, right there in front of Tim Horton's. "No,
Mikey," I said, "I just bet he isn't." Sometimes Mikey takes to
standing in the middle of the road cursing and swearing and
disrupting traffic, and then they hauls him off to the Mental for
a while.

Poor old Phonse. I knows now it was probably appen-
dicitis, but we were ignorant as fleas back then on the Cape
Shore. I seen Phonse by the door to our room the night
after he died, and nearly every night for a couple of weeks
after that. He'd just stand there for a minute or so, looking
kind of confused, like he wanted to climb in bed with me

and Brian but couldn't figure out how to do it. And then he'd just fade off, like fog on the water when the sun comes up.

After Phonse died, Mom got paranoid about me and Brian. She wouldn't even let us go down by the water, in case we drowned or cut ourselves or broke our legs, or something. That was real bad; b'ys oh b'ys, if you couldn't go down by the water, what was the use of being alive on the Cape Shore? Mom took to her bed in the fall and wouldn't get up for nobody, so the old man had to get Aunt Rose Dunne to come in and cook and clean for us. I used to go up to see Mom a fair bit; she liked having me come up to her. She used to pet me like a cat and say I had hair as black as a raven's wing.

One day when I was up trying to make her laugh, telling her about Uncle John O'Leary getting drunk the week before and standing up on the roof of his shed making a speech about effin' politicians to a bunch of us kids and his wife, who was bawling at him to get down out of it and stop making a goddam arse of himself, she got out of the bed and said, "Lift up the mattress, Jimmy Joe." So I did; underneath was all this money. It was from the old man working on the roads, Mom said. I never seen so much money all at once before or since, except the time I sold dope in Toronto. I knows now it was probably mostly ones and twos, but, b'ys oh b'ys, it looked like Scrooge McDuck's stash, all that money in the bank vault he used to roll around in. Mom gave me a two-dollar bill out of it because it was my birthday the next week. She always remembered my birthday even though we never had parties or nothing.

That two-dollar bill, though, well, it would be like someone passing you a twenty these days. I got Brian and we went down to the store and bought all the drinks and buns and candy we could carry, and the word got around about me and Brian buying up everything in Power's store—when we come out, there was about ten of the b'ys waiting for us. And we all went up the road, with me and Brian out in front like two kings, and we ate and drank ourselves sick up in the woods behind Uncle Joe Kennedy's. It was the best birthday I ever had.

That November they took Mom to St. John's, to the hospital. I wasn't around when she went, but I knew when I came in the house she was gone, I could feel it. That was the Christmas I found out there was no Santa Claus. Not how most kids finds out; you know, their Mom or Dad tells them or they hears it at school, but it's not so bad because they still get presents and everything. But when me and Brian went down over the stairs Christmas morning the year Phonse died and Mom went away, taking the stairs two at a time like we always did, pushing and shoving each other—it's a wonder we never broke our necks because there was no carpet or nothing on them stairs and they were as slippery as a gutting table—our stockings were as flat as pancakes; we could see 'em laying limp over the clothesline by the stove before we were even halfways down. I couldn't believe it. The old man never said nothing to us when he got up, and we never said nothing to him. The old bastard; dead to the world on Christmas Eve on all that money, and me and Brian laying awake for the longest time, listening for the reindeer to pitch on the roof.

One day in the winter the old man said that Aunt Rose Dunne and him were going to visit Mom into Town, and did I want to go. I'd never been to Town, even though it was only eighty miles away. Aunt Rose Dunne's husband had an old Chevy, and me and Aunt Rose and her husband and the old man got into it and took the Shore road to Town. Dirt road it was, and dirty to drive; worse in the winter with the frozen ruts, and the wind coming off the ocean and shaking that old car like she was a cardboard box on wheels. It seemed like it took us all day to get there. To the Mental. That's where they'd put Mom. In the Mental, like she was crazy or something. I can tell you one thing, take someone who's all broke up about something away from their home and family and put them somewheres like that, and they will go cracked sooner or later.

An orderly took us up to her room, and I thought he must have made a mistake. This poor skinny woman was laying on the bed with no blankets on her, making awful sounds and jerking around like a connor on the end of a jigger. A couple of nurses had ahold to her and one was trying to stick a needle into her. And the room smelled something awful. I looked at the walls and there was this brown stuff all over them. It turned out that Mom had been rubbing the walls with her shit when the nurse went in to tell her we were coming. So we had to leave until they got everything cleaned up.

The old man never did go back in, only me and Aunt Rose Dunne. Mom was laying there all quiet and the room smelled like Javex. When I went over to her she looked straight at me and said "Who are you?" I said, "It's Jimmy Joe, Mom, it's your son Jimmy Joe," and she said, "Jimmy Joe, Jimmy Joe, I never had no Jimmy Joe. I had Phonse, but he's dead, he's dead," and she started to cry, all low and soft. I started to cry too, but it came out of me like a police siren. Like someone else was making the noise. "Shh," Mom said, "get into the bed with me," and I did, and she petted my head and said my hair was like a raven's wing. And then we both fell asleep.

Aunt Rose Dunne woke me up later, and we went down and got in the car. Her husband and the old man were already in it; the Chevy smelled like a brewery. No one said a word all the way back to the Shore. It was dark by the time we got halfways there, and I remember Hank Williams was on the car radio singing "I'm so lonesome I could cry." I was in the rear with my head laid back along the seat, looking out the window. It was a clear night and all the stars were out, glittering on the snow. And I wished I could flick a switch and make them disappear.

I never seen Mom again after that. A while after, I asked Aunt Rose Dunne why Mom said she never had me, and she told me I come as a foster baby to the McGraths when I was six months old. My name was really Jimmy Joe Flight, she said, and I was born in Town, but everyone belonging to me was dead so they sent me down to the Cape Shore to the McGraths. I asked her if I could go somewheres else to live, and she talked to the old man. By the fall I was with another foster family up to Salmon Cove.

I don't know why I done that, left Patrick's Cove and Brian and Aunt Rose Dunne and Queen and the b'ys and Power's store and the school with the nice missus who let the dogs come in and flop around the stove. Sometimes I wonders what would have become of me if I'd stayed put. But then I thinks it's all laid out anyways, just like the patterns the stars make, laid out long before you ever comes down here, and there's nothing you can do about it except have a draw and a laugh. Other times, though, I wonders

when I goes out of the house if maybe it makes a difference if I turns right or left, what'll happen to me the rest
of the day. Generally, I tries not to think too much. It's not
good for you—the next time you're reading the paper, just
look down at the face of your dog and then take a look at
the face of some man on the front page, some poor arsehole who's trying to run the country or something. B'ys oh
b'ys, your brain will kill you if you lets it.

All I got to say about Salmon Cove and the Ryans is
that I hope they're all dead now, and if they are I knows
where they went and it's too good for them. They had two
of us foster kids, me and Billy Walsh. I didn't do so bad
because I never opened my mouth for five years except to
say yes and no. Billy, though, he didn't have any sense—he
wouldn't keep his mouth shut. He's got even less sense
now, because the Ryans beat him so bad he started to have
fits after awhile. Poor old Billy, sitting on the steps of
Atlantic Place in front of his cut down salt-beef bucket,
summer and winter. I heard they're talking about putting
him away because he gets right out of it sometimes and
goes after the businessmen and the tourists. Poor old Billy,
I wish he was like me. Tough as nails I am, all five foot four
of me; there's not enough pickaxes in Power's store to do
away with Jimmy Joe.

Once a year the government inspector came out to
Salmon Cove to check up on me and Billy, and the Ryans
would clean the two of us up and warn us not to open our
mouths or we'd get worse than what we already got. I can't
imagine what that would've been unless they planned to
murder us in our beds. We never had enough to eat the
whole time we was there, not even at Christmas, and they
worked us every minute we wasn't in school. And beat us

for something to do. And the oldest brother, me and Billy had to sleep with him and he done some awful things to poor Billy. He only ever come after me once, though. I twisted his balls so hard he couldn't hardly walk for a week, and he was too scared to tell his mother why. She would've beat both of us, only me harder.

One day when the government man was coming, Billy ran away. Old Man Ryan offered me a dollar to go find Billy. "Creep up on him and beat him over the head with a rock if you got to and drag him back here," he said, "so long as you gets him into the house before the government man comes." You had to creep up on Billy if you wanted to catch him because he could run like one of them skinny little birds that beats it along the shore; that's what he looks like, one of them small little birds that hops it the minute you gets anywheres near them. But I knew I wasn't going to see no dollar even if I did find poor old Billy. And I wouldn't never have beat him over the head anyways, like he was nothing but a sculpin or a half-dead rabbit in a slip.

I told Old Man Ryan I'd do it though; I wasn't that stupid. I found Billy down by the landwash, half under the Big Rock. He was sitting there with his arms around his knees, rocking back and forth and making the same noise as the sea; water was running down his cheeks, off the Rock and out of his eyes. It was one of the most pitiful sights I ever seen. I went back and told the Ryans I couldn't find him. Billy showed up on his own before the government man got there, though, and the Ryans were so happy they didn't even touch him after buddy left. That time it was the Welfare Minister himself who showed up. He was a nice guy: he gave us a quarter each. Not that we got to keep it.

115

I saw Billy at some guy's funeral awhile ago; he looked like one of them children that got that aging disease. He was helping them wheel the coffin up to the altar, and the tears were streaming down the cracks in his face. Poor Billy, he never had a chance, not like me. I'm tough, tough as nails, I am. They'll have to come with a pile of pickaxes to kill Jimmy Joe from the Cape Shore.

Me and Billy finally ran away from the Ryans, but we were sixteen so they couldn't come after us. We hitchiked into Town and got ourselves jobs at the biscuit factory. One night when we were down at the Bull and Bear—the Bull and Beer, they used to call it—there was a commotion out by the door, and some of us went over to see what was going on. There was this guy outside, arguing with the bouncer. "I ain't no fuckin' Portugee," he was yelling. "I'm from Harbour fuckin' Grace, you fuckin' arsehole." "That's almost as bad," the bouncer said to him. By then he realized the guy wasn't a Portugee, but you can't call a bouncer an effin' arsehole and expect to get into the club. The thing was though, buddy looked just like me. I got a real queer feeling in my gut, like I was looking at my double or something. He was dark-skinned—some of the b'ys on the Shore used to call me Nigger Jim—and about the same size, and his hair was real black like mine, only it was in tight little curls all over his head.

I went out of the door and grabbed him by the arm. He was so mad at the bouncer he nearly made a swing at me, but I gave him a shake and he straightened out. "Who are you?" he said. "I'm Jimmy Joe Flight," I said. "Who are you?"

"I'm Wayne Flight."

"Maybe we'd better go somewheres and have a talk," I said.

So we went to the Big B and split a large fish and chips. Turns out I wasn't an orphan after all; I had a mother and a father and a brother all along. I got the whole story that night from Wayne, my brother, who was reared up in a foster home in Harbour Grace.

Our mother was married to some guy named Flight, Wayne told me, and he died, and she put their three kids into the orphanage. And then she met our father and had the two of us, and when he went to jail for bootlegging she locked me and Wayne in some house they'd been renting and took off for Canada. I was two months old and Wayne was three years. One of the neighbours heard us bawling a couple of days after she left and called the Welfare, and off we went to the orphanage. And a few months later they split us up and sent us away like we was nothing but kittens out of the same litter. I went to the McGraths and Wayne went to the Morgans, up to Harbour Grace. When he was sixteen, they told him about being left by his mother, and that he had a baby brother. Wayne went knocking on all the government doors he could find when he first come to Town, but they wouldn't tell him where I was. I don't know what makes them tick, that government crowd. To tell you the truth, I don't want to know.

But Wayne managed to track our mother down, up to Quebec, where she was married to a Frenchie and had two more kids. "Mom," he said, "it's me, Wayne" when she come to the phone. "Wayne who?" she said. "I said, 'It's Wayne your son,'" Wayne said to me, "but I felt like I was lying or something." "I don't remember no Wayne," she said. "I remembers Brian. And little Jimmy." Turns out Brian was Wayne's first name, the one he went by until he got to the orphanage. Why the Brothers decided to call him by his second name God only knows. I guess it don't matter what you're called if you don't matter to them who has to sing out to you, even if it's just to tell you supper's ready. Anyways, Wayne said our mother told him never to phone there again because she didn't want her new husband and kids to know about us. Like we was scum or something.

I tried calling her myself once, but I got the same story. Crazy miserable bitch, she was. If anyone deserved to go to the Mental, it was her. But she was tough as nails, she was; you got to be if you're going to do what she did and get away with it. She died five years ago. Someone called me. As if I gave a fuck.

Wayne got our father's name out of her before she hung up, though. It was Joe Noseworthy, so I suppose by rights I'm Jimmy Joe Noseworthy. Wayne pointed him out to me one day; he was walking up one side of the street and we were walking down the other side. I used to see the old man from time to time after that, but he didn't know who I was. Queer thing, isn't it? Passing your son on the street like he was a stranger. The reason he never knew me was because Wayne phoned him up after he talked to our mother and the old man said to meet him at the Bull and Beer. Wayne said the old man was okay at first, but when he had a few in he said our mother was only a Portugee whore anyway, and we were nothing to him. It was probably true, Wayne said; Joe Noseworthy was tall and skinny and fairheaded. He died last Christmas, threw up his liver. I hope it hurt.

I don't know what our mother looked like. Maybe she was short and broad and black-haired, like me and Wayne. Or maybe there's some guy over there in Spain, dark and squat and wrinkled like an old toad, sitting on a beach mending nets and thinking about the other side of the ocean where he used to go fishing and drinking and whoring. Some old Portugee with scraggly grey hair hanging all down over his face, dirty old grey hair that used to be thick and black and shiny. Like a raven's wing.

Me and Wayne ended up going to T.O. together, but we got into trouble right off the bat. Wayne turned out to be a real hard case. We got in with these Hungarian guys who sold dope and ran a prostitution ring and I ended up in the Don jail for six months. Wayne never got caught, but he went back home out of it just in case. He got hit by a cab a couple of years later right in front of the Bull and Beer. It wasn't the cabbie's fault, though. My brother had a case of beer and two hits of acid in him when he died, which was what he usually had in him when he was alive.

Yeah, they're all dead now, all my so-called family. But that's no odds to me. I'm Jimmy Joe from the Cape Shore, and I'm tough, b'y, tough as nails. You just can't put a dent in me at all. A tractor trailer load of pickaxes wouldn't do it.

After I got out of jail I met this girl, Gail. The first time we did it she ran her hand over my head after and said, "Jimmy Joe, your hair is as black as the wing of a raven." "You're not the first woman who ever told me that," I said. She didn't like that one bit, but I never told her the difference, that it was Mom who used to say it. Gail's parents were real nice people. They gave me a camera the first Christmas we were married and I found out I liked taking pictures. So I went to photography school for a year and the instructors said not to bother to come back, I was that good at it. I set up my own gallery; Light Years, I called it, because I was light years ahead of the rest of them. And because light is everything in photography.

When I came back home, I went around and took pictures of the whole island. I even went down to the Cape Shore. That was a queer thing; I always thought the Cape Shore was a dark place, but the camera loved it. There was light everywhere, I just never seen it before. B'ys oh b'ys, there was some light down there, even off the water at night. The camera caught some strange old lights down under the water in the dark, too, though it might have been squid.

I read something about squid once. Apparently they talks to each other by lighting up and blinking off and on in a sort of code. And their one big eye is as good as a human's, only it's not attached to nothing but a gut and a tiny brain. Buddy who wrote the article said it was like putting a high quality lens on top of a shoebox and he couldn't see the point of it.

Squid are everywhere, in all the seven seas. I was thinking about that the other night, after a few beer and a couple of draws. What if squid were the eyes of the ocean? You know, what if the ocean was alive and it needed eyes to see what was going on all over it, and even on top? Then I got to thinking about people. Maybe people are like squid; maybe we're all just eyes for some big intelligence, and the light's just bouncing off our lenses so this Thing can see what's going on. Yeah, that sounds about right; just a bunch of eyes attached to a gut, and a brain the size of Old Man Ryan's heart.

Sometimes when the Welfare cheques are late, I goes down with Billy and does some panhandling of my own. People won't even look at you most of the time, although you gets the old sideways squid-eye from some of them. But even then they don't really see me; their brains has got it all made up beforehand.

Me and Gail had a baby, a daughter. She was some sweet. We called her Emma, after Gail's grandmother, Emma Jane. She must be about eighteen now. I came back home when Emma was four, after Gail divorced me. Turns out she was cracked, just like every woman I ever got in tack with except Carm, the one I lives with now. "Physical and mental cruelty" it said on the papers. Gail used to get mad at me just because I went on the beer the odd time, or had a draw, or maybe a few lines of coke. Sometimes I got on the needles when my head was real bad, all hot and confused so I didn't even know where I was, like the night Phonse died. I used to get that way when Gail called me a no-good piece of shit, standing there all cold and beautiful like the wicked stepmother in one of them fairy stories. They always says the same thing, the women. That I'm a drunk and a drug addict and that I beats them. Me, who wouldn't even hit Billy Walsh over the head with a rock for a dollar from Old Man Ryan that time in Salmon Cove.

I seen Gail at that funeral too, the one Billy was at. She had a young girl with her, a sweet-looking girl with black curly hair to her waist. I never seen Gail around here before. It was all pretty queer, it was. Carm was there too, and Carlos. And a lot of old women, you know, them ones who goes to anybody's funeral just for the fun of it. Carm was screeching her head off and I wanted to go over to her, but I never, I never went over to anyone, and no one come over to me. Maybe I dreamed it all.

Carm's my woman now. We lives in one of them boarding houses back of city hall, me and Carm, and this big black guy named Carlos who washes dishes at the Big B and sells a bit of weed on the side. Carm's the other side of sixty, and sometimes she puts me in mind of the north wind, she's that thin and cold to the touch, but she's a good woman all the same; besides, all cats are grey in the dark. And I got to have someone around, to bring me a cup of tea and to keep the old hag off me at night.

One thing about Carm, she don't go on at me about drinking and drugs. Although she tells me I'm going to over-do it one of these days. Don't you worry about me, my love, I tells her. I'm Jimmy Joe from the Cape Shore, and I'm tough as nails, I am. The Angel of Death will have to have some big pickaxe when he comes for Jimmy Joe. And don't you forget *it*, I says to her, like Quick Draw McGraw used to say to Baba Looey. That always makes her laugh.

Sometimes when I gets to thinking too much I goes up to Dunny's, and he always fixes me up. And when I puts that needle in my arm, I can go out to the seven stars of the Dipper just like Mikey, if I wants. Right out there on that glow, with the stars waiting up ahead smiling at me like I was their youngster. But mostly I goes down to the Cape Shore, and me and Brian and Phonse go out on the water, and we jigs for cod—the ocean is full of 'em, just like in the old days—and then we goes and buys every bun and bottle of drink in Old Man Power's store and eats and drinks our-selves sick up behind Uncle Joe Kennedy's. And the light, b'ys oh b'ys, it's some bright there on the Cape Shore then, even down on the wharf at night. You can look down and see the squid blinking off and on; they're talking about me and Brian and Phonse, I guess, and hoping we don't laugh so hard we falls right off the wharf and lands in the mid-dle of them.

The priest at that funeral I was at, he seemed like a good guy. He wasn't one of them snotty young ones, or an old crooked one you just know is doing the altar boys. No, he was

what you wants a priest to be, serious and stern but with a kindly way about him; a big, calm man, he was. He said that the
dead guy had been baptised into Christ when he was just a tiny
little baby, and now he was going back to God just like he was
a little baby again, all innocent and pure and full of light. I liked
that bit.

Light is everything.

Asking Jesus to Dance

When the boy opened his eyes, his mother was screaming again, or maybe she was still screaming. Her voice had been the bad sound against which he had pulled the quilt over his head last night, the quilt and the memories of the day to protect himself against the sound of the Voice in the kitchen under his room. He had been afraid that the sound would split the new ceiling and slice through the wires and the pipes and then the floor of his room, and rip through the rag mat by his bed. And then it would tear apart the air until he would have to leap out of bed and grab his inhaler because he wouldn't be able to breathe. The quilt was thin and the day had been thin too, but the boy filled his nostrils with the smell of the things that looked like sheets of toilet paper his mother put in the dryer to make the quilt all soft, and he breathed in the good smell of a new fart, and he put the sounds of the morning's hockey practice in his ears—the b'ys yelling and the coach's whistle blowing, and the thonk-thonk of pucks hitting the boards, and the deep boom-boom that all the noises made when they came together under the ceiling of Brother O'Hehir Arena.

The boom-boom was a sound something like the one you heard at Mass, the sound that happened when the priest stood up there like a big black crow and cawed all those words at the people sitting in rows like a bunch of pigeons on telephone wires; most of the people were too far away for the

123

words to hit them like pucks going into the net, but the grandmother always made their family sit up front because the priest was like her coach or something and she was deaf. Most of the caw-caws went up and up, up past the Virgin Mary Mother of God who stood behind the priest looking down over his shoulder, all serious and pretty, the way the boy's mother looked sometimes when she bent over him while he was doing his homework at the kitchen table. And then they went way up past the coloured windows that had ugly things in them, thorns and blood and a dead lamb and poor skinny Jesus on the Cross with his head hanging down on his chest like the boy's father when he was asleep in the chair in front of the TV after Sunday dinner. And then the caw-caws hit something when they got past Jesus and turned into the boom-boom on their way up to the ceiling.

The boy had never seen the top of the ceiling of the Basilica because you couldn't look up in church, you had to keep your eyes straight ahead or down; if you looked up the priest would catch you and you would probably get beaten with the handle of a broomstick across your knuckles like at school when the Brothers got mad at you. But sometimes the boy made his eyes go as far up as they could without bending his head back, and he saw things that looked like the rafters in the rink, but he still couldn't see the ceiling and sometimes he thought maybe there was no ceiling, that the inside of the Basilica just went up and up, up past the clouds and then the sun and out past the moon and all the stars and then maybe it got lost in the Silence before it got to God, and the boy hoped so because he thought that the noise might upset Him.

And then the boy didn't have to smell the quilt anymore or put the noise of the day into his ears to keep the Voice away, because he was sitting with the Virgin Mary in the

stands at Brother O'Hehir, and the net down below them
was full of crows; Alex Faulkner was hitting slapshots at
them and there was blood on the white ice like the blood on
the lamb but it was okay because the Virgin was holding his
hand and smiling at him. And then all the sounds, the Voice,
the thonk-thonks, the b'ys yelling, and the coach's whistle
and the caw-caws went up into the boom-boom and then
right up into the Silence so far above everything.

When the boy's family first moved into the new house, his
father and Uncle Ted had to fix something inside the kitchen
ceiling, and the boy had looked up into the hole they made,
and there was a room up there, a whole other little room
between his bedroom and the kitchen. The ceiling of the
secret room was made of white slats, only they were grey with
dirt and there was a thing for a light bulb to go in in the middle, and there were black wires wrapped in old cloth; the ends
of them were all ragged and dangly, and they hung down like
snakes over the hole in the kitchen ceiling. There were pipes
up there too, the colour of the roof of the Basilica or the
stuff you saw on the rocks in the woods up on the South Side
Hills, all mouldy greeny blue. And the smell that came down
through the hole was so old and strange that the boy had
never smelled it before, but he liked it because it reminded
him of being under the quilt. And the boy thought that
maybe the hockey cards were up there in the secret room,
wrapped in a pirate's map or in a black box with iron hinges.
Alex Faulkner's rookie card might be up there.

Alex Faulkner was the first Newfoundlander to make the
NHL, and he was on the same line with Gordie Howe, and
he scored three winning goals in his first year in the playoffs.
The boy had a picture of Alex Faulkner that Uncle Ted had
cut out of the newspaper in 1961; it was in his hockey card

box even though it wasn't a hockey card. The boy had asked
Uncle Ted—who wasn't really his uncle, he was his father's
best buddy—if he would lift him up so that he could climb
into the hole in the ceiling, but Uncle Ted just laughed and
said, "Your father would have me head if I did that." And
then the hole got closed over and he never got to look for the
cards, but Uncle Ted gave him a 1929 Newfoundland penny
he found up in the hole. And the boy put that in his hockey
card box too, after he polished it with Brasso so it was all
shiny like the buttons on his father's dress uniform.

The boy's mother's morning screaming had a different
sound than her nighttime screaming; it wasn't so bad because
it fit in with the banging of pots and pans and the traffic on
their street and the yelps the beagles were making out back
because they wanted their breakfast and his father was still in
bed; it fit in with his sister's whiny voice and his own stupid
laughing and clowning around that made the Voice go up like
he had twisted a knob on his mother's chest or something. It
didn't fit in at night, though, when they were all in bed except
his mother and his father who were down in the kitchen, and
she was yelling and his father never said anything; the boy
wished his father could find the knob on her chest that would
turn the Voice off, but his father didn't seem to know where
anything was in his own house, not even the cereal or his
underwear; it was like they were playing hide and seek all the
time and his mother was always It; everyone ran around saying where's my and what's this and did he call and can you
drive me with the Voice like a giant kettle whistling out all the
other voices.

If it was a really bad day, the Voice was like the big jack-
hammer the men had used to open the concrete wall outside
the boy's school last week. The boy had hoped there would be

something interesting inside the wall when they broke it open; maybe the hockey cards would be in there, Wayne Gretzky's rookie card, and of course Alan Faulkner's rookie card and all the old guys like Toe Blake and Rocket Richard, because they were heroes and even better than Spiderman or Superman because they were real. The boy thought they were even better than his father and Uncle Ted, even though they were firemen and saved people from burning buildings barely escaping with their lives, and they even got in the newspaper one time. Sometimes the boy felt bad about liking The Rocket better, but he thought maybe it was because he liked ice so much; it was cold and clean and you moved over it faster than a speeding bullet almost, and fire was bad and hurt people. And then the boy thought maybe there might be a dead body in the wall, a little girl, and he was afraid to look, but when he opened his eyes the wall was nothing but concrete all the way through, concrete with steel rods stuck in it, all rusty and twisted up like licorice twizzlers.

Today was Sunday and the boy and his family were going to Mass. They went to the Basilica, the closest church to their house except for the big Protestant one his grandmother called the Black Church, the Black Protestant Church even though it was grey like theirs. The boy used to think it was a church for black people, but there were only two black people in Town. One of them walked along the boy's street sometimes; he was going uptown, to the university, the boy's mother said; he was a huge big nigger and his face was the colour of a conker, like the dining room table after his mother polished it on Saturday morning. Before you got a conker you had to peel the green outside off, and it was all spiky like a sea urchin and it hurt if you didn't have a jackknife and you had to do it with your hands. And then you had to rub the white stuff off it, the stuff that looked like what was on his sister's underwear sometimes when she left it on the bathroom floor before she took it down to the laundry room in the basement.

The face of the nigger was carved like the coconut in the window of the corner store at the bottom of the second street over from theirs; he looked like someone had scratched him up with the ends of a compass or a jackknife or something. The boy's mother said that the nigger man had let people mark up his face on purpose because he came from Africa and that's what they did over there. And they could put a Voodoo Hex on you over there in Africa if they wanted to and make you into a zombie slave, which was a person who could walk and talk but their brains were gone right out of their head, they didn't know what was going on at all. The boy thought he never wanted to go to Africa if you had to let people hurt you on purpose, cut up your face and put the Voodoo Hex on you, and there was nothing you could do because it was the law.

The other black person in the city was an old woman who went along their street sometimes too; she was really small, like a midget or something, and black as tar, and she went along fast like a spider. She scared the boy more than the black man did even though the boy knew he could take her because she was only a girl and not much bigger than him. But he didn't know where the black woman was going because his mother never saw her, and he was afraid the woman would put the Voodoo Hex on him if he tried to follow her. The boy wondered about the Voodoo Hex and if the black woman had maybe put it on his mother because she never saw the black woman; she never saw a lot of things, like his father sneaking the flask of rum down into the basement every night and the Barbie in his sister's closet under a pile of sweaters, with its hair all cut off and scissor marks on its face and down below. Or the way his sister looked at their father sometimes like he was the Bogey Man, or the marks on the boy's own arms from where he scratched them all the time because it felt like something was crawling under his skin and he had to get it out. But his mother always knew where there was an extra pair of skate laces and where his inhaler was even if it was somewhere like down inside the couch.

Sunday morning breakfast was better than all the other breakfasts because his father had to get up to go to Mass, and the whole family sat down at the dining room table instead of the kitchen table, and sometimes Uncle Ted would come over and he would let the cat get up on the table and drink the milk out of his dish of Shreddies, and the boy's father would get mad but he couldn't say anything, so he would get up from the table and yell, "Come on, maid" and the boy's sister would have to get up even if she wasn't finished her breakfast and go upstairs with their father and wash his hair for him. And then the grandmother would leave the table and go into the living room to say the Rosary, and there would only be him and his mother and Uncle Ted and the cat; that was the part the boy liked best because Uncle Ted would always give him his left-over toast and say, "That'll put hair on your chest." Every Sunday night the boy looked to see if there was any hair on his chest, but there wasn't so far. Someday there would be, though, because Uncle Ted had lots of hair on his chest from all the toast he ate at their house on Sundays.

The boy's father wasn't from Town and neither was the grandmother. They were from Out Around the Bay, and that was why the boy's sister had to wash their father's hair for him and why his mother always had to make a cup of tea for his father even when she just got home from work and his father had been lying on the couch watching TV all day. And why the beagles could never come in the house even when the girl beagle had puppies in the middle of the winter and they froze to death, and why when their cat had kittens his father drowned them in a bucket of water in the middle of the kitchen instead of calling the Shelter to come get them. And it was why the grandmother sat in front of the living room window all day knitting and watching people walk by. If the boy was there, she always asked him who was this one and who was that one, as if he was supposed to know everyone in the whole city, but he felt bad all the same when he couldn't tell her, he felt like he was lying. One day the old black woman scuttled by the window like a June bug, but the grandmother never said a word and then the boy knew that the black woman had put the Voodoo Hex on the grandmother too. Maybe the Voodoo Hex only worked on women, or maybe the Virgin wouldn't let the black woman hex him because she knew he was going to be a famous hockey player some day, bigger even than Wayne Gretzky.

One time the boy asked his mother why they never went Out Around the Bay to visit his uncles, and she said, "My son, you wouldn't want to go there; sure, they'd eat the head off you, that crowd." And the boy had thought that Out Around the Bay must be something like Africa, except that the people there were white and spoke English, only not the same way as him and his mother and sister, but more like his father and the grandmother, who couldn't say the letter *h* when it started a word and put it on the beginning of words that didn't need it.

When the boy's father went upstairs after breakfast on Sundays, Uncle Ted would always go over and turn on the

radio, and then he would get up and do his Mick Jagger dance
with his lips all pooked out and one arm crooked back with his
hand on his arse, which was all pooked out too; his other arm
would be straight out with the elbow bent a bit and his hand
all limp and dangly. Sometimes Uncle Ted would grab the boy's
mother and make her go one-two-three, one-two-three all
around the dining room and even out to the kitchen and back,
only they never went into the living room where the grandmother was saying the Rosary because the grandmother might
be deaf but she wasn't blind. His mother would close her eyes
and lean her head against Uncle Ted's shoulder, and sometimes
Uncle Ted would stop counting one-two-three one-two-three
long enough to kiss the boy's mother on the top of her hair,
but when he did that she would look like he hurt her or something and she would say, "That's enough Ted," and they would
sit down and have one more cup of tea before it was time to
get ready. But the boy thought that maybe Uncle Ted wouldn't
come for breakfast this morning because last Sunday he had
gone too far.

Last Sunday, Uncle Ted had gone over and said to the statue of Jesus that stood in the corner of the dining room,
"Jesus, my son, would you care for a dance?" and when Jesus
didn't answer Uncle Ted said, "C'mon b'y, you looks like you
needs to boogie." And then Uncle Ted had picked Jesus up
and whirled Him around and dipped Him and everything and
the boy had laughed so hard he had peed in his clean underwear, but only a little bit, and his mother had laughed too and
the boy couldn't remember if he had ever heard her laugh
before, except the time his father fell face first into the pond
one year at the Regatta. But then the boy's father had come in
the dining room and started swearing at Uncle Ted, and he
had called the boy's mother the names that the old crazy

woman called all the women who walked past her. The crazy
woman sat next to them and the O'Reillys in church, in a short
skirt and white rubber boots and a knit hat; she never said a
word in church, but the rest of the time she walked all over
town calling all the women bad names and asking the men if
they wanted to do bad things to her. And Uncle Ted said "You
effin' bayman, you don't talk to her like that," and he punched
the boy's father in the face, and then he went out the front
door, which they hardly ever used, and he slammed it and then
he opened it back up and slammed it again.

And then the boy's father sat down on the chair in front
of the TV and put his head in his hands, and the boy's
mother turned on the Voice and the boy started jumping
around and a cup went smash on the floor. And the Voice
smacked him up the side of the head, and he felt bad, like
the time he forgot to take his cup to hockey practice and
Johnny Fowler said, "Here, b'y, use this Pepsi cap," and all
the b'ys had laughed and he did too, but he had felt bad, like
when his father drowned the kittens and the puppies froze
to death. And the boy went and sat down beside Jesus, Who
had ended up on His side next to the grandmother's knitting
bag, and he wondered if that was how He felt all the time,
except maybe when Uncle Ted had been dancing with Him.
And the boy felt sorry for Jesus, Who had to stand in the
corner of the dining room all day long, with His heart on
the outside of His chest where anybody could get at it.

Estate of Grace

Two crows woke me this morning; they were fooling around, bouncing up and down on the telephone wire outside my house here in Salmon Cove, and cawing loud enough to wake the dead. I was sleeping downstairs with my ancient mongrel, Spike, on his mattress in the studio when the crows started their Sex Pistols hymn to the morning. The studio is a fat bright room with a wood stove and generous windows. The windows are old and have begun to run a little: old glass is almost like ice, really, isn't it? Not at all as solid as it looks. When I was a girl in Scotland, I fell through the ice once, on the pond by the sheep byre. But my father, who was haying the sheep, came and drew me up through the splintered window in the pond and carried me back to the house, and wrapped me up and set me by the fire. The house we were living in then had a secret room under the stairs, with shelves full of Victorian novels. You couldn't tell there was a room because the door was made to look like part of the wall. I spent a lot of time there, reading all sorts of ghastly books with titles such as *Mrs. Mannerly's Folly*. That is all I remember of our time in that place, the cold water closing over my head and then being held tight against my father's body, and the smell of musty books in a hidden room.

We were as peripatetic as gypsies, our family; I don't think we ever stayed put anywhere for more than two or three years at the outside. We began in Scotland on the Isle of Islay, where I first fell in love, with our shepherd, Ian Crawford. Or perhaps I was in love with his dog, Ben Fleming; at three, such distinctions are not important. We finished, appropriately enough, at Land's End, where my father got on the ferry to Ireland one day and left us forever. I was twelve then. Twelve is when girls leave the long-legged larval stage and turn into mummies, all pale and pudgy and undefined, wrapped in baby fat and sullen shyness. In those days, we were also bound up in our first bras and girdles and stockings and garters. When I was fifteen, I emerged from my adolescent cocoon as what I am now, the quintessential Englishwoman, birdy nosed and horse-faced, shaped like an Anjou pear. Perhaps if my father had waited, I might have become something else, something as lovely to look at as he and my mother. But my father was not a patient man. And I have had my share of lovers, all the same. And even a husband, for a while.

Both my parents were beautiful, like movie stars. I have a favourite picture of them, taken on a beach in Spain when my mother was in her mid-thirties and my father in his late twenties. Mum looks like Grace Kelly; she is wearing a halter top and a pair of those wide khaki shorts that are back in fashion. My father is Cary Grant; he has on a light short-sleeved shirt buttoned only two-thirds of the way up, as usual, with a swatch of dark hair sticking out of it that looks like the Irish Moss they use to fertilize the gardens here in the Cove. When I was a child, that bit of hair sticking out of his shirts used to disturb me, like the odd trace of blood on the toilet seat. But now I sometimes run my finger over it in the picture.

The back windows of my studio look out on the waters of the Cove. My house is frighteningly close to the sea: some nights the spray comes flying at the glass like liquid porcupine quills. I saw a dead porcupine on a highway in New England once; it had obviously been run over several hundred times and looked like a decrepit hemp mat. That was the time I ran away from home, left my teenaged sons and headed south by myself, with two thousand dollars Canadian sewn into the lining of my jacket. I had to go, I don't know why, but I went all the same, all the way to Ecuador where I sat on a rock one night and watched the equatorial sun drop into the ocean, abandoning me like a bored lover. The next day I headed home, where my sons were waiting for me, three pretty lads all in a row. Actually, they weren't waiting at all; they had fled the nest for a grungy little flat in town where they could make as much noise with their drums and guitars and tambourines as they liked. And have adoring young maidens in at all hours.

The front windows of my studio face the road. I have made curtains for them out of one of my grandmother's Edwardian tea gowns, sewing thick cotton to its back so that no one can see in; a shocking thing to do to that dress, really, but its shape is perfectly suited to being a curtain. After all, it is not that I was ever going to put it on and sit in state in my garden, sipping jasmine tea while some man entertained me with outrageous lies of his exploits in the Sudan, of a vast fortune he made and lost on the Ivory Coast. Of his devotion to English womanhood, of which I was the crowning glory.

My grandmother sat listening to such a man once, and she married him within the month. They went to live in Ceylon, on a tea plantation, but she ended up back in

England with her two children before five years had passed; her husband, my grandfather, had a fashion of driving about on his motorcycle late at night, drunk and naked as a new-born babe. With a native boy in the same condition on the back of the bike. My grandmother could have abided the drunkenness and the boy, she told my mother, but not the nakedness—it was unnatural, no Englishman fit to be called one would allow himself to become that degraded, roaring about without a stitch on. He had made it impossible for her to retain decent servants, and without them the East was not fit to inhabit.

When my children were young, this studio was a family room: long ago, it was the only room a pair of newlyweds had to themselves. The room was newly wed itself then; it was built onto the house during the Depression. The bride-groom's father had no money for lumber, and so he cut down the silver birches that encircled the house and made this lovely room out of their ribs for his son and his son's bride. And here they have been ever since, the stooped old house and its squat consort, through sixty-odd thick winters and thin summers. When I bought the house from the family who had owned it for over a hundred years, the old part was gull grey and the new a sort of salmon, but I have painted both parts mauve, the colour of the three-part flame the Hindus say is in God's heart.

I have been sleeping with Spike in the studio to escape the ghost in my bedroom. Actually, it's more of a bloody incubus. Whatever it is, it makes such gentle love that I have awakened more than once all soft in my heart and my bones, with the hairs on the nape of my neck erect. But I have discovered that incubi, or at least this particular one, are no better than the flesh-and-blood members of their gender. Last week, a friend of mine came here from town for a few days to sleep off a bad affair. She slept for fourteen hours straight; it was mid-afternoon when I heard her get up and head for the loo. I was just pouring up the coffee when Miranda cried out, "Grace, come look at this!" and so I put down the pot and ran up over the stairs, reminding myself not to slip. There was carpet on them when we came here, but I took it off. Carpet is so filthy, and, besides, I like the old spruce stairs; they are the colour of butter and almost as soft, with a melted bit in the middle of each step. Sometimes I fancy I can see the imprint of my babies' knees in them.

In the mottled Empire mirror, Miranda and I looked at the fresh bruise on her neck. "I dreamt," said Miranda, "that I was floating above my body, and someone, a man, was making love to me, and it was so tender, so extremely tender and intensely erotic at the same time. And I *knew* him, but I didn't either—no one has ever touched me like that. He felt like the One, you know, *the* one true lover. Oh, God, Grace, do you think I'm cracking up? But where did this come from?" The bruise was pale fuchsia and spotted with tiny crimson dots where the capillaries had broken.

Miranda and I went downstairs and took our coffee out to the garden by the brook that runs out from under the road, down by the womb-shaped part where I have planted cress and mint and herb robert, and we talked about ghosts and men and women and Freud and Jung and men, and watched fluorescent green caterpillars bungee jumping on invisible lines from the chestnut tree. Above her long white neck with its stigmata of love, Miranda's face was as smooth as one of those beach rocks that look like eggs.

When the crows woke me this morning, I had been dreaming of my dead father. In the dream, I was walking up a curved staircase in a Victorian office building in London, and I met my father coming down. He was dressed in a business suit, something he had never worn in his life. He looked quite distressed. "Dad!" I said, "Dad!" and I ran up the steps between us, until I reached the one below him. "Hello, Grace," said my father, and he leaned over and hugged me. He smelt of Imperial Leather, as usual, but the scent of pipe tobacco was missing: I suppose the afterlife has gone no-smoking along with every-bloody-where else. I looked him up and down, from the Oxfords with their silly perforations to the ridiculous tie. Whoever had taught him to knot a tie, I wonder? The Archangel Gabriel? Mother Mary, perhaps. "It's so good to see you," I said. "But, Dad, why are you dressed like that?" He looked down at the Oxfords. "I have to be a clerk for seven years," he said. "On account of what I did." I laughed, and then the crows began their jam session and Dad disappeared.

A clerk for seven years. I wonder, is that God's time or only seven turnings of this green and blue atom? My father had three times seven years before his death to regret the relentless infidelity that led ultimately to the destruction of our family, if that is what he meant by "what I did." But the story we heard at his funeral in Ireland was that when the priest who was giving Dad the last rites reached down to anoint his forehead with holy oil, my father reached up and put his hand on the night nurse's breast. I wouldn't be at all surprised, although the Irish are terrible storytellers—not liars, really, just over fond of mythology. All island people are, even the English. Only they insist that their myths are history.

My mother came from money; she was at art school in London when she met my father. He was in the city trying to drum up money for his latest scheme, which was, at that time, a plan to grow Christmas trees commercially. He tried it, too, for a while, planting hundreds of blue spruce saplings on two acres in Devon. I went back to that place a few years ago: there was a handful of mature blue spruce trees there, my father's orphans, spiky of limb and indigo-coloured, obvious misfits in the pliant green English countryside. Next to them stood a row of stately elms, their heads bent a little, in the condescending manner of llamas. And Englishmen.

Nothing my father ever did lasted long, except for fishing in Ireland. And that, said my mother, was because he had to eat, and the Irish, being a nation of lazy confidence artists themselves, were not about to be fooled by my father's charm into lending him money for one of his schemes. The truth was, though, that the Irish women took him in like a prodigal son. I don't think he really did much fishing. He was well kept in Ireland, by barmaids and horse breeders and farm wives and fishermen's daughters. I wouldn't be at all surprised if they washed his feet with their thick Irish hair. Most women who met my father wanted to do that. Or something like it.

We all went to Ireland for Dad's funeral, my brother and me and even my mother. Mum went out of duty, she said, but of course she was under no social or moral obligation to go; she just wanted to know how he had been living, I think, and to see him one last time. She handled it like a proper Englishwoman, in thick black pumps and a black pillbox, nodding and smiling like the Queen Mum. She was exceptionally courteous to the woman my father had been living with when he died. Certainly, they were both old women by then, two tiny old women in widows' weeds, two latter-day

Widows of Windsor. I have always found it intriguing that people begin to shrink at a certain age, as though Death were a womb they were getting ready to fit into.

My mother never remarried after the divorce, although she was quite lovely well into her middle age. Beauty is excellent coinage when you are a woman: it can get you love and work and a handsome husband. But it is even better coinage when you are a man. All the women are yours then, and they will keep you so that you don't need to work. My father was as handsome and charming as Dionysus, and every woman he met became a Maenad on the spot, even the most respectable, the dullest, the plainest. Especially them.

My mother sent me off to boarding school when I was eight. "I can't look after you and your father both," she said. "One misfit is enough." I don't know why she thought I was a misfit. I was a very solitary creature, wandering the woods and fields with my dog and wishing I had the nerve to run away. I was quite sure I could survive on roots and berries; that's what comes of reading too much as a child, I suppose. My brother wasn't a misfit. He always took top honours at school and was sporty and popular. Later he became a barrister and married the daughter of a distant cousin of my mother's, a woman neither beautiful nor intelligent, but well-bred and well-to-do. Last year he shot himself when his wife told him she was leaving him for a young sculptor.

I remember my brother's wedding well; it was at St. Martin-in-the-Fields and the reception was in Chelsea, at the house of a second cousin of my mother's. At midnight we all went out into the garden to watch an eclipse of the moon. My brother and his bride danced underneath it, disappearing when the eclipse was at its zenith and suddenly reappearing with the moon, like the ghosts of ill-fated lovers. It is bad luck to marry during an eclipse, they say. I wonder when it is good luck to marry.

When I was seventeen, I went to art school for six months, and then I married a farmer from the Scilly Islands. What a ridiculous thing to do, my brother used to tease me, marry someone from the Scilly Islands. The joke rests, as most do, on a thin thing: one doesn't pronounce the *c* in Scilly.

According to my mother, it was the War that ruined my father. Dad's people were tenant farmers in Kent, and one April morning in the forties a German plane dropped a missile there. It was intended for a building that was being used by the British military for spying operations, but it missed and hit my father's school instead. Everyone was killed except Dad, another boy and two girls who had been pipping off. My grandfather beat my father for his truancy; shortly after, Dad ran away. He always said he went off to seek his fortune, but really he was a runaway. No one went after him, either, or put his picture on a milk carton. There were no milk cartons back then, anyway, and very little milk or anything else. We had rationing in England until the fifties— only of sweets, mostly, but still there was a pervasive sense of want, of shabbiness. I remember going to Exeter, and how shameful the places where the bombs fell seemed, as if the city had had its knickers pulled down. And all the interminable talk about the War—they were still at it when I left. Still fighting the Germans, and reusing wax paper until it crumbled like the skin of a three-thousand-year-old mummy exposed to sunlight. Now, I throw out leftovers just because I can. Except when my mother comes to stay with me, and then I eat warmed-over roast beef until I want to scream.

All my life, the thing I have noticed most about rich people is how stingy they are, cheating shopkeepers out of small change, shutting their doors in the faces of people collecting for charities, running off to auctions of the goods of the dead or the dispossessed in a feeding frenzy, mad to strip the bones of the downed of whatever is left on them. As a child, I once read a story in which a man asked God why, if he loved him, he had made him so poor. And God said, "I made you a poor man because if I had made you a rich man, you would not have been a good man, and I loved you too much to allow that to happen."

Not that my mother is rich any longer. My father went through her inheritance like an otter through a net, destroying the very thing that had attracted him in the first place, the lovely golden seine full of sovereigns and precious heirlooms, with my mother floating in the middle of it all like the nymph daughter of a river god. Now I am the only tangible evidence that my father ever passed through this vale of tears, me and a few blue spruce in Devon.

Where I live now, the coniferous tree is king. That is because they are survivors nonpareil, hanging on to the sides of the great cliffs here with their roots dug in like the talons of eagles. Some of them are practically horizontal from the beating they take in the winter, when the sea and sky thrash them day and night on end for months. But they endure. And in the summer, they come out all over with waxy cones, and their thin boughs drip with a myrrh as thick and sweet as opium.

If my mother had the greed of the rich, the hoarding, scrounging greed, my father had the poor man's greed: to get and get and spend and spend. To fill his pockets with whatever was at hand and then drink it up, eat it up, or throw it at horses and dogs and women. Getting was easy for my father; he had the instincts of a sleight-of-hand artist. I sometimes think he might have made an international jewel thief if he could have managed to apply himself to one thing. But only three things ever kept his attention for any length of time: my brother and I when we were small, things that were newly come up out of the earth or the sea or dropped from an animal's womb, and the conquest of a woman.

I went to Ireland to visit my father the summer I was fifteen. He lived in the southwest, in a cottage by the sea. His lover at that time was named Siobhan. Siobhan was not much older than me, but she was beautiful in the Irish fashion—long thick hair the colour of the sky in Mazatlan at midnight, a pale face with two red clown dots on each cheek and heavy black eyebrows. You sometimes see old Irish nuns in town with such eyebrows, improbably black and vital in those pale, untouched faces. I admire the eyebrows of the Irish nuns, I admire the stubborn energy of those shiny black quills shooting up out of the sterile flesh: it reminds me of grass growing up through cracks in concrete. My mother always plucked out her eyebrows and pencilled them back in; she could never stand the way they grew on their own.

Siobhan and my father made love every night of the time I spent in Ireland, love that absolutely rocked that flimsy Irish cottage. I was terrified that one night they were going to tear a hole in the skinny, shaky wall—more of a membrane, really, than a wall—between Dad's room and mine. I left a week early, I had to get away from that awful drumming and shrieking, away from the sounds of the nightly ride of my father and his wild *bansidhe*.

After Siobhan, there was Deirdre of the Sorrows; Moira the Fatal; Maeve, Queen of the Celts; Mary, Rose of the

World; Sinead of the Flaming Hair; Assumpta, the Ascended
One; and others whose names I don't remember, if I ever
knew them at all. In the end, there was Jean, a Scottish nurse.
I met some of them at his funeral. They make a lot of noise
at Irish funerals, laughing and crying and chattering like
magpies. And they eat and drink like bloody Vikings and
dance like bacchantes to the wailing pipes, the inconsolable
fiddle and the bodhran, the drum that is like the heart's beat.
When we got the funeral photos back, my husband, who had
refused to go, said, "Did someone die, then?" because in
most of them everyone was smiling and had their arms
around one other, even my mother, my brother, and me.

Some of those women must be dead themselves by now;
I imagine them all buried in the same spot like the nuns in
the convent graveyard in town, with my father's shadow
falling over them the way the shadow of the Basilica falls on
the small black cowl-like headstones. I wept for two months
straight after Dad died. Spike was a puppy then, and he used
to lick the tears off my face; it's a wonder he didn't die of
saline poisoning.

Once, I painted a picture of the Crucifixion. I left the
loincloth off, and it was easy to see why all those women followed Him around. My Jesus was an Arab, dark and squat,
and His cross was X-shaped. I don't know why I painted it.
I could never sell it or hang it; it is in my bedroom closet. St.
Augustine said that the Cross is the marriage bed. I guess the
opposite was true for Dad.

My mother is in her eighties now. I had a letter from her
last week; she considers a long-distance telephone call an
extravagance unless it is someone's birthday or there has been
a death. I called Mum the day after I got her letter. I could tell
she wasn't pleased to hear from me; rather, she was somewhat

pleased to hear my voice, but unhappy about the cost of the call. "You are so irresponsible, Grace. Guess what I had for dinner last night?" I said I hadn't the faintest. "When they delivered the compost for the garden, the most marvellous mushrooms were growing in it. And then someone ran a pheasant down on the road, right in front of my door. So I had a lovely meal of pheasant and mushrooms for nothing."

"That's great, Mum," I said, "So you're living on garbage and road kill these days?"

I don't know why she concerns herself with the cost of our calls; they're infrequent and short. My mother lives in the last village in England without street lamps, and she regularly threatens the council by post in case they are plotting to put them in. Her cottage is old and dark; its thatched roof is like a worn-out wig because she won't spend the money to fix it. All the remnants of my mother's life are stacked helter-skelter in the tiny rooms: dusty bone china, a few pieces of good furniture that escaped my father's eternal squandering; a lot of ancient, lying photographs. The cottage is unbelievably dirty because Mum is nearly blind now, not that she will admit to it. She reminds me of an old badger gone to ground, coming out to sniff the air now and then and root in the garden for something to eat. My mother has a lump in her side that she insists is nothing; the doctors say otherwise. I will not go to care for her when the time comes. It would destroy the rhythm of my life, and for what? A few reluctant words of gratitude from an old woman I barely know. Sometimes, I wonder if I will even weep for her when she is gone. I hope I shall.

I live on an island off the coast of North America now. It is a cold, barren place most of the time, except in July, when it has one great orgasm of beauty: the sea bursts with whales and little silver fish and the earth flushes all the greens of Ireland.

My sons have all gone from this place. They work in the music business, all three of them, running about all over the world, skimming through foreign countries as though they were the streets of the old town. They can never seem to keep wives or girlfriends for very long, but they never lack them either. They come back to me, one by one, or all together, once a year. They bring their women and their children and their instruments, and the old house shivers with the joy of it all.

Their father and I came to this island to farm turkeys, but eventually he went off to seek his fortune. I already had a son by him when I married him; he was eighteen at the time and I was twenty-one. I used to feel guilty because I took him like a bull calf to the slaughter. He balked a bit before the knacker's door, which is why our first son was a year old before we were married, but calf love and convention won out in the short run. Not in the long run, though. I had left art school and run off to the Scilly Islands, and I was living on the pecuniary equivalent of nuts and berries when I met Reg. He looked like a pirate, and, as it turned out, he was. I thought at first we could be pirates together, but the babies took the wanderlust out of my heart with their chubby hands. But not out of his heart: Reg left me and went off to seek his fortune in the unofficial capital of this country, a young, large awkward city that imagines itself to be the embodiment of sophistication— a fairly common illusion as far as North American cities go.

My ex-husband is a rich man now, with a company on the stock exchange and a designer wife. He has never once come back to see our sons or me, and he has never sent us any money, although he gave me a thousand dollars a year ago when I happened to run into him on the street in

Toronto. It was so odd, in that enormous foreign city, to see Reg walking towards me; it reminded me of the time I ran my car into a pole. It seemed to take forever, the car and the pole coming inexorably closer to each other like figures in some old, slow folk dance, and finally meeting in a light, formal embrace. Reg was surly at first, in the way men often are when guilt is buzzing around their hearts like a horsefly, but he relaxed when he realized I wasn't going to bite him. Why would I? I never really liked his taste even when I thought I loved him. So we had coffee, and then he bought me off and I went to the Queen Street boutiques.

The thing I got that day that I liked the best was a sea-green skirt with beaded and sequined dolphins on it. It didn't really suit me when I tried it on, but it was such a beautiful thing, I had to have it. I have hung the skirt like a tapestry at the foot of my bed, and when the moon is in the right place the dolphins turn into fantastical creatures, gleaming chimeras of the Ocean of Paradise. It is the most frivolous thing I have ever bought for myself.

I haven't had a lover in eight years now, if you don't count the incubus. The last one, Gavin, was the darkest man I ever met. He was tall and spindly, and his face was like the one in *The Scream*. He used to tease me with stories about how he tortured insects as a boy. He looked like an insect himself, like a praying mantis; it was like embracing a rake when I put my arms around him, a rake or the skeleton of some upright carnivore, a grizzly perhaps. But he told me I was beautiful, and that he would never leave me. "Only strangers travel, owning everything," he said. "I have nowhere to go." Later I discovered these were lines from a Leonard Cohen poem.

Gavin must have loved me a little, at least, or he would-
n't have squandered Cohen on me. He was not a generous
man. He made the most beautiful stained glass, though, as
delicate as the shell of a razor clam and finely tinted,
although the shapes in it were queer, twisted. After three
years, he left me for my best friend. She and I have never
made it up, although people used to mistake us for sisters.
Goneril and Regan were sisters.

The last time I thought of Gavin was a year ago at a
poetry reading. The reading was held out of doors, on a spit
of land that is the closest point in North America to Ireland.
It is an ancient, derelict place, with only a small lighthouse as
a candle against the dark. A slender young girl with hair like
a veil sat astride a cannon left over from the War and read an
old Irish poem about a woman forsaken by her lover. The
end of the poem went like this:

> *You have taken the east from me; you have taken the west*
> *from me;*
> *you have taken what is before me and what is behind me;*
> *you have taken the moon, you have taken the sun from*
> *me;*
> *And my fear is great that you have taken God from me!*

I wanted to weep, but I had one of my grandsons,
Nathan, with me. Nate is five. You can't cry in front of children—or men, or even some dogs—because you'll scare
them. Nate is easily frightened; he was a colicky baby. Nate's
mother was a singer in my middle son's band. She sang with
the band until her seventh month, sang and strutted among
the raging guitars and brutal drums with poor Nate hunched
in her belly like an infant Jonah. Nate has asthma; lately, they

are saying he also has attention deficit disorder. Nate's mother lives in town and his father lives in Wales, which is not an island although it would like to be. My son has asked me to come and live with him there; he says I could paint the mountains, and he and Rhiannon, his love of the last two years, would fatten me up on leeks and potatoes. No, I said, I cannot leave my garden. I did not say, I cannot leave your son, who needs tending even more than my delphiniums. Someday I might say this to him, but not yet.

Nate loves Salmon Cove; it is his enchanted country, his Never-Never Land, his Narnia. When Nate is here with me in the Cove he breathes much more easily. "Look, Nanny Grace, I am running the whales!" he says to me when we are down by the water, and he gallops into the North Atlantic with his head down like a newborn lamb butting its mother's flanks. Nate makes me promise over and over that I will never sell the house in Salmon Cove. I won't, I tell him, one day I'll give it to you.

"And where will you go, Nanny Grace?" Nate says. "I hope you will stay here with me." "I will," I say, "always and forever. Or at least until all the seas run dry and the rocks melt with the sun." That's a promise the Scottish poet Robert Burns made to a young girl once; he put it in a song, a lovely song that my sons sing sometimes when they are here. Not that he kept his promise to her. Or to any other woman.

Poor old Dad, a clerk. Well, I hope They had the sense to stick him far away from the secretarial pool. I imagine it was necessary to chain him to his desk. But perhaps it is worse than that; perhaps part of his job is to help keep track of the angels. Once a day he must get up and look out his window and count them: lush Rubenesque angels tickling marvellously rotund cherubs, ethereal Giotto angels stroking the strings of gilded Celtic harps, tarty Toulouse Lautrec angels stroking one another, all the glorious company of heaven at play in the fields of the Lord, under a sun that is young always. I sometimes wonder if Dad can see Nate and Spike and me down on the beach in Salmon Cove, running the whales and singing in our chains like the sea.

I hope he can. And I hope that it grieves him more than the sight of all the angels in heaven he cannot touch. Perhaps one day I'll paint a picture of his grief. Or have my sons make it into a lovely song.

Roses and Rationalists

Yesterday I went to Martha Morgan's with my sister, Elizabeth, and her cat. "Are you going to tell her about the roses?" I asked Elizabeth while we were sitting in the waiting room, sandwiched between an anorexic woman with a blind Siamese shivering at the end of a leash by her feet, and a fat man who was making circles with his forefinger on the brow of an orange tabby kitten asleep on his shoulder. "Depends," she said. "On what?" I asked, wondering if the man with the three chins was trying to open the kitten's third eye, or it was just a nervous habit. "If the subject comes up or not," she said.

I thought that was a fair answer; after all, you never know with Martha where a discussion is going to end up, or even what route it will take to get wherever it's heading. If you like the conversational scenic route, Martha's your woman. Although some might find the rapid acceleration from ear mites to the real possibility of a Virgin Birth in light of quantum physics a bit of a rush. Not me, though. Or Elizabeth, although I think she mostly tunes out, not that you can tell. Elizabeth's charm is legendary, and the better part of it consists of not opening her mouth except to show her flawless teeth in a smile that is on record as the quickest known way to vaporize a human being if you discount exploding nuclear reactors. I've often seen the molecules fly apart as

152   IN THE CHAMBERS OF THE SEA

Elizabeth's laser lips do their thing, never to reassemble in quite the same form. Especially male molecules.

Martha is the best vet in town: if they ever hold a Veterinary Olympics, I'd bet the shop on Martha to come home with the gold. She only treats cats, not because she doesn't like dogs—Martha loves every creature that creepeth upon the earth or flies in the firmament, and those that move upon the face of the waters and under them—but she sticks to cats to keep her business small. "Small is best," Martha says, "like a country doctor's where they know the name of everyone who comes in through the door. And nobody says 'Would you like a rectal exam with that?'"

The only living things I have ever heard Martha slam are the teenagers who break her clinic windows from time to time and write graffiti on the walls of the building. "The vermin," Martha says. "With apologies to the members of *rattus rattus*." Martha told me she wouldn't even mind about the graffiti if it was amusing, but it's only tiresome stuff like "There's too much blood in my alcohol system" and "No beer, no pussy." Sometimes there's even upsetting things like swastikas and "nigger" marring the silhouette of the cat on the door when she arrives in the morning. "At least when we were young," she said to me, "we put some thought into what we were going to say before we hauled out the markers."

"Yeah," I said. "Remember 'God is dead—Nietzche' with 'Nietzche is dead—God' underneath it?"

"Who could forget that one? Did you know there's a band in town called Nietzche's Children? Thank god; at least not all the young have rotted their brains out on Big Macs and Xbox. Well, I'm in a white bread and bologna neighbourhood and I'll just have to take the consequences. But 'No beer, no pussy' is not great for business—'Marge, look what it says on the vet's—times must be some hard—she's holding the cats for ransom until someone goes and gets her a six pack.'"

Nora, my sister's cat, was the victim of a hit-and-run driver. She went missing for two days; on the evening of the second day my brother-in-law heard her crying at the back door. When he opened it, Nora was lying on the deck he had just finished making, a thin line of blood running from her hindquarters down over the steps. "Nora," he said, "Nora Dora, what has happened to you?" And she went towards him, moving like a seal along the fresh pine boards until she got to his feet, and she laid her silver head on the top of his tartan slippers. Somewhere in the city a man or woman who ran over a small animal and drove on is not thinking about Nora lying on Martha's table, crying in thin little pieces while urine is being expressed out of a bladder that no longer knows when it is full.

Nora used to love Martha; she would stand on her back legs and put her front paws on Martha's breasts and kiss her eyelids; now she snarls and spits when Martha walks into the waiting room. You would think Elizabeth had a Tasmanian Devil in the blue plastic carrier on which her daughter Bess has stenciled sixties flowers, big daisies all the colours of the rainbow. Martha has to wear two leather gauntlets to handle Nora, as if she was a wild creature, a falcon or a feral cat. That's the downside of Martha's profession. "I should have been a dentist," she says sometimes. "At least I'd know my patients were guilty of something when I have to hurt them."

When my sister and her husband, Daniel, were in France last month they went to Notre Dame and lit a candle for Nora.

"It cost two Euro dollars," Elizabeth said. "The thing I like about Euros is that they're like loonies and twoonies so you have a better sense of how much you're spending."

"What was Notre Dame like," I asked her, "was God there or what?"

"It was the kind of place you could sit down and stay forever in," she said. "Like a movie theatre where all they show is *The English Patient*."

My sister's father-in-law died in his sleep last week, after the third stroke in as many months. Elizabeth felt bad because they didn't light a candle for him. "We forgot," she said. "We were jet-lagged, I guess. Maybe he wouldn't have had the stroke if we'd remembered."

"No," I said, "you weren't meant to do it. God and Daniel's father already had their minds made up, and they're both stubborn cusses."

Daniel's father was an atheist and a utopian socialist. The latter is something that can easily happen to former Methodists if they're not careful. When your religion comes as dry as a rusk with a bit of low-fat margarine on it, it's not unusual to toss it away. And then go elsewhere to satisfy the craving for ultimate meaning. But a utopian socialist? Obviously the man never spent any time in MallMart. I always feel like an anthropologist when I'm in there, not that I go often. Only when I have to, to pick up stuff you can't get anywhere else. Like the kind of bras you buy when you're between lovers. If I have to spend more than half an hour in MallMart I end up leaving with a bad case of sensory over-load and a strong desire to go live on the smallest Aleutian island.

Nora originally belonged to Elizabeth's father-in-law: she and Daniel took the cat after Mr. Godfrey had the first stroke and ended up in a home. They had wanted to take him too, out of the hospital and into their upstairs back bedroom, the dormer room that used to be Bess's when she was a baby, with moons and stars holding hands around the windows and a big Happy Face sun grinning on the ceiling, things Daniel had painted to keep his daughter company at night. But Mr. Godfrey refused. "Too much strain on the family unit," he said. "It's not ethical."

"If there hadn't been any such thing as an old-age home for Daniel's father to go into," Elizabeth said, "I'm sure he'd have hopped on an ice floe and demanded to be pushed out to sea, for the sake of the greatest happiness of the greatest number."

But the greatest number wasn't at all happy about his decision. Daniel was miserable because he wanted his father under the family roof, and Elizabeth was miserable because Daniel was miserable. And Bess missed her grandfather, whom she got to see only on Sunday afternoons because they didn't allow children at Noonan's during the rest of the week. And when all four of them were together in the common room of the home on Sundays, it was like visiting with strangers, Elizabeth told me, because no one swore or farted or got annoyed or ignored anybody, they all just sat there and drank tepid tea and watery juice and pretended they didn't see the people who were talking to themselves or playing with dolls. Or hear the ones crying for their mothers. Those people never lasted long in the common room on visiting days anyway, Elizabeth said. There was always some staff member hovering, ready to pounce and stick them back in the beds that were like cribs, with railings on the sides to keep them from wandering out and aggravating the adults.

Elizabeth told me that sometimes dogs were brought into the home for therapeutic reasons. "I was at the home one day when the dogs were there," she said. "These two chipper young fellas were making their rounds—you know the type, Aryan youth with earrings—with two German Shepherds—canine Aryan youth, no earrings—dogs and guys all smiley happy, tongues lolling out of their mouths. And then they came to this old woman who was sitting in a rocker picking at the snags on her housecoat. 'Good day, ma'am,' they said. 'Would you like to pat Rune and Franz?' And the woman looked up at them and yelled, 'I don't want your goddamn dogs, I want my dog, *my* dog, not *your* goddamn dogs!' And then she started wailing like a banshee. It was awful. But at least she put a temporary dent in all that happy home for seniors crap. Although Daniel's father seemed to like it at Noonan's. Mostly because he was so smug about not being a burden to society. Only to his family."

Yesterday, Nora started to dribble all over the house; Martha says she won't need to be catheterized again for a week. And that it looks like the nerves in her back are going to heal and Daniel won't have to make a little cat wheelchair for her after all. He would have, too. My sister won the matrimonial stakes big-time when she bagged Daniel, even though Aunt Bride threatened to go to live in Ireland with her brother the Brother because her niece was going to marry a black Protestant.

When Elizabeth and Daniel brought Nora to The Cat Clinic on the night she crawled home, Martha put some holy oil from St. Anne de Beaupré on Nora's forehead. A client's husband had brought it to her the night before his wife's favourite cat was going to have surgery. "There he was," Martha said, "sneaking in the door with a bottle in a brown paper bag at ten o'clock at night when the clinic is usually locked up tight. I can only imagine what the neighbours thought. Well, at least the bag had an image of the Quebec cathedral on it, not a red circle and crossed-out car keys."

On the window-sill of Martha's waiting room there's a small bronze church that you wind up with a key on the bottom to make the cross on top of it spin. Martha lets Bess play with it while she's waiting for her mother and Nora to come out of the examining room. Next to the church is a little crêche with "It's a girl!" written on a pink banner strung across the manger. The church and the crêche were gifts from some nuns with a weird sense of humour, Martha's friends from the convent she spent three years in before she decided she didn't want to be a Bride of Christ after all. "I figured He had enough wives already," Martha said to me, "and I'm not really the marrying kind. Besides, there are no cats in convents. Not four-legged ones, anyway."

It's hard to imagine Martha as a Sister; there's no odour of sanctity about her at all, only the smell of antiseptic and hand cream. Sometimes beads of sweat ring Martha's forehead like a diadem, and that's when you know she's really upset; her face is broad and smooth and stays that way no matter what's going on—hysterical cats, hysterical owners, urban graffiti piss artists. Death coming through the door at all hours.

When my cat died on the way to Martha's clinic one night, she gave me a globe with a tiny Virgin in it; you shake it and Mary is suddenly lost in a snowstorm. It was snowing hard the night I took Danny Boy in, but I ran every red light until I got to an unholy crossroad, MallMart on one side with

McDougal's kitty corner to it and a Zoobie's across from them. And I didn't have enough faith in God or the Virgin or even my own driving skills to take on the legions of snarling cars roaring between those bastions of Mammon. So Danny died a block away from The Cat Clinic and I went in crying with his body cradled against my chest, and Martha said, "He would have died anyway, it wasn't your fault."

Danny was a diabetic; I used to have to give him needles twice a day, but he didn't mind—you'd swear he was a junkie, standing there with this dreamy look in his eyes while I injected him. He was a strange cat anyway: every night he used to watch invisible objects flying around the ceiling over my bed, sitting there slowly rotating his head while I pulled the covers over my face and told myself to quit being an idiot—there were no such things as whatever he thought he was looking at. Although my daughter Becky thinks there are probably cat angels as well as the ordinary kind. "There must be," she said to me, "because how else did Danny Boy get to Heaven if one of them didn't take him? You know he wouldn't let grown-ups pick him up."

Martha took the globe with Mary in it out of a drawer and shook it over Danny's body, which was lying on the counter on an old yellow towel I had wrapped him in, and I watched the fake flakes swirl and wished I was inside the glass, under the blue folds of the Virgin's robe. And then we went into the back room and drank some vodka, and Martha told me about the time she got her arm stuck in a cow. "You can't imagine," she said, "what it feels like to have your arm up the anus of a cow, and it tightens its sphincter muscle until your hand goes numb. I thought I was going to have to spend the rest of my life with my arm up the arse of a cow." "How did you get it out anyway?" I asked her. But she changed the subject, so I guess there was probably an electric cattle prod involved.

When I was leaving, she told me to take Mary with me, and then she pulled a little cross made from a palm leaf from between the pages of one of her medical books. "You can bury it with him," she said. And I did. In my father's backyard, even though it's against city regulations. My father says that after he dies whoever buys the house will probably call in the Constabulary once they start digging in the garden. All the bones of thirty-odd years of family pets are there, plus those of a dead seagull Becky found in the parking lot of Tim Horton's one afternoon. She put it in the basket of her bike and sang "Don't Cry for Me, Argentina" all the way home, in case its spirit was still hovering and needed some inspiration to get moving to wherever it is dead seagulls go.

After Danny was in the ground, wrapped in a piece of black satin that used to be part of one of Becky's Halloween outfits, my father and I sang, "O Danny Boy, the pipes, the pipes are calling/From glen to glen, and down the mountainside" over him three or four times. Neither one of us could remember any of the other lines—we must be the only RCs in town with that particular form of musical Alzheimer's because you can't go a week around here without hearing "Danny Boy" being belted out somewhere. My cousin Pat, a guy about half the size of one of the front-end loaders he drives for the City, sang it at Elizabeth's father-in-law's funeral last Thursday.

Elizabeth and Daniel gave Mr. Godfrey the full Catholic send-off at St. Paul's. The Archbishop made a cameo appearance, and Aunt Bride sang the "Ave Maria" from the upper balcony after Cousin Pat finished giving "Danny Boy" a truly operatic going over. And then they buried him in Mount Carmel Cemetery in our family plot. Mr. Godfrey's wife died a long time ago in Maine, where both of them were from—they were divorced anyway. Daniel says it was because his mother was as crazy as a coot, even though she was a very nice woman nevertheless. Elizabeth says she bets Daniel's mother was perfectly sane before she married Daniel's father.

Mr. Godfrey had left a sheet of paper in the drawer of his nightstand at the home stating that he absolutely forbade any kind of religious funeral service—if so much as one prayer was said over him he would be extremely displeased. And he wanted his remains donated to science. Elizabeth showed me the paper—"I'm going to frame this," she said. "The old fool. Atheist to the end, and yet he was going to throw a hissy fit—where? in the ninth circle of utopian socialist hell?—if someone said a Hail Mary or two over his dead body. Over his dead body indeed."

"But don't you feel guilty," I asked her, "about not following his last wishes?"

"No," she said. "He didn't care about Daniel's and my wishes, and we were alive when we made them. Besides, I tried. I called the medical school and they said they didn't want him. Apparently they're crawling with old cadavers. The ghoul on the other end of the line said, 'What we could use is a few children's corpses,' and then he said, 'Oh dear, was that out loud?' No, I told him, it wasn't and have a nice day. So we did what we thought should be done. Besides, he liked it."

"What do you mean, he liked it?" I asked.

"Well, you're going to think I'm nuts, but about an hour after we got home from Mount Carmel, the whole house filled up with the scent of roses."

"No way," I said, and Elizabeth said "way," with the smile that got her crowned Miss Stella Maris High fifteen years ago, and six years after that brought Daniel to his knees with a proposal on his perfect lips.

"I got my knickers in a knot right off the bat," she said, "because I just bought a big jar of rose oil from that really expensive boutique across from the downtown Kentucky Fried, and I figured Bess had taken it out of the cupboard in the bathroom and dropped it on the floor. But Bess and her father weren't even in the house: they were out on the deck with Nora, helping her practise walking. And when I went upstairs and opened the bathroom cupboard, the jar of rose oil was sitting there as big as life and twice as beautiful."

"Wow," I said. "Neat."

"Yeah," said Elizabeth, "too cool. I started snivelling and then I went and told Bess and Daniel to get in the house. Daniel's first words were 'Lizzie Dizzy, don't you think you've gone a little heavy on the rose oil?' And then I told him. 'It's a miracle,' I said. 'It means your father has finally smartened up. He had to die to do it, but better late than never. Maybe Bride belting out the "Ave" loud enough to wake the Muslim dead over in Iraq helped. Otherwise, he'd probably still be unconscious, because he was one mule-headed man.

"But, Jesus, is Daniel ever his father's son. 'Mizzy Lizzy,' he said, 'hold on a moment. Just because we're experiencing a collective olfactory hallucination doesn't prove anything. And it's not like my father was fond of roses. Now if it was carpenter's glue. . .' 'I like roses, you jerk,' I said to Daniel, 'and your father always got me a bunch on my birthday, which was lucky for me because I would have spent my married life rose-deprived if I had to depend on you.' But before things could degenerate into a common or garden domestic brouhaha, Daniel said he had some research to do and went up to the study. And Bess and I sat down on the couch and cuddled up, inhaling the scent of roses and passing the tissue box back and forth. After a while the smell got fainter and I was just getting up to put dinner on when Daniel came down over the stairs, his eyes the size of two of Bride's bakeapple pies. 'What's up with you?' I said. 'Get out some wine and I'll tell you,' he said. Days of wine and roses, I thought. Was that a book or a movie, by the way?"

"Movie. Jack Lemmon and Lee Remick. It ranks right up there with *Lost Weekend* as the biggest AA booster ever."

"Anyway, I went and found the Newman's Port Aunt Barb had brought for the wake, and we sat together on the couch drinking from the same glass. Daniel had his shirt off. And as much as he pisses me off sometimes, my husband is one hunk and if the day ever comes that I am denied, through death or divorce, the feel of his bare skin next to. . ."

"Elizabeth," I said, "would you mind cutting to the chase just this once because I bought a bra in MallMart this morning. You know, the kind with the print on them that looks like wallpaper."

"Oh," she said. "So things didn't work out with Luke?"

"I am going into the convent next week," I said, "and if the Mercy Sisters don't want me, Martha said I could come work for her, which amounts to the same thing."

"Sorry," she said. "Anyway, Daniel had been surfing the Web, researching supernatural phenomena, for Christ's sake—I have never met a more Protestant Protestant in my entire life. 'I found it,' he said. 'It was on this woman's site, she's doing a doctorate in England in psychic phenomena. And she has half a dozen reports from credible people who smelled roses after a death even though there wasn't a rose bush—or a jar of rose oil—within fifty miles.' 'So that proves it,' I said, giving him one of my special ear-lobe nibbles— Bess had gone back outside to supervise Nora. 'No,' he said, 'but it must mean something.' And then he gave me that look, you know, *that* look, and he said 'Let's send Bess over to Bride's for the night; she won't mind, seeing we're recovering from a death and. . .' 'Roses,' I said, 'recovering from a death and roses,' and then I put my hand underneath. . ."

"Shut up, Elizabeth," I said in the tone of voice that had gotten me suspended for a week by the principal of Stella Maris twenty years ago, and she said "Sorry sorry sorry."

My sister's husband is truly a hunk. I know I shouldn't think of him like that but it's hard not to, especially during bouts of celibacy that get longer as I get older, months when the desert of denial seems positively sub-Saharan, when each beckoning oasis turns out to be yet another mirage, an arid sinkhole down which my overeager heart goes tumbling (head trailing far, far behind). And I think maybe I should just go to Martha and ask if she'll take me on as her assistant, and we'll live happily ever after, fixing felines and discussing how Sartre was not so much a ground-breaking philosopher as a disappointed romantic. And no sex ever again, no sins of the ignorant flesh and the half-witted heart.

Sins as in errors, big fat mathematical mistakes, one and one adding up to zero no matter how hard I try. At least cats are somewhat predictable and moderately faithful. Not to

mention seriously self-sufficient—and self-cleaning. And
Martha hasn't had a decent assistant since Amazing Julia left
her for a South American entomologist. Martha showed me
the most recent picture of Julia and Raul and their three kids
yesterday. "There she is," Martha said, "the best veterinary
assistant in the history of the trade—Julia could hold down
a twenty-five pound unneutered tom with one hand while
applying that violet mascara she used to wear with the
other—and what does she do? Gives it all up to chase bugs
and children around in some country with a name that
rhymes with *silly*." I looked at the photo; beside Julia, in her
capri pants and funky purple T-shirt with a sneering jaguar
on it, stood the South American version of Daniel. Tall, dark
and handsome, just the way the clairvoyants call it.

"Wonder what came over her," I said, and Martha looked
at me as if she didn't know whether or not I was kidding.
"What came over her was not unlike what came over the
Holy Mother before she got married, I imagine," she said.
"Although that didn't end too badly, all the same." And then
she asked me if Nora's name was from Ibsen. No, I told her.
As far as I knew, Mr. Godfrey had named the cat after the
wife of a fifteenth-century English earl from whom he could
claim descent on the distaff side. "That was going to be my
next guess," she said.

Raul and Daniel: they both look like a boy I met when I
was travelling in Italy once, except for their hair. The boy was
long and lean, broad-shouldered and narrow at the hips, his
black hair waist-length even though long hair wasn't fashion-
able then. (But he was the kind of boy who is always in fashion; like Peter Pan, he was one of those to whom the secret
kiss belongs, the kiss that neither Mrs. Darling's husband nor
her children could ever elicit.) Long trailing clouds of sultry

hair, long agile fingers stained with nicotine. Long ago and far away, once upon a time.

We were waiting for the same train; my friends couldn't pry me away from Florence—specifically Michelangelo's *David*—and they got fed up and went on to San Gimignano. The boy told me he had been sitting in a field outside Florence the week before, drinking wine, and he had run out of cigarettes. A dog named Bacchus was with him, and he said to the dog, "If you can get me some cigarettes, Bacchus, I'll name my firstborn after you." And the dog walked away and the boy followed him; a couple of yards later he stumbled over a carton of Rothmans. Which happened to be his brand. "But it was only a dog," the boy said to me, "so I don't have to keep my promise. Besides, I'm a rationalist."

I said to the boy, "You are in an ancient country, thick with old and powerful gods, and you were drinking the holy thing that Bacchus gave to humanity to relieve its myriad sorrows, so you had better name your firstborn after him, even if it's a girl. Even if you were so drunk you just forgot that you had brought a carton of smokes with you and hid them underneath the nearest cypress." He looked at me for a moment, and then he leaned over and put his lips on mine. It reminded me of a part in a John Wayne movie I saw once, John standing there all lanky and cool in his white Stetson while this woman harangues him from underneath a poke bonnet. And suddenly he roars "A woman's mouth is only good for one thing." And he grabs her and plants a big wet one right on the place where all those shrill words were coming from. Only the boy was so quick and soft as he stole the kiss I didn't know I had that it took me a moment to realize what had happened. Well, if a man doesn't want to listen to what a woman is saying, there's worse ways to indicate it, I guess. Especially if he is young and beautiful and so is the morning in a train station in Tuscany.

And that's why my daughter's name is Becky. It's the closest I could come.

Ladies Wear

My first cousin is rich and I am poor; that is the way it has always been. Not always, not when we were kids. If we hadn't been kids together, we wouldn't even know each other now.

Some of my friends say that my cousin makes a god out of money, but I tell them to spell that backwards and then they'd have it right. Raina uses money for insulation: she lives behind its barricades and sends it out like a good dog to retrieve the things that keep her secure inside her house that is as big as the Giant's castle in *Jack and the Beanstalk*. Art for its walls, for instance, the kind that is bought because of its resale value, or to complement the colours of oriental rugs and silk draperies, a practice that can have unfortunate results sometimes. Raina told me she was at a dinner party once where a reproduction of Gustav Moreau's *Salome* was the most prominent thing in the dining room. "I could hardly force down my sushi," she said to me. "Although the gore dripping from the severed head of John the Baptist really set off the crimson motif in her tablecloth."

Money brings Raina period furniture and the latest imitations of period furniture; it gives her the gardener who tends to her imported trees and titled flowers. It regularly summons a depressed middle-aged woman called Mrs. Mahoney to come in to clean, and to get paid under the table so that she won't lose a precious cent of the six hundred dollars a month Welfare gives her for her rent and her utilities, and the bread and eggs and sardines she lives on. It is responsible for the two vehicles in Raina's quadruple garage, one big enough to contain the entire cast of *Cats* (as long as they kept their tails tight to their bodies), the other as small and chic as one of Raina's purses. But the most important thing the good dog money brings Raina is her wardrobe. Raina's closets could hold most of the world's homosexuals in denial, and each one is a transvestite's dream.

I, on the other hand, wander the world like St. Francis of Assisi, who went barefoot and half-naked in all seasons because he wanted to experience God as intimately as possible. Of course, I have a lot more clothes than St. Francis ever did, but in my cousin's world I am considered as naked as a jay bird because I don't own a single stitch of designer clothing. Except for some of Raina's cast-offs, but she is so much smaller than I am that most of these end up going to Jessie, a schizophrenic woman who lives around the corner from me. Jessie begs on the streets sometimes, and I worry that one day Raina will see her in one of her old Dolce and Gabbana dresses, and then all hell will break loose.

But Raina is rarely in my neighbourhood. It distresses her even to pick me up there: the sights and sounds and smells of poverty put fear into her belly. But Raina, I say, just look at the people, look them in the eyes, why don't you—come for a walk with me and I'll introduce you. To Connor, who plays the fiddle as though he invented it, taunting the strings until they get angry enough to throw back his own rage at him in a wild wild tune, or weep out the memory of his wife's suicide. To Billy, who got his head beaten in so many times in a foster home in Salmon Cove that he is the best tea leaf reader in town—he can pull your future right out of the air as if it were a dandelion spore floating by. To Jessie, who is as mad as three waltzing mice and funnier than Jerry Seinfeld. And to Martha, who would love you like a child. Her daughter was killed by a drunk driver when she was three, and you are so tiny and thin and big-eyed you could be her girl grown up a little.

Raina tells me I am crazier than Jessie for even suggesting such a thing.; she thinks poverty is contagious and doesn't want to risk catching it. So usually I take my bike or the bus and meet her at the shops. This is because, in my mind, on the rare occasions Raina does pull up in front of my house, she is driving a Brinks truck and motioning wildly with a pistol for me to hurry up, hurry up, get in. And then we speed away out of what she refers to as "the ghetto." It hurts me to go tearing off like that because I love where I live; I love the people, even the ones I don't particularly like. Maybe because it is easier to look through the rags of poverty and see who is under there. You can hardly ever get the rich out from inside their suits and dresses, or their cars and houses. And you can never get into their country unless you have a designer label on what you are wearing. The labels are like bar codes: the rich swipe you with their eyes the same way the check-out girl at the supermarket runs the bar code on the thing you are buying over the scanner to find out what it's worth.

When I first moved into my neighbourhood, people were suspicious of me because I spoke differently and had more stuff. They thought I was a spy, a spy in the house of the poor, but now they know I'm not anyone at all in particular. "Who are you?" an in-law of Raina's once asked me at one of her parties. "'I'm nobody, who are you?/Are you nobody too?'" I said to him. He looked at me nonplussed: he had wanted to say "I am the king of all I survey," only it would have come out something like "I'm Charlie Escott, Escott Motors." But I hadn't given him the right password; instead, I had confused him with some Emily Dickinson. So he turned away and went looking for one of his own kind, but I didn't mind. I was busy with a tray of canapés; that is one of the things I miss most from the old days, decadent food: escargots in nests of puff pastry, scallops in bacon strait-jackets, and inverted mushroom caps coy about their contents, hiding them under a delicate sprinkling of parmesan cheese. And good wine.

Although wine is always good, even when it's a bottle of cheap Australian sherry named after a flightless bird—if a bird can't fly, can you really say that it is a bird? Technically, of course, you can, but what I would like to know is if emus remember, in their species consciousness, or even more deeply, in the racial consciousness of all winged things, what it is like to be light and high and far away from the clutch of the earth and its heavy possessions, the furniture of forests and mountains, the broadloom of prairie and wheat fields, the big-screen cities, the titanic swimming pools that are the oceans. And if that dim unconscious memory is what gives them the eyes of malnourished children, or the anorexic wives of the rich.

Whenever Raina is driving me, she always slows down when we cross the road that is the demarcation line between Raina and Them, between East and West Belfast, between Israel and Palestine. Not much, though; Raina never really relaxes until we are inside the Great Mall. And why does Raina the Rich take her poor cousin shopping with her? One of the reasons is that neither of us has any sisters, or brothers for that matter, although everyone always thinks we're sisters. Our families lived across the street from each other in the suburb where we grew up. Her mother and mine were the sisters, twins joined at the soul from birth. When they

married, even their husbands couldn't separate them and
they ended up living a stone's throw from each other.

Their daughters couldn't separate them either. Raina's
mother and my mother spent more time with each other
than with us, although we were often with them when they
were together, especially when we were small. But there was
such a thick, brilliant web connecting them, and we were
never more than slight objects on its perimeter, quivering on
gossamer-thin lines. I was happy with the Kool-Aid and
cookies we got when I nagged often enough and loud
enough, but Raina usually didn't even eat hers. She was a thin
child and so was I, but eventually I took on a woman's shape.

I guess I didn't really care that much about my mother. I
suppose I loved her; I was sad when she died, and I think of
her often, but she was always too far away to be meaningful.
And besides, the world was big and rich and warm and full of
things to attach to, for a moment or an hour, or even years
sometimes. One summer's day when I was ten, a blue and yellow butterfly spent part of an afternoon on the back of my
hand; it would go away and ruffle the skirts of my mother's
roses, her Madame del Bards and Charlottes, her Ravels and
Annas, but I kept my arm outstretched and it came back to me
three or four times. I hardly breathed while it sat on the back
of my dirty brown hand; it was so lovely and foreign and fragile I couldn't understand why it wanted to be with me. At
school we sometimes played a game called statues during
recess, so it was fairly easy for me to stand without moving,
like a tree or the wrought-iron Pan that my mother had placed
in the middle of her rose garden. Even when I was a child and
didn't know he was the god of wild things, Pan seemed incon-
gruous to me standing among the rows of tailor-made blos-
soms. He looked as though he was at the wrong party.

The feel of the blue and yellow butterfly on the skin of
my hand is the only thing I remember about that summer,
although Raina says it was the summer we got our first two-
piece bathing suits and thought we were the coolest chicks at
the neighbourhood pool.

Even when we were kids Raina was planning her getaway
to the new suburbs walled like medieval towns. While I was
down playing in the graveyard at the bottom of our street
because it had trees big enough for climbing and a brook with
water spiders blurring its surface in their haste to get away
from my outstretched fingers, Raina was in her room reading
Vogue and *Vanity Fair* and *Chatelaine* and all the other magazines that told her what to eat and wear and do to end up like
the women in the ads. The ads were Raina's favourite part of
the magazines. I found the sleek, sure, remote women in them
intimidating; I also thought they were like Sleeping Beauty,
lovely but sad because they had to stay as still as statues, locked
up between the pages of a magazine until the prince came.

Occasionally there was a man in the pictures. Usually he
was standing to one side gazing in awe at the woman's beauty,
with a rose in his outstretched hand; sometimes he was behind
her with his hands resting lightly on her waist, but he never
had his arms all the way around her because then you would-
n't be able to see her Chanel bathing suit in all its glorious
detail. That's how I knew he wasn't the prince, only a courtier.

The other reason Raina asks me to go shopping with her is
because I carry her bags and keep tabs on where she lays her
Prada purse and her Alfred Sung sunglasses, not that she ever
asks me to. But I do it anyway because she becomes so forget-
ful in the shops; she moves in a trance from piles of sequined
blouses that cost more than I make in a week to racks of dresses so fantastically constructed that you know they could go

dancing without anyone inside them; indeed, they look as though if you did get inside them you would be lost because they are so much more than you are; you must fit their shape, move to accommodate their darts and kick pleats, perhaps even cut your breasts and fill them with plastic so they will sit high and tight on your chest and not interfere with a neckline that is as wide as the Amazon and plunges to the navel; no, these dresses are not about to make allowances for you.

Raina moves up and down the marble floors of her temples of haute couture as though she is walking underwater; she moves as one bewitched, in thrall. One day I watched her stand for fifteen minutes looking into a glass case at jewelled butterfly hair clips and tiny gauze-covered handbags with enamelled dragonflies on them. I once saw a Brazilian butterfly that was as big as a bird and the colour of the sky in the Yukon, where I taught on a reserve years ago. But the butterfly was dead and under glass like the hair clips. If I had Raina's money, I would go to South America and find that butterfly, clipped to the throat of some gingko-green tree deep in the rainforest. (Perhaps I would even stretch out my arms and hold my breath.) Raina hardly ever goes anywhere though. If she does, it's on a cruise ship, or she and her husband fly straight to a compound in some hot country where he can golf and she can lie by the pool in her Ralph Lauren suit, wearing enough sun screen to protect her from the radiation of a million nuclear bombs.

Yesterday's outing was a dose of what Raina calls "retail therapy."

"I'm really down," she said when she called me, "can you go shopping?" Raina had been to the funeral home the night before: her husband's partner's mother had died.

"I didn't know you knew Harry's mother," I said. "I'm sorry you're upset."

"I never laid eyes on the woman," said Raina. "There was a picture of her on top of the casket, though, from when she was in her forties. She looked kind of like Vivien Leigh back then."

"Why didn't they put a more recent picture of her on it?" I asked, but Raina didn't answer.

"What I'm upset about," said Raina, "is that Harry's wife had on that black Misura suit I was going to buy; you know, the top and pants with the gold lining and the ribs down the front."

"Oh," I said. "I didn't think she shopped at Mavericks and Molls."

"I didn't think so either," said Raina," but it's the only shop that carries that line. She *must* have gone in there." Like a thief in the night, I thought to myself. Raina owns Mavericks and Molls even though she doesn't really, but she is the only one in her set who wears certain clothes from certain shops, and woe betide anyone who dares to encroach on her territory. I almost felt sorry for Harry's wife, but like everyone else, I was born with a finite amount of compassion and I decided she didn't really need any of mine.

Actually, we are all born with an infinite amount of everything, but for some reason each of us decides we are in the red in some area. Compassion is my area. I've given a lot of it away, and some days I think I can feel my nails scratch the bottom of the barrel when I reach down for more. I'm like some nineteenth-century outport shopkeeper, worrying about the flour and the sugar and the salt beef running out before the ship carrying provisions can get through the ice in the spring. But then Billy comes over and makes tea, and after we drink it he rips open the bag and dumps the grounds in my cup, and tells me to flip it over and spin it around three times. And then he turns the cup right side up and looks in it, and says he sees a rainbow and the bluebird of happiness. And I feel the barrel start to fill up again.

Raina found the suit Harry's wife had on at the funeral home: there was one left and it was in her size. Mavericks and Molls had had only two of the suits to begin with; there are never more than one or two of anything in such shops. The people who buy their clothes in these places are the kind of people who don't want to meet themselves on the street. That was a favourite expression of my mother's. "If you get that dress, you'll end up meeting yourself on the street," she'd say when I was a teenager and she and Raina's mother and Raina and I were out shopping. I loved that expression; indeed, I even liked the idea of meeting myself on the street. "Hi," I'd imagine myself saying. "Want to go get a Coke?"

"I'm just going to try it on," Raina said, "come on," and we both went into one of the dressing rooms. I'm not comfortable watching Raina undress, but I can't tell her this, and I can't say that the dressing room is not big enough for both of us because an entire third-world family could live there quite comfortably. The dressing rooms in Mavericks and Molls have faux Chippendale chairs and mirrors that are slightly smoky and lit so that even I look like Miss Cosmic Universe in them. And big terra cotta urns full of pussy willows, which someone has sprayed with gold paint. "Who would paint the lily," I said to my cousin, "or gild refined gold?" "What?" Raina said. But I didn't answer because I knew she would forget I had ever spoken in a matter of seconds.

The reason I don't like to see Raina naked, or seminaked, is because Raina is forty-three but she has the body of a fourteen-year-old. And there is not a mark on her face, not a wrinkle or a line or a spot of discolouration. But Raina has never had surgery and she rarely exercises. And she lives on toast and salads. But there she is, with her adolescent breasts and her unblemished skin, and her tiny face under the black bob that makes her look like a French urchin. I saw a foetus in a bottle once, floating in formaldehyde with its rudimentary thumb in its undefined mouth; its skin shone like Raina's does. She says she owes her skin to Clinique, but I tried some of Raina's leftover Clinique once and my skin is the way you would expect a forty-three-year-old woman's skin to be. Perhaps I didn't have enough faith in it. "Because of the savour of thy good ointments thy name is as an ointment poured forth, therefore do the virgins love thee" I tell her, and she rolls her eyes. Sometimes I say, "I know you made a pact with the devil, what did he look like?" "Like Ralph Fiennes," she says, or "Mel Gibson." Or I say, "There's a picture in your attic, isn't there, and it probably looks like Bette Davis the night before she died." The answer to which is "I don't *have* an attic. Attics are passé."

I have an attic; my house is one hundred and four years old and looks it. Its attic used to be the maid's quarters, but I have made it into a study where I mark the papers of the men and women in my adult literacy class. They were once children who had to go out to work, in factories or on fishing boats, or as ladies' maids and scullery boys to the wealthy. And now when their grandchildren ask to be read a bedtime story, the black marks on the white page look like something they have left dirty, and the shame of it sends them to me. One of the papers I read last night had tear stains on it. It belongs to Mrs. Frances O'Leary, who cried in class once, after she had written her signature for the first time.

Raina said, "So how does it look?" The suit fit her like a glove; or, rather she fit the suit as if it was her mother's womb. "Perfect," I said. I always say this, because it is always true. Raina is built like a hanger and the clothes love her for it. "Does it look better on me?" said Raina. "Of course it does," I said, even though I hadn't seen it on Harry's wife. But I've met the woman; she's in her early thirties and slim enough, but her two babies poked her belly out a bit while they were in residence, and they pulled her breasts down when she was feeding them, and so she is a little bulgy here and there.

Raina put the suit back on the rack and tried on a blouse that made her look like the youngest daughter in the BBC production of *Pride and Prejudice*. One of the clerks came over and whispered, "You know, that line of blouses is the favourite of a famous pop diva," and then he named her. "That slut can't even sing," I said to him, and he stared at me in horror. "But she's one of the richest and most powerful women in America," he said, and then he looked at Raina for confirmation. She nodded. "Do you like the blouse?" I asked her. "Do you?" said Raina. "Yes," I said, "but just remember, you'll be sharing it with a lesser individual." Raina sings like a lark in the morning, and she's never been a slut.

Raina's husband is only the second man she's ever slept with. The first one is a secret she won't even tell me. There was a boy once, one summer when we were in our late teens. He was tall and slender, and he had black hair like Raina's and the same pale face; they even walked alike, two swans moving over a lake. The boy liked to draw; he went away in the fall to art school and never came back. In Raina's bedroom there is a sketch of a young man's naked back; above his shoulder is the arched neck of a young woman. Her face is not in the picture, only the edge of her cheek, a strand of

black hair defining its curve. Raina says she picked it up from
a street vendor in Cuba.

Neither Raina nor I have children. I just never got around
to it and Raina can't have them. She tried, though, ten years
back: she tried so hard. She even spent thousands of dollars
on in vitro fertilization, and endured the pain without a murmur. Three times. She was so sad that year that we didn't even
go to New York to check out the summer lines.

"Why don't you adopt?" I asked her.

"Because no one gives up children any more. I'd be old
enough to be a grandmother before I got one."

"What about going to China and adopting a little girl?
One less for the garbage pail in the abortionist's clinic."

"I haven't got the energy," she said. Sometimes, though, I
think the real reason Raina didn't go to China is that she wanted a child from her own genetic line, a designer kid, not some
Chinese generic. But maybe not; maybe she just broke her
heart over trying to catch a baby, lying there so still and hope-
ful while they put the fertilized eggs inside her. And then waiting and waiting for life to swell up her belly and her heart.
And life rejecting her, as if she wasn't a proper address.

Before we left Mavericks and Molls, Raina asked me if I
wanted anything. I almost said, "Sure, I'll take that lamé gown
in the corner, the one that says fifteen hundred dollars on the
tag, even though between you and me and the wall, I know
for a fact that if you take the middle man, or men, or women,
out of the equation, it would say fifty bucks." Which would
be mainly the cost of the fabric. Every time Raina tries something on, I see tiny brown hands stitching it up around her.
Children's hands, hands that should be catching water spiders
or whatever children's hands like to do in those countries.
Sometimes the hands belong to small women with glass ban-

gles on their wrists and naked babies clinging to their legs. But I never say these things to Raina any more. It only distresses her: she says, "Well, what can I do about it? That's the way the world is; how would it help anyone if I walked around nude?" And then I think about Sumeria and Babylon, and Persia and Egypt, and Greece and Rome, and the United States of America, and I marvel at the great cycles that change the face, but never the heart, of humankind.

But Raina is very soft underneath her Vivian Westwood jacket, at least when it comes to those she loves. When I was in the hospital for six weeks last year, she came every night even though she has been terrified of hospitals ever since her mother died in one. And when her fifteen-year-old Portuguese water dog, Dali, kicked the bucket, Raina wore a black band around her arm for a month, even though people thought she was protesting something and stopped inviting her to parties for a while.

Dali had been sick for a long time, sick and senile and deaf and two-thirds blind. On the morning of his death he started barking uncontrollably and dragging himself by his front legs around the house, urinating as he went. He didn't recognise Raina or her husband. "It's time, Raina," her husband said, but she said "Oh no, he's just having a bad day." In the end, Raina's husband made her go to their bedroom so he could pick Dali up and put him in the back of their SUV, after he put plastic down over the flooring. He collected me on the way to the vet's. Raina called me after, crying. "How did it go," she said, "was it quick?"

"He was asleep in fifteen seconds," I said. "By the way, they'll have his urn for you on Friday."

"Oh." she said. "You know, I was thinking that we should go out and buy a really nice container for Dali's ashes.

I saw some wide-mouth bottles made of milk glass at one of
the craft galleries, with angels on their lids, don't you think
one of those would look perfect on the mantelpiece?"

"Perfect." I said. "A sarcophagus fit for a prince of dogs.
And the queen of mantelpieces."

I lied to Raina about Dali's death. The vet was a young
man, an Egyptian; his eyes were a lot like Dali's, and by the time
the dog was dead they were overflowing like the Nile in spring.

Raina's husband carried Dali into the clinic and put him
on the table, handed the vet's assistant his gold card and left.
I told the girl I was staying and she went back to the reception area. And then I went to Dali: he was lying still with his
eyes closed, and I cradled his head in my arms and said,
"Never mind Dali, it's all right, it's fine, you're a good, good
boy." The vet took a needle from his cabinet and filled it with
a clear liquid, and then he came and stuck it into the dog's
leg; a few moments later I felt Dali go limp. The vet and I
looked at each other over the body and made sad faces, and
he started to take off his gloves.

And then Dali raised his head and looked straight at me, his
black eyes full of anguish. And a noise crinkled the antiseptic
air: the thin high keening of one betrayed. I put my arms back
around him and began crooning a lullaby Raina used to sing to
him when he was a puppy, but he wasn't buying it. Before I
knew what was happening, the dog gathered up all the strength
he had left in his dying body and made a great lunge, and we
both toppled from the altar of compassionate death onto the
thin linoleum underneath. And suddenly Dali wasn't senile anymore: he was watching the vet with eyes like a hawk's, and
every time the poor guy got within a foot of him, Dali twisted
in my arms and shook and moaned. The vet was sweating and

so was his patient; I was dry as dust because I wasn't really there. It didn't seem like the place to be, after all.

"I can't believe this," said the vet. He crouched down and put an empty needle inside another vein in Dali's leg; when he removed it, it was full of what looked like strawberry jelly. "His blood is so thick," the vet said, "that the narcotic couldn't get to his heart. I don't know why he's lived this long."

"Because his mistress loved him," I said, "and Love is stronger than Death."

"Well I have got something here that is stronger than love or death," said the vet. "It is designed to kill an elephant or at least a cow." So he got the biggest needle in the clinic and filled it full, and I had to practically sit on Dali while the vet stuck it straight into his heart. And when he did, the dog slumped over and the sphincter muscle in his anus relaxed and I got shit all over my jeans, but I was happier than I'd ever been in my life, or at least within recent memory. The vet and I embraced and I took his tears home with me on my cheek, and when I got there I drank the bottle of Dom Perignon that Raina had given me for Christmas. I was saving it for my friend Sam's wedding, but death can be like a wedding sometimes.

Later I went over to Connor's. He lives across the street from me in a run-down Edwardian with his three-legged dog, Laslow. Laslow growled when I went in because I forgot to change my jeans. "You're drunk," Connor said, and I said "Yeah, but not drunk enough." And then I told him about Dali and he went into the kitchen and got a bottle of sherry and two glasses and we went up to his bedroom. The last thing I remember before I passed out was Connor playing "She Moved Through the Fair" and me trying to sing it, but screwing up the last stanza, on purpose I guess, who knows?

I dreamt it last night that my dead dog came in;
So softly he entered that his feet made no din.
He lay down beside me, and this he did say:
"It will not be long, love, till our wedding day."

I had taken off my jeans and Laslow was in bed with me; I sang it to him and he licked my face. Raina would like Laslow, although she'd probably want to get him a prosthetic leg. By Givenchy.

The next morning Connor made me put on his ratty old robe and then he lifted me up in his arms and carried me down over the crooked stairs, murmuring into my hair, "You are the snowflake that never touches the earth, you are the linnet in the spring," and other things he used to say to his wife until the night she hanged herself while he was with another woman. Jessie was in the kitchen making scrambled eggs and I thought I was going to throw up, but then she turned around and said, "Look, look what I got at the Sally Ann this morning for *two bucks!*" It was a rhinestone brooch, and she had it on the lapel of a plaid woods shirt; the shirt hung down over a pair of purple harem pants that were busy serenading the plastic violets on the table. And the sun was shining in through the stained glass window somebody had scrawled "Jesus Never Fails" on with a black marker; there were rainbow butterflies all over the walls, and suddenly I felt like dancing. So I did, with a three-legged dog and a crazy old woman. And a man who can play "Mary's Wedding" and step a credible jig at the same time.

I bet Tommy Hilfiger can't do that.

A Day at the Races

One must have a bit of Chaos in oneself to give birth to a dancing star.

— Nietzche

Natalie is walking beside the harbour with the wind at her back. The wind is very obliging; it changes direction whenever Natalie does; it is a strong wind that she can lean against a little to steady herself, and it is as warm as a man's naked chest.

The harbour is small and shaped like a kidney bowl; it is rotten with untreated sewage, the blood of the mother toxic with the waste of her delinquent children. But still Natalie comes down to the water's edge; the harbour is her only access to the sea, and she must put salt air on the wound in her heart. Otherwise it might heal.

Matt has been gone for three months. A month after he left, Natalie had her hair cropped off as short as she could get it to go without shaving her head. Her friend Claire told her she looked like a cross between Sinead O'Connor and Joan of Arc.

"That's okay," said Natalie. "They're both admirable women."

"Yes," said Claire, "but neither is exactly the poster girl for *joie de vivre*."

"I don't speak French," said Natalie. "*C'est dommage, mais c'est la vie, n'est-ce pas?*"

"Can I shake you till your teeth rattle?" said Claire, putting her hands on Natalie's shoulders.

"I don't think they would rattle," said Natalie. "After all, they are teeth, not maracas. When I die, you can make maracas out of them if you want to."

"No thanks," said Claire. "I have an aversion to percussion instruments."

"Me, too," said Natalie, and Claire gave her a kiss on the cheek that felt like a pinch.

Once, when Natalie and Matt were living together and he didn't come home for two days, she had cut her long black hair off herself, cut it all ragged and crazy; what she had really wanted to do was carve a line down the side of her face so that the hurt could run out.

When she heard Matt coming up the apartment steps on the third day, she had gone and opened the door before he reached the top. He had stood there looking up at her with narrowed eyes, as if she was too bright, or wouldn't come into focus. "What did you do to your hair, Nat?" he said. Natalie looked down at him, and replied, as if he was the postman, "I wanted to be ugly, so when you came back, you'd go away again." And Matt's eyes had opened up like a time-lapse film of big blue cornflowers coming into bloom, and Natalie saw that they were blemished with guilt and pity and she felt bad for bringing ugliness into the world. She had wanted to go down to him and reach up and run her hand over his face until his eyes cleared, but she'd had to stay hanging onto the doorframe because her legs were as weak as if she had been making love all night long.

And Matt had said to her, in a voice so low she could barely hear him, "You could never be ugly, Nat, not you, not even if you broke yourself all up and shaved yourself bald,

because you are so beautiful inside, Nat, so pure and good
that God would send an angel to put you back together
again." And then he had come the rest of the way up the
steps and lifted her up in his arms, and he had carried her to
their bed and bandaged her up in the quilt that Natalie's
mother had made when she was Natalie's age. And he had
lain down beside her and put his hand on her tattered head,
saying, "shh, shh," because she was crying by then, and her
hands were shaking so badly she thought her fingers were
going to fly off. Or fly up into his face and draw a picture of
her pain on it with her nails. But the part of Natalie that
needed Matt's blood to stream down his face like tears had
drifted so far away since he had come to live with her that it
was like the memory of a dead woman she hadn't known
very well.

The next day Matt took her to the hottest hair salon in
town and bartered one of his handmade belts for a cut and
perm. "She tried to do it herself," he told the stylist, "but
hairdressing is not one of her many talents." When Natalie
came out into the waiting room an hour later, Matt was talking to a girl who had green and orange hair and a round face
with bits of metal dangling from various sites, like a codfish
with hooks in it. "Hey, Matt," said Natalie, and he had turned
away from the fish girl; his eyes were nearly cobalt, the
colour desire turned them—for me, Natalie told her new
face, curl-capped and tinier than it had been, in the mirror
behind the desk; not for her, for me.

"You look like a faun, Nat," Matt had said, "like a little
pixie: those bones can take anything can't they?"

"I have strong bones," said Natalie, "like my mother. But
even hers got brittle eventually."

"If you stay with me, I'll keep your bones strong, even if I have to coat them with crushed calcium."

"Would that work?"

"Yes, but only if the moon was full and one of us was wearing fishnet stockings."

"Really?"

"Absolutely," he had said, and then he had bent down and kissed her nose. The green-and-orange-haired girl watched them with the eyes of a fish struggling on the bank of a river, drowning in the air.

The man who owned the hair salon had chosen the Banana Belt from the selection Matt offered him. It was wide and made of red oxhide, and its brass buckle had a yellow enamel banana on it. The banana had eyes and a nose, and a smiling mouth underneath a Hitler moustache; Natalie thought it looked like a leering Man-in-the-Moon.

Matt made his belts when he wasn't working in the inner-city backyard terraced like a Japanese garden where his father grew flowers and herbs for the tonics and potpourris he sold in his shop. Matt had a workroom in the back that smelled like leather, and dill and fennel and other plants that had been hung to dry from the roof beams and even the curtain rods, obscuring the windows so that it was always like a High Arctic midnight in summer inside; the only source of illumination was a naked forty-watt bulb hanging from the ceiling on a long black cord.

Once, Natalie spent the night there with Matt, on a pile of burlap bags covered with old coats, and she thought she had never been in such a beautiful room, not even that time in Quebec when she and Claire had stayed in the hotel with Godiva chocolates on the pillows of their canopied bed; every night before they went to sleep they had hung out the hotel window, half-cut on the contents of the mini-bar, yelling, "Fie on thee, scurvy wretches!" at the people below. But Matt hadn't been there, with his golden hair all long and loose like Rapunzel's, saying, "Lay your sleeping head, my love, human on my faithless arm." And Natalie did, looking up into his face to see if he really meant it about the faithless part, even though she knew it was a quote from Auden. But he put his hand on her cheek and told her to go to sleep, and his hand seemed to be sincere, so she took it and placed it over her heart.

On weekend nights Matt played the drums in a band called Nietzche's Children. "I didn't know Nietzche had children," Natalie said to Matt once. "I sort of hoped he was infertile."

"No," said Matt, "he was very fertile and spawned a lot of us. But I am his favourite."

"I was my mother's favourite, but then I was her only one," said Natalie. Only one, lonely one.

"You are certainly my favourite," Matt said. "The favourite of discerning men everywhere."

And your only one, your only one, Natalie had said to herself, crossing her fingers on both hands as tight as they could go without breaking.

Besides the Banana Belt, Matt made a Bible Belt, an Irish Belt, a Fan Belt and one called Orion's Belt, which had three rhinestones on its black buckle. Matt had given Natalie an Orion's Belt for Christmas last year, only he had put three small diamonds on the buckle. And the belt was made of dyed doeskin instead of a strip of cow. "The poor deer," Natalie had said.

"The deer," replied Matt, "would have died anyway, for her meat. At least this way she has a sort of immortality.

There are men who would peel off whole stretches of their skin to wrap around your waist, you know."

"Are you one of them?" asked Natalie.

"No," said Matt. "When I die, I want my skin to be a drum."

"A snare drum?"

"No, a big Irish bodhran; I think I have enough skin for that, don't you?"

"I think," said Natalie, "that you have all the skin there is. I never notice other people's anyway."

"Honey," Claire had said to Natalie a few nights after Matt came back, "you know how the joke goes."

"Yeah," said Natalie. "What's the first thing a drummer does when he gets up in the morning? Goes home."

"I guess he didn't get up for two days then," said Claire.

"Or nights either," said Natalie, and then she and Claire had laughed the laugh peculiar to women when men have lived down to their expectations. Later, Natalie threw up outside the pub she and Claire had been drinking in; projectile vomiting, it was called; the beer had shot out of her and hit the sidewalk like a liquid bomb before she even knew it was coming up. But no one saw except the moon, who had a star dangling from one lobe like a rhinestone earring.

Natalie hasn't worn earrings since Matt left, except for the small pewter crosses that used to belong to her mother. Sometimes she looks at the profusion of glitter in her alabaster jewellery box—gold and silver, beads, glass and feathers—and remembers how she used to dance when Matt's band played, shimmering like the Milky Way in mirrored shifts or fringed blouses and embroidered jeans, with peacock feathers or glimmering latticework hanging from her ears. She had danced for him like an East Indian woman, her hands making mudras of love all of their own volition and fashion, her body undulating as though it were at home in bed under his.

Last week, Natalie emptied her lingerie drawer and stuffed everything into a long net bag and buried it in the back of her closet. Natalie had never owned lingerie before she met Matt. Her breasts were as small as her hands, and her hips barely knew that they weren't her waist. But a few months after Matt moved in with her, he started bringing home things he called frillies—transparent teddies and slinky slips; camisoles, fantastical bustiers—and all manner of strange hosiery: fishnet stockings, stockings with lines up their backs, pantyhose with the middles gutted out of them. And he had dressed Natalie in these things the way she used to costume her Barbie dolls. Sometimes he put the stockings on his own legs, and wrapped his long body in satin and silk and lace. Natalie had found this disturbing at first, but he was so beautiful, as beautiful as a god, and who could fathom the ways of a god? They descended upon mortal women in many forms, even as bulls and swans; Natalie preferred Matt's approach. But sometimes it made her feel bad when he was done up like that; he was so big and powerful that Natalie felt her small sexuality slipping away like a little green grass snake, seeping out of her the way it used to in high school when she was around the dangerous girls, the ones with black lips and tattoos, and half-exposed breasts that they aimed at the boys like Uzis.

Natalie had met Matt one Saturday night when she and Claire were out roaming the downtown. They had strayed away from the small pubs, the ones that held them like friendly hands when they were inside, where they knew the bartenders and the bathrooms and which pool tables were

slanted so that it was easier to put down the balls. The bar
they went into when it was starting to get thirsty out was big
and dark and full of troubled music. "It sounds like Wagner
on acid," Natalie said to Claire. "Vag who?" said Claire.
"Never mind," said Natalie, "let's just go"; the hymn to
chaos was making her palms sweat and the tips of her fingers feel prickly. But then the band went on break, and the
drummer came and sat down at Claire and Natalie's table. He
was tall and blond; a gold stud in his right ear winked at
Natalie, and she had winked back. "Hi there," he said to her
in a voice that took its own sweet time, "I'm Matt, and I
would really like to know who you are."

"I'm Natalie, and this is Claire," said Natalie. "This is
Matthew, Claire."

"Matthew? Are you aiming to make a saint out of me?"
And the gold stud had stopped winking at Natalie because
Matt had lowered his head like a bull, and his long ponytail
had fallen across the flirtatious ear.

"No," said Natalie, "why would I want a saint? Saints are
celibates, or so we have been led to believe."

"Well, then, I'm Matt."

"But I don't know what Matt means. Something to walk
on, something to lie on?"

"Something simple. But you can walk on me any time
you like, so long as you're wearing high heels."

"I never wear high heels. They hurt."

"Too bad, because you sure do have the legs for them,
legs like a yearling filly, Nat."

"My name is Natalie. And horses don't wear high heels."

"They do in Texas," said Matt. "All the females in Texas
wear high heels, even the ladybugs." His face had been as
straight as a board when he said this, and for a moment

Natalie entertained a vision of all manner of fauna line-dancing in high heels in a Texan bar the size of a city block. And then she looked up, and Matt was grinning at her, and she burst out laughing. And she had taken him home, even though before they left the bar Claire had slipped her a napkin on which she had used eyeliner to draw a stick figure playing a drum; a circle ran around the figure and a slanted black line cut it in half.

"It's only for tonight," Natalie had whispered in Claire's ear, but Claire had put up her left eyebrow, the eyebrow that knew it all. The eyebrow had been right on the money, too; Matt had gone back to his father's the next day, but he was on Natalie's doorstep by suppertime with his clothes. And the set of drums that sat in their living room like a pagan shrine, except on the weekends when it went off to be beaten by the children of a dead German existentialist.

"Why did you come here?" Natalie asked Matt's father, Bill, one day when she was helping him pick lavender; picking lavender made Natalie's fingers smell like her great aunt Lydia, whom she used to sleep with sometimes when she was little. Aunt Lydia had lived to be one hundred, dying the day after she got her congratulatory telegram from the Queen. The one from the Prime Minister arrived on the morning she was to be buried, and Natalie's mother had read it to Aunt Lydia in the funeral home. Just in case, she said to Natalie.

"Well, when Reagan got elected, I decided it was time to put on my boots and head north. When Matt and me got here, I figured it was far enough. And it seems to be," said Bill, and he had grinned and reached down and tickled Natalie's nose with a lavender sprig.

Bill had been at Woodstock. "Was it really. . .?" Natalie asked him.

"Yes, it was. Really and truly. But don't expect me to explain it to a sweet young thing like yourself. That time is gone and will never come again. Only the music is left, and I hope and pray that it will go down through the generations so that time won't be forgotten. I listen to that music every night—Janis and Joe and Jimi—just like an old Reverse Holocaust survivor, not to be disrespectful of the Jews or anything. But there was more love in that place, more love in the last three days of that time than there ever was before or since. Only we thought it was the beginning of something, not the end. But people are like that. They're always mistaking endings for beginnings. Do you want some lavender to take home?"

"Thank you, Bill," said Natalie, "I would love some. If you put it on your pillow, you will dream of your true love, you know." Bill looked at Natalie, and his blue eyes had been as pale as anemones on a grey day. "I don't know if love and true belong in the same sentence," he said.

"Sometimes they do, Bill. Sometimes they just have to." And Natalie had reached up and tugged his ~~thin grey~~ ponytail.

That night Natalie crushed the lavender on her side of the bed, and she dreamt that a strange city and she was climbing an iron back of an auditorium. She opened a rusty was Matt, doing a striptease to a packed ho pitch black inside and the audience was a formless, faceless mass; Natalie couldn't tell if they were women or men or aliens. A naked forty-watt bulb hung above Matt, who was down to a G-string; beside him was a small heap of sequined frillies and a pair of red shoes like Dorothy's in *The Wizard of Oz*. It was so quiet you could hear a pin drop. Natalie looked at Matt's face, and it was exactly the way it always was the moment before he ejaculated, like the face of a dying man praying for salvation or someone steeling himself for a blow. Natalie woke up and threw her pillow onto the floor. Matt was sleeping on his back, and she dove under his arm and pulled herself up onto his shoulder, lying there until the conch-shell sound of his blood moving under her ear slowed her heart.

The day after Bill gave her the lavender, Natalie asked Matt about his mother. "I never had a mother," said Matt. "Bill grew me in one of his big pots; he crossed a runner bean with some fireweed, and there I was."

"Seriously," said Natalie.

"I am serious," said Matt. "As serious as I get." And then he had said, "Okay, Nat, I am going to say this once and then I am never going to refer to the subject again and neither will you if you are as smart as I think you are. You want to know about my mother, the woman who gave birth to me? Because that is basically all she did, propel me out into this shitty world and walk away wiping the blood off her legs while I cried in Bill's arms. And then my Aunt Lou came and took us home to Texas. My father and mother were living in some hippy dippy heaven in California, where everything was shared, the food, the clothes, the women, the children— the cats the rats the elephants—anyway, it didn't work out. And do you know why it didn't work out? Because when that woman was carrying me, my father had some twisted epiphany that carried him somewhere off to the right of J. Edgar Hoover. He wanted to marry my mother and get a job and a house and have more babies. And she just laughed in his face and disappeared like yesterday's news."

"What was her name?" asked Natalie.

"I don't remember," said Matt. "It wasn't Nat, though. Do you want some more spaghetti? I put the oregano Bill picked yesterday in the sauce."

"Yes," said Natalie, "yes, I would." A fly was trying to climb the mound of spaghetti curled up like a nest of baby rattlers on her Blue Willow platter; she caught it and took it in her cupped hands and let it out the back door.

Last summer Natalie had taken Matt to Salmon Cove to meet her mother's people: it was the first time she had been there since her mother died of cancer eight years before. Natalie's father lived in Florida with the woman he'd been having an affair with during the last five years of his marriage. The affair had broken Natalie's mother's heart and melted the flesh from her body; so toxic was her sorrow that in the end it had corroded her very bones.

When they pulled up in front of her uncle's house, Natalie's Aunt Myrtle was standing in her front garden in exactly the same spot she was in when Natalie had last seen her. "I didn't mean to be away for so long," Natalie told her aunt, who was saying Natalie's name with a mouth that had tears running around its perimeter. "Anyway, it was nice of you to stay put," said Natalie. And then she had hugged her aunt until both of them said ouch.

Later, while Matt was having a beer in the shed with Uncle Hubert, Natalie's aunt said to her, "My dear, I don't want to trouble you, but are you sure he's all right? I didn't like the way he slyered at Jennifer when she came out dressed for the Legion dance."

Jennifer was Natalie's first cousin, once removed. She had just turned eighteen, and Natalie had had to be reintroduced. "Oh, Aunt Myrtle," said Natalie. "Matt grew up in Texas and he's got a permanent squint from the sun down there." But when Matt came in from the shed and said why didn't they stay the night and go to the dance at the Legion, maybe the local boys would let him jam with them, Natalie told him that they'd better get back because she thought she'd locked the cat out.

On the way home, Natalie said, "Well, Jennifer sure has grown."

"Which one was Jennifer?"

"The one you slyered at."

"Slyered?"

"It's a local term."

"Speaking of local terms, did you know your uncle keeps a specimen of a very rare breed of dog out there in that shed?"

"You mean Rupert, the Cockled Spaniard? Rupert's not rare; there are at least half a dozen Cockled Spaniards in Salmon Cove."

"You are rare, as rare as the orchid that blooms once every ten years on the brow of Mount Olympus."

"Could it grow in this climate?" Natalie moved her hand to lie along his thigh.

"I can make it grow here." And Matt had put one arm around her neck and slid his hand down over her breast, stroking the nipple until it rose up hard and pushed against the cotton of her T-shirt, looking for the full weight of his hand.

The moon flew like Pegasus above the car all the way home; when they got there it was hovering outside the bedroom window, making the tail of the cat asleep on the bed shimmer like a ten-cent sparkler.

Matt left Natalie on a Monday afternoon. Natalie had been at work, in the section of the library called The Browsery. Natalie loved The Browsery because it was always full of old people, and she got to have them all to herself once a week. At three o'clock the phone had rung. "Hello?" said Natalie, and then she remembered and said "Good afternoon, Public Library."

"Hello, Nat," Matt had answered: his voice was far away and flat.

"What's up?" said Natalie, but her hands already knew because they had started to tremble; she hoped they wouldn't get really out of control because they could when they were frightened, they could skim off into the air like startled swallows and she needed them to keep holding on, to the phone and to the corner of her desk.

"I'm leaving for Ireland in an hour."

"Oh," said Natalie. "Oh. Who is she?"

"Jesus, Nat, does there have to be a she? Okay, yeah, there is a she, but it's not like that. I mean she's just this chick who's been hanging out with the band, but her parents live in Ireland and she can get me over there on air mile points and I can stay with her for nothing. For Christ's sake Nat, you know how much I want to go to Ireland; it's not like I'm never coming back, can't you just let me go with the flow without making a big deal out of it?"

"Do you know what, Matthew? You are just like your mother," said Natalie. Later, when she was in the rest room giving her lunch to a toilet, she wondered whose phone he had thrown against a wall.

Natalie turns away from the harbour. Up on the high street the specialty shops are waiting like anxious bears. It has not been a good summer for tourists; if they don't come soon, some of the shops will be dead by the winter. Natalie passes the maple that marks the border of boutique country. The tree is wearing earrings, big, dangly yellow ones, and its green head is all funked up with short curly leaves. As Natalie moves under the tree in her black T-shirt and cut-offs, she thinks she feels it shiver.

Over the last six months Natalie's wardrobe has darkened and lengthened. "I wish you'd get out of mourning," Claire said to Natalie last Saturday while Natalie was paying for a grey ankle-length skirt. "I'm not in mourning," said Natalie. "I just get cold a lot lately." "And I am the Queen of Rumania," said Claire. "Are you?" said Natalie. "I can never remember where that is."

When Natalie rounds the corner of the high street, she sees that it has been closed off to traffic; striped pavilions line half its cobbled length. She wonders if the Downtown Development Commission has arranged a medieval tournament to lure people to the shops, and she hopes there will be a joust. And then she sees Claire. "Claire!" Natalie yells, but Claire doesn't turn around. Claire is tall and curvy, and quite unfashionable at the moment because she looks like a forties movie star instead of a female kickboxer. Today she is wearing a classic little black dress and a pair of black patent slingbacks.

Natalie starts to run; she has forgotten about running, how she loves pushing the air away, how satisfying it feels as the balls of her feet thrust themselves into the asphalt, which gives way a little because it has been cooking under the August sun. The brown orthopaedic sandals Natalie is wear-

ing cost more than any of the high heels or slides or slingbacks Matt had liked her to wear, but they make her spine
glad; she feels as if she is eating up the ground like a runaway
horse; in her ugly beautiful sandals Natalie will soon catch up
to Claire, who is undulating down the middle of the high
street like the Queen of the Nile. Or the Queen of Rumania.
"Claire!" Natalie yells again, and people turn their heads, but
just for a moment, because there's nothing very interesting
about a small dark girl shouting out a name. And then she is
right behind Claire, but Claire must have her Walkman with
her because Natalie yells "Claire!" one more time and Claire
still doesn't turn around.

Natalie reaches out and grabs Claire's arm. Her fingers
grip strange terrain: Claire's upper arm is as muscular as
Matt's, which is ridiculous because Claire has arms like the
Venus de Milo, except that Claire's are intact. Claire turns her
head, and Natalie says "Jesus Christ" and jumps back.

"What's the matter, darling," says the man in the blonde
wig and padded dress, "never seen a drag queen before?"

Natalie looks at him until he is not Claire for sure, and
then she says, "No, I never have actually. I thought you were
a friend of mine."

"I can't imagine someone like me having a friend like
you." The man's lipstick is smeared, which detracts from his
sneer; his voice, though, is as pointy as his heels.

"Well, thank you very much," says Natalie, and she turns
her back to him, but he reaches out and grabs the bottom of
her T-shirt.

"I'm sorry, it's just so stressful, you know? Every year, I
think I'm going to be on top of things, but I'm always late,
and the race is going to start in fifteen minutes, and I can't

find Jimmy or even the tent, for god's sake, and these panty-hose are right up my crotch."

"What race?" says Natalie, because the man still has the tail of her T-shirt held hostage, prisoner of two fire-engine-red fake fingernails.

"The Imelda Marcos Hundred Yard Dash."

"Oh. Why is it called that?"

"Because you have to wear high heels to enter."

"Didn't Imelda Marcos have any flats in her collection?"

"I don't know. I don't have any in mine, anyway. By the way, my name is Julian."

"By the way, my name is Natalie. Can I go now?"

"No," says Julian, "you're going to enter the race. I know you dykes would rather sleep with Rush Limbaugh than take off your Birkenstocks, but it's Gay Pride Week and that includes all of us girls, sweetie."

"I'm not wearing Birkenstocks and I'm not a dyke," says Natalie, and before she can stop it, one hand darts out like a hummingbird and stings Julian's face. "Ow!" says Julian. "Well, I guess I won't need any rouge on that cheek."

"I'm so sorry," Natalie says. "I don't usually do things like that. I'd go in the race to make it up to you, but I'm not wearing heels."

"Well, you will be when I find my tent."

"But I take a ten, my feet are way out of proportion to the rest of me—do you have tens?"

"Honey, I *only* have tens."

"Look, we're here," Julian says, stopping in front of a rainbow-coloured tent; inside, a dog is yapping hysterically. "That is not a Cockled Spaniard, is it?" asks Natalie. "No," says Julian, looking at her quizzically, "she's a Mexican

Hairless. Jimmy and I brought her back from California last year."

"Patsy," Julian coos, pulling aside the flap of the tent. "Daddy's here!" A diminutive dog with the bare pink skin of a young pig springs up into Julian's face like a canine gymnast; around its neck is a rhinestone collar attached to a pink leash. "Wait here," says Julian to Natalie, "until I get you the appropriate footwear." He slips inside the canvas rainbow and reappears with a pair of gold platform shoes that have three-inch heels, and straps that go around the calf. The straps are snakes whose heads form a clasp that joins them under the knee; they have red glass eyes. "You're kidding," says Natalie. "No," says Julian, "I'm very much entirely and completely serious." And then he helps Natalie put them on; they feel like lead weights. Or something Minerva might have worn into battle, but Natalie is not a Greek goddess, she isn't any kind of goddess or even an Amazon. Before she can explain this to Julian, his relentless red talons have dragged her to the starting line.

Julian and Natalie are standing in front of a bank with Corinthian columns. They are in the middle of twelve other people, men and women, one of whom is on stilts with high heels drawn in charcoal on the bottoms. Hundreds of people line the high street, and Natalie hopes that Claire is not among them; the thought of explaining any of this to Claire makes her feel tired. And then, "On your Marcos, get set, go!" yells the mayor of the city, who is slightly drunk and tottering on a pair of white nurse's pumps. The young man in the buckskin loincloth and turquoise stilettos next to him draws a bow and shoots an arrow with a gold-coloured Christmas tree ornament shaped like an apple attached to its tip; as it begins its ride on the rays of the noon sun down the

A Day at the Races

high street the onlookers roar like lions and the line of high-heeled contestants breaks up into multicoloured particles that rush along in the wake of the gilded plastic fruit.

Natalie jumps into the air and throws one leg out in front of her as far as it can go and then sends the other after it; her hands are pushing hard at the air to make holes for her to slip through and her head is down like a swimmer's; the asphalt is a slow dark river under her and she is moving over it like a Kansas tornado. After nine or ten strides, it occurs to her that her ability to run in high heels is akin to the flight of a bumblebee, aerodynamically impossible, but the bees did it anyway. And she was doing it anyway, she was the Flight of the Bumblebee, she was the Queen of Rumania, she was Natalie, the Fastest Woman on High Heels in all the Known Worlds.

A tall thin man in a cotton candy pink wig and a fuschia bridesmaid's dress with matching satin shoes jumps into the corner of her eye, his dress flapping like the wings of a flamingo. Natalie looks up and sees that he is about to overtake Julian, who is in the lead. "Go, Julian, go!" she yells, and he does, accelerating until he looks like a wind-up doll on amphetamines. And then Julian is passing the finish line in front of Just Cats Pet Salon, and the crowd whistles and hoots like a bunch of lunatics as he bends over and pounces on the arrow tipped with the golden apple lying on the other side of the rainbow ribbon he has breached with his latex breasts. Natalie slows down, letting the twelve other contestants flow past her—eventually she bumps into Julian's broad back and he turns around: his face is streaming with tears and sweat, and he is saying, "We did it, we really did it, we did, we did." And then Julian picks her up and tosses her in the air; Natalie closes her eyes and hopes he doesn't forget her, up there among the startled pigeons. But Julian doesn't

forget; he catches her without even digging the nails from
hell into her bare arms.

"Come in and sit down," Julian says, holding up the flap
of the tent, "you were marvellous, darling," and he pats
Natalie on the top of her head. Patsy is asleep on a pile of
dresses; her eyes are moving back and forth under the lids
and her paws are twitching, and Natalie wonders if the dog
is chasing Mexican cats around a dusty piazza in her dreams.
She sits down on a wooden deck chair and looks around; it
is dim in the tent and it takes a while for her eyes to adjust.
And then she sees a Banana Belt draped like a snake pelt over
a stool next to Patsy's sleeping quarters; the Man-in-the-
Moon slyers at Natalie as though she is something he would
like to tickle with his moustache. Natalie tries to pretend it is
any old belt, but her fingers start picking at her cut-offs.
Julian sees her looking at it and he says, "Pretty cool, huh?
Just a little souvenir of a night to remember, and speaking of
the *Titanic*, he went down like. . ."

"Was it Joe, the guy who owns the hair salon on Raglan
Street?" asks Natalie absently; the smell of Matt's groin is in
her nose; it is the smell of the floor of the forest, of dead
leaves and young ferns and Indian pipes.

"Joe Sullivan, that old queen, are you out of your mind,
darling? What in heaven's name made you say that?"

"Oh, I saw him wearing one of those once," says Natalie,
"that's all. I wasn't thinking."

"Well," says Julian, "for starters, this guy was a Texan,
and for finishers. . ."

"A Texan?" The floor of the forest tilts; dead leaves suddenly cover Natalie's face and she can barely breathe; black
spots begin a saraband in front of her eyes. "Not an old
Texan with a grey pony tail?"

"Natalie, are you on some kind of medication or do you routinely say absurd things?"

"No and yes," says Natalie. Her fingers have curled into her palms and hidden under the hem of her T-shirt; even though her nails are short, they hurt when she digs them into her Mounts of Jupiter.

"He was a young Texan, and he had blond hair, and he was taking a walk on the wild side, honey; you know, officially straight, but bent a little too much to stay that way all the time.

"They're my favourites," Julian continues, fondling the gold medal hanging from a rainbow ribbon around his neck. The mayor had placed it there as if he had been bestowing an Olympic award, and then he had kissed Julian on both cheeks; Natalie had wondered if there was a municipal election in the offing.

Julian sits down with his back to Natalie, smiling at himself in the mirror in front of him like the cat that caught the canary. "I guess," says Natalie, staring down at her hands lying across themselves in her lap like two dead doves, "that if he was a Texan, it must have been your big hair that attracted him." She wonders how the words got out onto the air, because her mind is hollow and her mouth seems to be full of pennies, or something that tastes like them. "Actually, sweetcakes," says Julian, "it was my big. . ." But Natalie doesn't hear the rest because she is kneeling on the floor retching; the bile burns her throat and mouth when it comes up, and it comes up so fast and hard that there is barely room for her to breathe between spasms. "Oh dear oh dear oh dear," Julian says, "I knew you were too thin to run in this heat. Come on, get up, we're going two blocks over and Uncle Jule is going to make it all better." And when Natalie gets rid of the last of the poison, Julian helps her stand up on the golden heels like someone steadying a foal not yet used to its legs.

Natalie and Julian are in a bar called The Ganymede; she is still wearing the snake shoes and there is a gold medal on a rainbow ribbon around her neck. "I forget where my real shoes are, Uncle Julie," Natalie says, leaning against his black silk shoulder; "I love your dress," she whispers into his ear, her lips tangoing with a strand of blond wig. Natalie has drunk a number of large glasses of something called a Marilyn. The drinks are the colour of pink lemonade and the rims of the glasses are sugared so that they seem sweet at first, but there is an aftertaste that is as bitter as gall.

"Actually, I have seventy-five dresses," says Julian. "After all, I came out of the closet when I was seventeen."

"Was it your mother's closet?"

"As a matter of fact, it was," says Julian, and he looks for something at the bottom of his Marilyn. "Anyway, your real shoes are not real shoes, Natalie my dear. You are going to have to go out and get some real shoes, aren't you?"

"I will, Jule in an Ethiope's ear, I truly will," says Natalie. "Not high heels though."

Julian smiles, and leans over and kisses her on the mouth.

"I didn't know you guys did that," says Natalie.

"What, kiss girls?"

"Yes."

"You're not just a girl, Natalie, you're Natalie."

"I guess I am," says Natalie, and she leans over and kisses Patsy, who is wrapped around Julian's neck like a stuffed toy with Velcro attached to its paws.

"I didn't know you guys did that."

"What, kiss dogs? She's not just a dog, she's Patsy."

"That she is. She is Patsy, even though she is also my girl. Do you know what an Englishman said to me when I was out walking her one day? He said, in that horrid snotty accent of theirs, 'You know, young man, my genitalia are bigger than that dog.'"

"Did you hit him?"

"No," says Julian, slyering at her. "I took him home." And Natalie and Julian laugh and laugh until Natalie gets the hiccups, and then Julian scares them out of her with his Marilyn Manson impression.

When Natalie opens the door of her apartment, the phone is ringing. It is three a.m., and her heart moves down towards her belly to find a hiding place because only bad news comes over phone lines at such an hour. But she will have to answer it because it is, in the long run, better to know the truth, when you can. The phone is a portable one and it is plugged in beside the couch where Natalie has been sleeping most nights. She bends over and makes a grab for the receiver, but the Marilyns and the gold heels send her tumbling. Lying on the rug in a moon pool, Natalie reaches out and picks up the white receiver: it gleams like a piece of a skeleton, like something from the carcass of a dead deer, and Natalie doesn't want to put it against her face, but she does. "Hello," she says, crossing her fingers on her free hand and not letting bad things come into her head, because if you do, they can spill out and take shape right in front of you.

"Nat?" says Matt's voice in her ear.

"There is," says Natalie, after a time, a time that moves like a video tape on fast-forward—Matt's gold stud winks at her; she is crying alone in her room, her heart and head all shorn; she and Claire are laughing in a bar; Bill is filling her hands with lavender; she is running in a noise like a raging current; the Man-in-the-Moon is slyering at her—"no one here named Nat." And she jabs the glowing green button on the phone that will take Matt's voice out of her living room, jabs it three or four times just to make sure, like those people who shoot other people repeatedly in the head. And then Natalie unplugs the phone and puts the receiver on top of the drum as an offering to the dark gods; this is the last one, she tells them in a firm voice.

Upstairs, Natalie looks at herself in the long glass on the back of her closet door. She removes her T-shirt: underneath it, her breasts are bare, her nipples like little thorns. And then she takes the *Woodstock* CD Bill gave her for her birthday from the pile on top of the player and she slides it in and moves back to the closet door. And she watches as her hips start swaying to "I'm Free" and her arms move away from her body so that her hands can begin their mudras of delight for the snake-shod goddess in the mirror.

Swimming to Lourdes

I would swim over the deepest ocean,
The deepest ocean
To be by your side.

— "Carrickfergus" (traditional)

The rock is covered with lichen, small round verdigris spots the colour of neglected copper; some of them are jagged-edged and have black hearts. Bernadette is lying on the rock with her head against its dappled flank. At the rim of the ocean there is an iceberg; it would be nice, she thinks, to swim out to it, not that she would make it, it is too far away and the water is lethally cold. The iceberg is spired like a cathedral; most of them are shaped like something. One that looked like the Virgin Mary had glided by the mouth of the city harbour in the 1950s; you could buy a picture of it in the local shops. The photo was taken by an amateur; it is black and white and somewhat grainy, and the Virgin looks a little sullied, a little worn. One of her hands is extended as though she is blessing the townspeople on her way to dissolution in the south. If you looked closely, you could see tears on her cheek; people said they were tears, but they looked like cysts to Bernadette. As if the Virgin's pity for humanity was trying to push its way out through her skin.

Swimming out to the iceberg would be like going to Lourdes on your knees the way penitents used to do

because you had a better chance of getting what you asked
for if you managed to get there kneeling all the way. If she
could swim out to the iceberg without drowning,
Bernadette would ask it to send him back to her. Or for
peace, but Bernadette didn't see where the peace would
come from if he didn't come bearing it in his arms like the
risen Christ. His peace had been the peace of the forest for
her, the peace of the forest lying next to her in human
form; once, when she was the first to awaken in the morning, she had looked at him and thought she saw vines growing in his hair, but it was only the sun through the curtains
making patterns on his head. She had reached out her hand
and moved her fingers in the chiaroscuro of his hair, and
she had thought that there didn't need to be another
moment after this one because whatever came next would
be superfluous. She had been sure that even the gods must
see it, and that they would have to end the world. But they
hadn't, because another moment came, and then another,
and they piled up into hours and days and months, and
then one afternoon when the moments were seven years
heavy, they fell over and destroyed the play of light and
shadow that had been the two of them.

     Bernadette is trying to hear what the rock is saying, in
this place where she and her lover used to sit on Sundays listening to the voice of the world shorn of the utterances of
its human creatures. She has read that stone is capable of
absorbing and storing the vibrations made by human voices,
that people have heard ancient walls in ruined towns murmuring, the cadences of dead lovers speaking of their love
in dead languages; she wants to hear the rock say her name.
In his voice. But the silence is being profaned by a man in a
baseball cap sitting a few feet away from her. He has a cigar

sticking out of one side of his mouth; out of the other side
runs a stream of words like an oil spill.

"So Ciaran was e-mailing some girl in San Francisco
who visited his Irish web site and wanted him to come
down and help her start a female hurling team. Anyway, one
Saturday morning there was a knock at the door, and when
he opened it there was this vision in a mini-skirt. About
twenty-five and built like a brick shithouse. 'Who are you?'
Ciaran says, after he thanks God and St. Patrick. 'I'm
Tiffany from San Francisco,' she says, 'and I've come to join
the Celtic Renaissance.' Like it was the Celtic Resistance or
something and Ciaran was the leader. Poor old Ciaran, a
middle-aged Irish ex-pat living in a fousty basement apartment with only an old dog for company, and he doesn't
know Van Morrison from the Van Allen Belt. But he must
have piled it on thick for the American, because there she
was, with a knapsack full of Pogues CDs and Celtic crosses
tattooed on both arms. She even had a snake tattoo, but
Ciaran didn't find that out until later. 'Where are you staying?' he says. 'Here,' she says, and Ciaran thinks God, you
are one shite sometimes, sending me the quintessential
blonde bombshell, only she's from the HIV capital of
North America. So he says, 'Fine, there's your room, that's
mine, and we'll talk later.' He goes back to bed, but then he
gets up again and goes out into the living room and there's
the American walking around without a stitch on. Ciaran
thinks well, we all have to die sometime, so he goes over to
her and starts to say, 'Would you like to come have a lie-
down?', but she's got about a foot on him and he discovers
he's at eye-level with her nipples."

Bernadette closes her eyes and thinks that if she finds
the pieces of her lover's face and puts them back together

like a broken icon, the man's voice will cease when she has finished. It has been a long time since she has seen her lover, but every night she lies down with his shadow and runs her hands over it and makes it flesh. The cells of Bernadette's body keep him intact for her: in the skin of her hands is the texture of his skin; her tongue still knows the ridges of the roof of his mouth; the scent of the back of his neck is in the atoms of the flesh of her nostrils. Bernadette's mind is less accurate than her body; it has kept his voice for her so that they can still talk to each other, but his likeness is starting to get pitted, like the rock she is lying against, like the picture of the iceberg Virgin.

It is easy to remember, though, how her lover's eyes had looked on the last day; they had been those of a medieval executioner who has spent time with his victim, perhaps even holding her when she trembled in the dark Tower. And then one day he puts on his black hood and disappears, except for two anguished eyes and the terrible blade, the blade that will cleave her heart, cleave it in two so that it will be like his, only Bernadette is not that kind of animal, one that can live with two hearts beating in discord, drumming to separate rhythms. *And as they sat on yonder hill, his heart grew hard and harder still/He had two hearts instead of one/She said, "Young man, what have you done?"*

Bernadette takes her lover's mouth from a day they had kissed for a long time in the sanctuary of a small storm, the rain and the liquid from his tongue running down her throat like sacramental sherry. His nose is easy to find because it is perfectly aquiline and slightly skewed from having been broken once. And there he is, floating in the air in front of her like the Cheshire Cat, except that he is not grinning. Hello, she says to him in her mind: isn't the iceberg lovely? I think that I will never see an iceberg as lovely as thee, he replies, and she laughs, but not out loud.

But the bump and grind keeps coming out of the heavy lips of the man in the baseball hat; his cigar wobbles around like Everyman's erection. He thinks it is a good story, he thinks he is amusing her, entertaining her: he is well-known as a raconteur. Bernadette almost wishes he had brought her here to kill her with the spade that is lying between them, the spade that will be used to root up a young fir tree for his garden. But he will not kill her even if he has considered it while they were making their way through the brush to get to this place. Bernadette is almost sure that the thought of killing her has passed through his mind once, though, even if he wasn't conscious of it, even if it was like the bird that had flickered through the trees a mile back so quickly that they couldn't name it. All men have blood on their hands—the venous blood, Venus blood of some woman—mother, wife, sweetheart. And so did her lover, in the end. The blood of her heart, lying under his words like a slaughtered lamb. "I will never love another woman. But I have to go; if I stay, there will be more pain. And I will always know where you are on the face of the earth. There will be other women, but in the end, there will only have been you. And someday I may come back." Three years ago he had said these words to her: after two years, she had stopped believing the last ones.

The cigar man's voice saws into her lover's voice and Bernadette is almost grateful. "So Ciaran hasn't got a word in his mouth what with being stared at by the biggest pair of hooters he is ever seen, but the American leans over and takes him by the hand and says 'Come on, boyo, show me how they fuck in Ireland.' 'Well,' says Ciaran, 'I can only show you how they do that on the south side of Dublin, if that's okay with you.' And I guess it was, because none of us heard from him for a week. And after he surfaced, he wouldn't shut up about it for a month. 'She was a real free spirit,' he said. 'I took her out to Logan's Bay and she ran along the cliffs buck naked—ah, that was a sight to see. And when I taught her how to say "My name is Tiffany" in Gaelic, she played my flute like it was never played before.' Are you asleep?"

Bernadette can feel him move closer to her, so she sits up quickly, turning towards him and folding her arms.

"No."

"Come on," he says. "We'd better get moving before I get stiff." And then he laughs at his *double entendre*, which isn't a *double* at all, only an *entendre*. Or perhaps neither: it may be a remark too crude to be civilized by a French expression.

Bernadette met the cigar man at the bar she and her friends go to every Friday night. He is a science teacher, but he isn't allowed to teach anymore, only encourage the children to learn. Which they didn't want to do, refused to do, and there were no more thick black straps to make them do it. And so they didn't know a semi-colon from a semi truck, and they thought Crab nebulae were something you got from unprotected sex.

The protagonist of the story the man has been telling Bernadette is a retired English teacher. And it had made him bitter, in the end, not being able to show the children how all the tedious rules brought you, like thickly brambled paths, into the clearing that was *Paradise Lost*. And how as the fine words and great poems and sublime stories sank beneath the tide of the new cartoon culture, so did the things they kept in their care—honour and truth and love and glory, and the folded wings of the Holy Ghost. So Ciaran supplements his pension giving Gaelic lessons, and the people he teaches must memorize tenses and declensions, and Ciaran harnesses their tongues with harsh criticisms so that they move gracefully to the precise rhythms of the strange language they would desecrate had they had not been so fettered.

"Thank God for Mel Gibson and even the end of education as we knew it," Ciaran had said to Bernadette one night in the bar. "Owing to the latter, the stupid young shaggers don't know Scotland from Ireland, and thanks to *Braveheart*, they all want to be Celtic warriors. I picked up five new clients the week that movie was released." And then he had drained his glass of Guinness and asked her if she would recite Yeats' "Sailing to Byzantium" for him. Bernadette had looked at Ciaran and said, as if it were something she had just been thinking about, "That is no country for old men. The young/In one another's arms, birds in the trees. . . ." Ciaran had kept his eyes closed until she got to the part that went "An aged man is but a paltry thing,/A tattered coat upon a stick, unless/Soul clap its hands and sing, and louder sing," and then he had opened them and smiled at her. "Bernadette, *aingeal*," Ciaran said when she had finished, "*Go raibh maith agat*—thank-you," and he had brushed the side of her face as if she was his old spaniel.

The cigar man puts his hand out as Bernadette begins to rise from the rock, but she tells him no, it's okay. She knows that he wants to touch her more than help her, and that he probably won't let go of her hand once she gets to her feet. They start to head back along the path that leads to the rock with the sea beneath it; Bernadette turns around and takes a last look at the iceberg; perhaps she should just make a run for it, a run and a jump into the freezing water. And let the waves zip themselves up over her body, freeing it from the abyss of bereavement where it huddles in numb night, waiting for his hands to reach down and pull it back into the living world.

Bernadette's skin burns constantly, as if a small electrical charge is travelling along it; waves of exquisite anguish run down her arms and pool in her hands. Her doctor has told her that this is normal. "Your neurological system is out of whack from grief," he said. "The heart and the mind are not separate, even though many have tried to wrench them apart. In the name of science. Or philosophy. Or even God."

Bernadette's doctor was once a priest, and then a pilot; now he is a psychiatrist. "Did you choose professions that begin with *p* on purpose?" she asked him once, before she saw how they were connected. Dr. O'Brien has a small plane that he flies sometimes in the mornings before his clinic. "When I am in my plane," he said to Bernadette one day when he had just come from the airport, "perfectly poised between the worlds of matter and spirit, I feel that I am on the Cross, that the cockpit is the cross. And when I ride in and out of the clouds, flirting with the sun, I want to stay there forever."

"And if you couldn't go up there, life wouldn't be worth it, would it?" she said to him. "No," he said, "no, it probably wouldn't," and he had looked over at a model of a biplane on top of his bookcase, a gift from a man who had suffered from paranoid delusions involving the CIA and crows. When the man's mother had been dead for a year, the delusions had gone away.

"Well, I felt like that in his arms, in his arms or even just when I was in the same room with him: when he left, it was as though he shut off the light of the world. But if I. . . go, I'll have to pay, won't I, I'll suffer even more than I'm suffering now. If that's possible." The doctor had looked at Bernadette across his desk, and his eyes were those of the Jesuit he had been before he had gone up into the sky one day in the north country, and had looked down at the hands of the bush pilot and had seen that they were a miracle, two living gods holding two men between two worlds, and it came to him that all flesh was holy, and he would no longer be able to preach of its sins.

"I think," Dr. O'Brien said to Bernadette, "I think that there would be a deep sense of regret, of great loss, and you would have to live with that for a long time, a time that is outside our comprehension. And if you wait, you will be healed someday, I promise you. For are not the very hairs on your head numbered, numbered and cherished?" And he had reached over and made the sign of the cross on her forehead.

Bernadette is grateful for her doctor's faith. She has lost her own; not even the rosary beads of her childhood give her any solace; she has taken them out and tried to get back to the place of safety that had been her parent's home on Sunday nights, all of them together, her mother and her father and her seven brothers and sisters saying the Hail Marys and Our Fathers until the last bead was done. But her old rosary is only a tawdry necklace now, a string of broken lies.

On her second visit to Dr. O'Brien, Bernadette asked
him if he was ready to give her a diagnosis, and she stiffened
herself against the label that was about to be pinned to her
hurt. The doctor she had gone to before him had told her
she was suffering from a chemical imbalance. She had taken
the pills he prescribed, but they had only numbed her; some
days she could hardly force herself out of bed to feed the
cat. After a few weeks, she flushed the rest of them down
the toilet. And the doctor had chided her for non-compli-
ance, saying she should have given them more time. "I don't
think I have enough time left," she had said to him. "And
what is left is so heavy, I don't know if I can carry it around
much longer."

"Your spirit is broken," the new doctor said to
Bernadette. "Come see me once a week, and we will mend
it in time. Together." And he had given her a moonstone to
take away with her, a stone that was clear except for a cloudy
spot in the middle that marred its translucence. Dr.
O'Brien's desk is like a lapidary's, silly with stones; there is
even one from the Great Wall of China. And another from
a valley sacred to the Hopi, a piece of sandstone Bernadette
holds sometimes; the sandstone remains cool no matter
how long it is in her hands, cool and heavy even though it is
so porous; its heaviness is not a physical weight, but some
kind of essence the stone contains and shares with her; it is
a grounding stone, absorbing the pain in Bernadette's hands,
leaving her mind free to move with Dr. O'Brien's through
the ritual of healing.

Bernadette goes to him every Wednesday, and they talk
about St. John of the Cross and the dark night of the soul,
about Saint-Exupéry and his Little Prince, about fiery
branching nebulae and how new stars drop from them like

celestial fruit. Human beings, Dr. O'Brien has told
Bernadette, are birthed from the dust of stars also, and go
back to them in time, a Time that is neither linear nor
absolute. Dr. O'Brien has also told Bernadette that sometimes when mundane love is transcended with another and
the other leaves, it can make a rent in the soul that is like a
black hole, an inverted sun. "But a black hole is not an empty
space," he has said to her, "it is heavy and thick with com-
pressed life." In Dr. O'Brien's office, Bernadette sometimes
feels as if she is pregnant with new constellations, but when
she gets home the stars start to go out one by one; by the
next day there is only the void.

Bernadette and the cigar man enter the shabby forest
that grows next to the ocean. Many of the trees are dead or
dying, particularly the tallest ones; they have been defeated
by the sleet-slinging north wind and the soil that is too thin
to bear great growth. Underneath, though, the forest is green
and vibrant with small things, mosses and ferns and improbably minute plants with star-shaped flowers. It is a country of
small life forms, except for the whales, but they are tran-
sients, leaving before the winter comes; they are not bound
like the trees in earthen stocks, to be starved and beaten for
the sin of reaching too high.

When Bernadette and the man have gone half a mile or
so, he says that they should rest. He sits down on a rotting
log and lays the spade at his feet, and pats the log to indicate
Bernadette's place, which is next to him. She sits down several feet away. In the dim light that is just barely able to
thread its way through the web of branches that are naked of
needles but thick with matted strands of witch's moss, the
man's face looks like the faces you see sometimes in the bark
of trees.

"I was teaching out West one year, when Anne and I were first married," the cigar man says to Bernadette, "and some rich people asked me to a stag party. You should have seen the spread they put on: wall-to-wall T-bone steaks and twenty-five-year-old Scotch. And then in came the stripper, not some tarted-up old hooker, but a real class act. She was so perfect she looked airbrushed. But the amazing thing was, after the show, they had a draw, and whoever won got to spend half an hour with her in a back bedroom. And I won! The man who never wins anything snags the prize of a lifetime; you should have seen her breasts—they were real, too, and so was her red hair, I know, because. . ."

"What did your wife say about it when you told her?"

The man looks at Bernadette as though she is a dog or cat that has suddenly become invested with the power of speech. He doesn't answer her at first; after thirty seconds or so he says, sullenly, kicking the guiltless spade at his feet, "I never told her." And then he says, throwing the words at her hard and fast, a shower of pebbled consonants and vowels, "You think you're too fucking good for me, don't you? Then why the hell are you here with me today?"

"I wanted to sit by the ocean," she says, looking at his belt buckle, which has a horse on it, "and my car is in the garage." And my friends say I should be with a man sometimes, and you never told me these kinds of stories in the bar, only funny ones about your students, and dumb jokes that made me laugh, and one night you said you wanted to kill yourself after your wife left you, and I pitied you so, she thinks, but she will leave the spoken words as they are.

"And I was good enough to get you here, right?" The man gets to his feet and moves towards Bernadette as he says this, moves rigidly; his fury has clenched his body, he is a fist looking for something to embed itself in.

"Not really." The slow, icy molecules of Bernadette's words hit the heat in him and he lunges at her, but she is on her feet and has the spade in her hands before his hands can reach her. Bernadette knows how to slow time down: she simply remains unmoved in the face of its motion, which is all time has, is. "I contain neither fear nor desire" she says to still the illusion that is time in all its turning; as she speaks these words to herself, the angry man moving along the trajectory leading to the point where they will intersect is infinitesimally paused: even the air holds its breath. And when it exhales, Bernadette is standing straight and strong, holding the spade against her shoulder like a softball bat.

The man drops his hands and laughs. "You don't have the balls," he says, and then he falls backwards over the log without saying anything else. Bernadette turns her head away from where the man lies moaning like a small sad wind in the unyielding face of a pock-marked cliff; she hadn't meant to hit him so hard, she hadn't meant to hit him at all, to make the blood run out of his head into the subtle moss and the innocent flowers. She will have to start running now, she must get away before he gets up. But what Bernadette really wants to do is lie down on the floor of the forest and curl up until she is as small as an unawakened fern. She has never hurt another creature intentionally before; the impact of the metal against the side of the man's head has intensified the pain in her arms; she wraps them around her body and holds on tight, wishing they were someone else's arms, even those of the man lying on the stained carpet of the forest. And suddenly the pain reverses its normal direction, moving out of her hands and up through her arms and shoulders and then down to her disabled heart; when it gets there it hits something that cracks on impact.

Bernadette cries out; she lets the spade fall from her hands and begins to run. Witches' locks lick her face and her feet confuse themselves with bracken and hidden stones, but in time, a time she does not, cannot, measure, she emerges in the clearing by the sea. The wind has picked up while she was in the woods; the iceberg has moved farther south. It no longer looks like a cathedral: it is a white cruise ship, turning away from this bleak place; its passengers, their bags full of toy puffins and photos of iceberg Virgins, are lying two by two in their bunks, sailing to sleep in each other's arms, sailing to Byzantium.

Bernadette lies down at the edge of the rock; tears stream down her face and into the lap of the sea, salt water into salt water; the blood of her soul is dissolving in the great briny matrix, but the sea remains impassive, unchanged. She should follow them: it is the only way she will ever get free of the burning in her skin, her heart. She is so tired she can barely lift her head, she is like the poor thin star flowers in the woods, their stems bent over with the effort of holding their faces up to the light. Bernadette slowly removes her thick fisherman's jersey; the air is bitter against her skin but the sun is bright and it has reproduced itself a million times upon the water; the sea as far as the horizon is a galaxy of tiny suns, a field of celestial daffodils. She will float among them and be at peace. "And therefore have I sailed the seas and come/To the holy city of Byzantium." *Consume my heart away; sick with desire and fastened to a dying animal/ It knows not what it is.*

There is a sound behind her: a large animal is moving in the woods adjacent to the rock face that slopes down to the sea. Bernadette wonders why the cigar man has come after her, all the long way through the trees with their crossed arms, over the stolid, stony ground; his pride must be stronger than his pain. What will he do to her, now that there is barely any survival instinct left in her? But Bernadette is suddenly indifferent to his coming; she will be gone before he can get to her. This thought constricts her to the point of invisibility; even if he does arrive before she slips into the water, he won't be able to see her; even God can't see her now because she has moved in her mind outside the realm of His consciousness, which contains only life and not the gap in between that is death.

Bernadette pulls herself to her knees and looks into the sea, which is shrouded by the shadow of the rock; beneath her, a jellyfish is contracting and expanding, struggling to move its fragile body through the heavy medium in which it lives. It reminds her of a photograph in one of Dr. O'Brien's astronomy magazines, but she can't remember the name of the object in the picture, only that it was transparent and gleamed against the black of space like the jellyfish upon the dark water. As Bernadette watches, a sudden surge of the tide lifts the animal off course, but it keeps pulsating like a quasar until it is back upon its chosen path. It is a small jellyfish; it would fit in Bernadette's hand. Such an insignificant thing, setting itself against the innumerable waves of a vast ocean; so sure of its own being. Around its bell are crimson tentacles as fine as hairs. Bernadette counts them: there are four. And they are suddenly precious to her; they may be the last thing she will

ever see, and they are so soft and beautiful, so red and
thick with life.

· Bernadette begins to feel as tender as a mother towards
the frail creature in the water; it is as though her heart is beating only to assist its pilgrimage along the dark path of the
shaded sea; she wants to reach down and push it away from
the sharp edges of the rock and out onto the field of light;
go, she tells it, go away from here and shine on the face of
the sea, be a light to lighten the darkness, a beacon to obdu-
rate hearts and stubborn souls.

And then a great wave of comprehension runs its
length over Bernadette; in its wake comes the image of a
God Who is the living world itself—fire, earth, air, water;
star, stone, wind and sea. Even the frail, flickering thing
that is Bernadette herself. And compassion for this
unimaginably brave deity, suffering birth and death a billion
times in the span of a single human day, begins to trickle
into the place in Bernadette's soul that is torn, mending as
it comes; she no longer desires to take a life that is Life
itself; she wouldn't harm a single hair on God's head for all
the tea in China. An enormous sense of relief floods
Bernadette's mind and carries off the tumorous thoughts
that have been there for three years. And in their place
comes an intuition of what might be at least the promise of
peace on its way to her; she will stay and wait for it. But first
she will put her sweater on, because it is damn cold and she
is not a jellyfish.

A voice behind her says, "Bernadette, what are you
doing, are you praying?" And then a hand touches her
shoulder. Bernadette feels her body shifting; a realignment
is taking place; relief turns into elation as her heart changes
poles, goes nova, bursts up through the last seal of pain like

a great glowing phoenix. *Set upon a golden bough to sing/ To lords and ladies of Byzantium.* She says, without turning around, "No. Yes. I don't know, I was going to swim to Lourdes, I was going to. . . How did you know, how did you know where I was?"

"Lourdes is rather a ways off, isn't it?" his voice says. "And I have always known where you were. Especially on Sundays. But it wasn't time."

"But it is time now, isn't it?" says Bernadette. Her voice rises in the air of the morning like a canticle, so soft and vibrant she barely recognizes it for her own.

"Yes," he says, his hands cupping the sides of her face. "It is time. Now."

Some months later in the Gulf Stream, a small piece of ice that once was a cathedral relinquishes its being: its cool silvery particles spread out and are soon lost in the vast Atlantic; not lost, but conjoined with others so that it has a new shape; nothing has been lost; an ocean has been gained. High above, strange southern birds cry out in exultation and the sun throws down a handful of gilt.

In the north, two people are being married on a lichen-covered rock by the sea. After the ceremony, the bride stands with her back to the ocean and tosses her bouquet over one shoulder for the mermaids to catch. And then her husband picks her up in his arms and jumps into the sea, which is not warm and never will be, but it is warm enough with the two of them holding hands and thrashing around trying to tread water; they are laughing and spitting the salt sea out of their mouths like a pair of weird whales, and the bridal party is laughing too; their cameras go click click click, and then Dr. O'Brien and Ciaran help Bernadette and her husband climb out of the place of their nuptial baptism.

When the pictures are developed, one of them has a small white spot shaped like a cathedral on it. "Too much light from the sun on the water," her husband says, and Bernadette agrees with him. But only because it doesn't matter now.

The Quality of Mercy

When Sara wakes up, there is a man is in her bedroom. She thinks she might still be asleep and dreaming, because he looks like the Michelin Tire Man, but without the indents that signify tires. And she had gone to sleep very drunk on cheap wine, the kind cherished by winos and students, rumoured to engender pink elephants and possibly even ridiculous advertising logos. A quarter of a century ago, this wine gave Sara Milton's *Lycidas* garbed in luminous commentary, making her beloved of professors, queen of their pedantic wet dreams. Or it would spill its glamour over some fellow graduate student until he looked like Lancelot, and Sara would stroke his hair and say, "'O what can ail thee, Knight at arms, / Alone and palely loitering?'" But Sara is middle-aged now; perhaps the muse of the alleyway drunk has become tired of her, like everyone else. When Sara's bedroom finally comes into focus, though, he is still there, filling the entire space where her closed door should be, and he has a holster with a gun in it, maybe two.

So Sara decides he's probably a cop, not the Michelin Tire Man after all; the wine was still her friend, it just hadn't had much to work with. The man has little definition because he is wearing a bulletproof vest under a thick uniform jacket; a spherical head that seems to lack a neck rests on top. Now that she is entirely awake but still quite drunk, Sara thinks he looks more like an old-fashioned

deep-sea diver than the Michelin Tire Man; he is missing
only the helmet and the metal umbilical cord that would
allow him to survive in a foreign environment. Like the
depths of the ocean, or a strange woman's bedroom. Or
perhaps he's an astronaut, a space cowboy; why aren't you
out floating around somewhere off Alpha Centauri she
wants to ask him, but his eyes are like a gerbil's so she
doesn't.

When she was younger, she might have. More likely,
though, she would have said, "What the fuck do you think
you're doing in my room?" Your mouth, her father used to
say to her, is going to get you killed one of these days.
Maybe today is the day, but Sara hasn't said anything. Yet.
And then she says, "What?" to the cop, in the voice she
would use if he were her daughter, Angel, waking her up in
the middle of the night, neutral with some sullenness
around the edges. Angel is sixteen now, and Sara resents
her intrusions. She still expects a small blond child in a
nightdress with bears on it when she hears Angel's voice
through the cracks in her derelict sleep. But always, when
she opens her eyes, a wraith with black hair and lipstick to
match is bending over her—a changeling, the old hag—saying, "Mommy, Mommy, can I get in with you? Frankie
broke up with me." And Sara moves over and takes this
creature into her bed and her arms, and it stops shivering
after awhile, and they both go to sleep. In the morning
when they wake up, Angel glares at her mother and leaps
out of the bed, as though she had been abducted in the
middle of the night, stolen from her red and black room
full of the potent mojo of adolescence and confined in the
place of her childhood fears.

When Sara says, "What?" a face appears on each side of
the man; now he is Cerberus, the three-headed beast that
guards the gates of Hades. Neat trick, Sara thinks, neat trick,
but I liked you better when you were an astronaut. One of
the faces is a woman's, the other a man's. They both have
police hats on top of their hair, which looks as if it has been
freeze-dried and stuck on their heads. "You're coming with
us," says the female head, and Sara tells her okay, although
what she really would like to say is you are out of your fucking mind and please get the hell out of my room and my
house right now.

Twenty-five years ago Sara did say something like that to
a cop when he had aimed and shot you're-coming-with-me
at her. After she said the thing, Sara had run like a little kid
who had just stolen apples from the tree of an old scare-
crow man; she had run under the winking moon, frost gnats
stinging her lungs, laughing to beat the band—it was too
funny, too ridiculous, someone coming up to her and saying
something like that. The cop caught Sara before she had run
the circumference of the building she had been standing in
front of because she had thrown herself into a startled
snow bank, out of breath from laughing and the weight of
the wine, and the pleasure of pursuit under the conspiring
moon. Sara had lain there in the cool arms of the snow
watching loosened flakes feather the face of the moon,
waiting for the cop to catch up to her: perhaps he would
lean down and tap her on the shoulder and say "You're it."
Sara didn't mind getting caught; after all, she hadn't been
doing anything, just hanging out with a friend in front of
one of the dorms, drinking beer and necking a bit, to keep
her face warm and because the boy had told her that she
reminded him of Portia. But it turned out that the cops had

thought Sara and her friend were selling dope, because it was five o'clock in the morning. That's what one of them told her later: We thought you were selling dope because it was five o'clock in the morning.

Sara hadn't been able to find the logic in that at all, even though she was minoring in philosophy. "Socrates is a man; Socrates is a pig; therefore, all men are pigs." Which was a logical fallacy, of course, although that didn't mean it wasn't true. The cop who caught Sara had picked her up with hands that had felt like the teeth of a large herbivore; both of her wrists had four forget-me-not bruises on them the next day. And then he had punched her, on the head so there wouldn't be any visible bruises; a ring on his middle finger had gotten caught up in her hair and he had twisted it, pushing the ring into her scalp until she squealed. And Sara had kicked his leg, and used a word she normally refused to utter on political grounds, because it was the worst thing you could call anyone, a slang term for female genitalia. You could call someone a prick and it didn't take their dignity away, but if you called them the other thing it meant they were the lowest of the low.

There were no good terms for what was between Sara's legs, although the Elizabethans had had one; it was "moss pouch." Sara used to think that one day she would have a lover who would say to her, "Mistress, I love thee not only for thy moss pouch with its jade clasp, but for thy sweet reason and constant heart." She would have to give him these words, of course, but he would receive them gratefully, and send them back to her as though they were his own.

The cop had hit her again after she kicked him, hit her on the cheek; Sara could feel the calculation in the blow, the necessity of making his anger known coupled with a reluctance to mark her. After all, she was only, and particularly, a female. And then he had handcuffed her and put her in the cop car, on the floor in the back. Sara had been wearing a long muskrat coat that belonged to her grandmother, and she had thought, lying there on the floor with the cop's boot wedged in the small of her back—not hard, or if it was hard she couldn't feel it because the thick, soft fur and the wool of her sweater kept her flesh unaware of the boot, except as a slight pressure—so this is what it is like to be a dead animal that some men have killed.

Sara's mother had come to the lock-up a few hours later, in a mink that came to the tops of her Gucci boots, and she let the cops know that there were two more cars in their driveway on Prince Albert Crescent like the big black one that was parked outside. While her mother spoke, in the high clipped accents of an affronted female of the upper classes, Sara looked out the barred basement window at the beams of the headlights her mother had left on: they were streaming valiantly across the parking lot, twin meteors signalling the birth of a hero, or the release of a princess from a tower.

On her way out, Sara had said to the cop at the desk, "I hope the Holy Ghost knocks your wife up and she bears kittens," which was a mangled version of the last lines of a poem they had been doing in one of her English courses. The desk cop had thrown back his head and laughed, but then he had been okay; he had come to talk to Sara when she was in the cell; he had even given her a cigarette, saying, "You're more grown up than that," because Sara had been swearing like a longshoreman and hitting the bars of her cage with the flat of her hand. "There are other prisoners here besides you, who are trying to get some sleep," he told her, looking at her the way her father did when he was trying to knock some sense into her head. Sara had felt ashamed, but she didn't say she was sorry. She can't remember why she cursed him on the way out, only that it had something to do with the smell of her mother's Chanel #5.

The boot cop telephoned Sara's parents' house the next morning at seven-thirty; when Sara answered, he called her Miss Crowley and asked her if she was all right, so she knew he was scared. "I'm okay," she told him. "But tell me, if I had been a guy instead of a girl, what else would you have done to me, would you tell me that, off the record, and can you tell me how it feels to hurt something smaller than you because I have never done that and it makes me sick thinking about it."

"I'm sorry," he said, "I'm sorry, it was five o'clock in the morning and we thought you were selling drugs."

"And that would have made it okay then," said Sara, "that would have made it fine, to do what you did?" The cop said he was sorry again, and that all charges had been dropped.

"What charges?" said Sara.

"Resisting arrest and assaulting a police officer."

"You're nuts," Sara said, and hung up the phone.

Tonight, though, she would say nothing. Because no one would come for her if she did.

"You'll have to leave while I get dressed," Sara tells the two male cops.

"She'll stay with you," the Michelin Tire Man says, and the female cop comes out from behind his left shoulder; the two men go downstairs. Sara's cat, Parsifal, who looks like a miniature albino musk ox in his long winter coat, jumps off the bed and goes over to the cop, purring. The woman says "meorrrwww" in the tone of an angry tom, and then laughs when the cat runs under the bureau. How very professional of you, Sara thinks, but the words don't leave her head. The woman watches as Sara pulls on her jeans over a pair of Angel's black panties; Sara forgot to put hers in the wash today; stiff socks and limp pieces of underwear litter the bedroom floor, the butt ends of Sara's chronic ennui, the evidence that she is no longer able to shepherd the minutiae of her existence. Sara is not sure that this is a criminal offense, however.

The female cop suddenly moves closer to Sara, and Sara folds her arms over her breasts. But the woman only reaches out and takes Sara's arm; strong nails embed themselves gently in Sara's flesh. Sara doesn't move; she stays still on the end of the hooks, hoping the woman will think she is dead and go away. But then the cop releases her, saying "You have a tattoo."

"Yes," says Sara. On her upper right arm is a sideways eight, the symbol for infinity, the Mobius strip.

"What does it mean?" asks the woman.

"It means what goes around, comes around. Eventually," says Sara.

"Oh," says the cop. "My friend has a rose on her ankle."

"My love is like a red red rose," croons Sara, "a blood red rose, that's newly sprung in tune, I told my love I told my love, I told him all my heart . . ."

"Come on," says the cop, and she takes Sara's arm although Sara is still trying to button up an old cashmere sweater; the buttons keep changing places, teasing her until she wants to weep with frustration.

"Outside," the woman says, and they leave Sara's bedroom and descend a flight of stairs, its thin carpet stained
with the contents of Parsival's stomach, larval fur balls in an
acidic wash; the short grey pile is grizzled with white cat
hairs. On the next to last step a small glass bead glitters like
a magpie's trinket; it is one of Angel's nose ornaments, abandoned in favour of a new brass stud.

At the bottom of the steps, Sara says, "Wait," and she
goes to the hall closet and reaches in for a jacket. As she
pushes her thumbs through the crowd of fabric, her mother's mink brushes against her hand; she strokes it twice
before continuing her search, once for luck, the second time
because she is seeking the solid form of the woman who
used to inhabit it. But the fur is flaccid and filmed with dust;
Sara pulls her hand away, and then she closes her eyes and
takes the first jacket that rubs its nap against her bewildered
fingers.

"Come on," says the cop. "I haven't got all night."

"I have," says Sara, "and all day too, and all night, and. . ."
The cop pushes Sara out the door, a good-natured shove,
something Mark would have done, or Angel when she was little. Angel girl blue, come blow your nose, the sheep's in the
meadow, the fork ate the rose.

Outside, the night is cool, the sky tarred over with a thick
covering of cloud. Sara and the female cop get in the back
seat together; the woman lets Sara move as far away from her
as she can, over against the locked door that has no handle.
The two male cops are in the front seat, separated from Sara
by a stiff steel seine that makes two compartments out of
the trap in which Sara is being transported. Sara's breathing
is not right, the air will not come in and go out in a balanced
rhythm; she looks out of the window, up into the night sky,

seeking diversion. And the clouds part for her; there is a fluttering of small stars and then Capricornus the Goat leaps at her over the hills of the harbour. Sara restrains an impulse to wave to him.

When they get to the hospital, the Michelin Tire cop leads Sara in by the arm. The others do not come with them; the second man and the woman drive off under a lover's moon which has managed to slip through the clouds; it is high and bright, full as a tick. Sara has her suede jacket on, the one she got at the Sally Ann for five bucks. It is a good jacket, because the people who give clothes to the Sally Ann only wear them a few times and then they get bored and go out and buy new stuff. Sara hopes everyone at the hospital will think she has bought the jacket new, although she doesn't know why she wants them to think this. Sara doesn't usually care what anyone thinks unless she loves them.

Sara's daughter and her daughter's boyfriend are sitting in the Emergency lounge. Neither Angel nor the boy with half a head of blue hair look up when Sara and her cop go by. Well, it was a weird place to be in the middle of the night if you weren't sick, Sara thinks; maybe she and her daughter are supposed to be strangers here. Still, she feels sad, as if Angel and the boy are conspiring against her. A conspiracy of those whose gods have betrayed them. An abbreviated coven of refugees.

Angel doesn't like Sara much these days. Not all of it is because her hormones are pulling her down into the Charbdyis of childhood's end, breaking the back of her innocent child's love against the rocks of sex and drugs and rock and roll. Angel hasn't really forgiven her mother for letting her grandparents die, her grandfather especially, who had become Angel's champion after Sara divorced Angel's father. (Who went far away into another country, into another woman; Angel hasn't heard from him in three years, says she doesn't care. But his picture is still in the left-hand corner of her bedroom mirror, underneath an old Spice Girls sticker.)

And Angel can't understand why there had been no money left in the end, why Sara's parents' estate had been as bare as bald bones; she doesn't know about the debts and the stock market losses, doesn't know that Sara's father, who hadn't even owned a computer, had gambled heavily on tech stocks and lost; now Sara and Angel's legacy is drifting around in cyberspace, insubstantial as the ashes of her father, which Sara and her mother had scattered one smoky October afternoon across his favourite golf course. Sara's mother had been buried beside her own parents, in a cemetery where they let the wildflowers have their way. "I would give you some violets, but they withered all when my father died: they say he made a good end." Ophelia and her flowers; did she mourn her father or her lover more? It is hard to unravel the skeins of mad thought, harder still to wind them up again.

Angel has liked Sara even less since Sara lost her job two years ago to downsizing. Angel no longer comes home after school to roast beef with potatoes around its perimeter like new-laid eggs, or to fresh cod nursing on goat's milk, or salads with shy strawberries hiding under spinach leaves. She must eat the victuals of the poor now, and Sara makes her call the meal by its proper name, supper; she corrects her daughter if Angel lets "dinner" slip when she asks if the no-name macaroni and cheap meat patties and frozen orange juice are ready yet. And Sara puts these things on the table at the ordained time for supper, five o'clock, and imagines her mother turning over in her grave, going around like a macabre rotisserie chicken, shaking her skeleton's head in disapproval.

Sara's family had always eaten at seven, a tenet that had been as sacred as the Apostle's Creed. "It isn't my fault," Sara says to Angel when she's had too much to drink. "I didn't do it." Angel doesn't believe her though; she is still young enough to think her mother arranges the world. When Angel was small, she once thanked Sara for putting the moon outside her window as a sort of celestial nightlight. But now she knows that her mother can't even afford to pay the hydro bill and buy enough good food for them to eat in the same week. Knowing is not the same as believing, though.

"So," says Sara to the cop who is guiding her along the corridors of the hospital as if they were navigating a foreign embassy, "would you tell me please, what is going on? I don't remember killing anyone. In fact, I don't remember being outside the house at all tonight." Sara's voice is too loud, too jocular: the hollow air in the late-night hospital does not like being assaulted by Sara's forced bravado; it distorts her syllables in revenge. The cop looks at Sara, but she can't make out what kind of animal is hiding in the crevices under his brows. And then she remembers: a gerbil.

Sara laughs, trying to make the sound friendly, engaging. "Would you mind raising the blinds on your eyes a little? I'm starting to get lonely," Sara says; she even tugs on the sleeve of the cop's jacket; it is good to touch the arm of a man again, even if it is a man who has broken into your house and dragged you off by force, a man who looks more like Sancho Panza than Zorro. But the cop is not buying Sara, she's not young or cute, and the neighbourhood in which he found her has not been reached by the developers yet; its genteel poor Victorians are forced to take in roomers to pay the bills, immigrants and prostitutes, chronic derelicts and the nouveau poor.

"Between you and I, your daughter said she found you in bed with a butcher knife and she thought you were trying to commit suicide," the cop says finally, in a disgusted tone.

"Well, I wasn't," said Sara. "And it wasn't a butcher knife, it was a bread knife. Butcher knives don't have serrated edges." Sara hates it when people don't know the things they should know, like the difference between a bread knife and a butcher knife. Or that "between you and I" is a particularly obscene solecism.

"I couldn't get the bottle of wine open; I had to use the bread knife to cut the vinyl off." Sara has a vague recollection of hacking at the obstinate black band encircling the neck of the pretty cherry red bottle, slender as a dancer and full of the water of forgetfulness; she had prayed that there would be a screw cap underneath instead of a cork because she couldn't remember if she still owned a corkscrew, or where it would be in her raggle-taggle house. Or even if she was strong enough to use it. Mark used to say to her that she had wrists like a Gibson girl's, fit only for holding up a parasol.

"So why were you asleep with it in your arms?" asks the cop; he doesn't sound curious, or even accusing; his voice is that of a patient coach.

"I don't know. I don't remember. Probably because it reminded me of my ex." Sara grins, but the cop takes out a notebook and writes in it. After he finishes he looks up at Sara and says "What about the two suicide notes?"

"Suicide notes? What did they say?" asks Sara. She is fascinated by this turn of events; she feels as if she is in some Canadian cop drama; you can tell it isn't an American one because the cop is not handsome and the hospital is old and grungy; also, there are too few extras. But two suicide notes? Sara's character is thorough, if nothing else.

"There was one on the floor inside the door that said you were going to see your psychiatrist, probably for the last time." The cop and Sara are in an elevator now. An elderly couple standing next to Sara stares at her; she smiles at them but they turn their heads away. Sara says to the cop, who is looking at the elevator buttons as if he might like to press them all at once, "I left that for my daughter so she would know where I was if she came home early. All it meant was that I was going to quit seeing my shrink if she made me wait for five hours in her cheesy waiting room like she did the last time, and the time before that. She makes me wait, she makes all of us wait for up to six hours to see her—can you imagine what that's like, sitting in a cramped little room for hours and hours, looking at fucking Hallmark posters—Smile at Someone Today! Kiss Your Dog!—afraid to go to the bathroom in case your name gets called while you're gone and you'd have to wait another hour? And she cancels appointments at the last minute. She did that to me yesterday, after I'd waited three weeks to see her, only her secretary phoned at the last minute and said to come in. So I went, and when I got to see her after four and a half hours of listening to people talking to themselves and crying, I told her to go screw herself. The first time I saw her she said I could depend on her, that she would be there for me every week—she said I had to trust her, and I did, I trusted that slut like she was

my mother, and she fucked me over." Sara has not meant
to say half of what she has said, especially not in a voice
louder than any she can remember using recently, except
for the time Angel had come home drunk and stoned, her
lip bleeding; "Frankie hit me, Mommy, he hit me, I never
did anything."

The elderly couple has taken refuge from Sara's voice in
the back of the elevator; Sara notes their absence and feels
tears start to well up; she bites the inside of her lip until the
delicate flesh swells. And then she looks at the cop; he has-
n't believed a word of what she has said, even though it is
true. But Sara is not real to him: her psychiatrist, whom the
cop has never met, is more real because she belongs to the
system of which the cop is a part. Sara is an outsider, and
not a blue-chip one either. Chipped around the edges,
cracked down the middle. "Speaks things in doubt/That
carry but half sense: her speech is nothing."

"What did the other note say?" asks Sara after she knows
the tears will stay put. Sara and her cop have come out of the
elevator into the basement of the hospital; each door they
pass may be the one to the morgue, or a room where pathol-
ogists dissect and examine the diseased parts of the people
who are asleep upstairs, floating at the ends of IV tubes,
their immortality secured for now. We murder to dissect,
Sara thinks, but she can't remember which poet said this or
what it means. The words seems highly significant to Sara at
this particular moment, however, potently charged with a
thing that is vital to this time and place, and so she lets them
wind around in her head, glow-in-the-dark Mobius strip
words; their cadence soothes her like the old lullaby Angel
used to love even though she was too young to know what
most of the words meant. "And Holy Mary pitying us, in

Heaven for grace doth sue, sing hush a-bye lou la lou la lamb,
hush-a-bye lou la lou." *Lamb* was enough, and her mother's
voice in the shifty-eyed dark.

"You wrote a poem," the cop tells her. "It was on your
bedside table. It said something about digging a grave and
a tombstone with a dove on it. And dying for love." He
blushes a little when he says this; dying for love is not
something he says often. Sara looks at him in amazement;
she has not written poetry since her undergraduate days,
long intricate sonnets on the nature of god and man and
the inexplicable runes of existence. No dove had flapped
its feeble wings in their austere passages, and if love had
ever tried to gain entry, it had been treated with contempt
and hung on the pillory of Sara's savage young heart. But
then a tune starts up in Sara's ears; it is a familiar dirge, Sara
can hear fiddles and a woman's voice given up to melodi-
ous lamentation. And then the "The Butcher's Boy" trick-
les over Sara's lips, haltingly at first until she is sure she can
remember the words, and then it comes in a steady stream
from Sara's memory, which is like a small Sargasso Sea;
many curious objects are entangled in its weeds, of no
value or use really, but Sara is a collector; she cannot bear
to throw away even the most insignificant piece of flotsam,
what the clerk at the corner store had for lunch last
Tuesday, an obscure word for ring. Or rotted bits of
sunken love.

"Haven't you ever heard of 'The Butcher's Boy'?" Sara
asks the cop. "I mean that song is as old as Murphy's goat."
Because that is what the cop is talking about, the words to
an old Irish song they used to play in all the pubs when this
bastard Irish city still longed for the motherland, a song
that never made Celtic chic: it was too naïve. Sara must

have written the words to it down on the pad she keeps by her bedside table to record her dreams on, but she can't remember.

Sara doesn't do that much anymore, delve into the pools of her subconscious searching for clues with which to uncover the meaning of her surface existence; she doesn't have any symbols for the malignant static that is all she usually remembers of her sleeping when she wakes. Sara suspects the pills may be causing it, but she is afraid to stop taking them. Because if she does, the real nightmares will come back. Unreal nightmares: Mark choking Angel with the cord of a VCR he gave Sara one Christmas, Sara's mother walking into Sara's house naked, encrusted with grave dirt, saying "Sara, Sara why did you leave me?"

But the cop isn't as old as Murphy's goat; he's only twenty-something, and he tells her no, he never has. In a tone that says *ergo*, it does not exist, even if you are standing there singing it. Sara is intrigued by her inability to move this man with her explanations, intrigued and annoyed. And another thing, a thing that feels a bit like fear. But Sara is in a hospital, there is nothing to be afraid of; hospitals are sanctuaries, havens, places where nurses with cool hands soothe fevered brows and doctors say kind things to you about your condition. Even if it's terminal.

After the wine bottle was two-thirds empty, Sara had started thinking about Mark, whom she had loved so much that she had once actually considered leaving Angel to go live with him, although Angel doesn't know this. Sara would never have done it, because she loves Angel more than anyone has ever loved anyone else in the history of the world. Sara would die for Angel. Sometimes she gets tired of living for her though.

Mark hadn't wanted Angel, only Sara. And when Sara had gotten broken, Mark hadn't wanted Sara either. He had left her a year after she lost her job, when she started to sleep most of the day. When she started to cry in front of him. When he couldn't give her orgasms anymore. Sara starts to sing "The Butcher's Boy" again so she doesn't have to think about Mark, but the cop tells Sara to shut up and sit down. Sara sits, but she hums "The Butcher's Boy" to herself, low and soft. Beneath the threshold of the cop's hearing, on a frequency where only another betrayed lover can hear it.

Sara and the cop are in a small room: there is only one window in it, which looks into the next room; on the other side of the glass doctors and nurses are doing things, talking to patients, dowsing with stethoscopes; a pregnant woman is crying by herself in a corner. A young foreign girl in a white coat is seated at a desk, leafing through a sheaf of papers; from time to time she glances at Sara through the glass. Sara resists the urge to make fish mouths at her, guppy pouts, or the grimace of an offended cod, pulled up from the dim depths of its late fall torpor. After they have been there for fifteen minutes, the girl looks at Sara's cop and raises her hand. The cop tells Sara to get up and come with him; they leave the room and go into the place where the girl is. It is hot in the hospital, but Sara hasn't taken off her jacket; she thinks she may have gotten the buttons on her sweater wrong in the end.

The foreign girl, who has a thick black braid down the back of her white coat, turns out to be the doctor, a psychiatry resident; she will be looking after Sara because Sara's case is not important enough for the psychiatrist on call to be woken up. Sara sits down on the small wooden chair that doesn't have any arms; across the desk from her, the girl

leans back in her seating system. Both of them look at each
other for a moment, and then the girl says, "I wonder if you
would answer some questions for me?"

"Of course I will," Sara says. She likes the doctor: the
girl's eyes are large and intelligent; her face is unmade up, but
her lips are carmine-coloured anyway and her skin radiates
health and goodness; small silver representations of Ganesh,
the Hindu god of joy, dangle from her ears. But Sara likes
her mostly because of the braid, hanging like a stout rope
over the side of a slim boat: it seems to Sara to be something
you could use to pull yourself up out of a tight spot, something you could hang onto if you felt faint or weary, the way
Sara is feeling now.

The girl and Sara play two hundred questions for half an
hour, and Sara wins; she has always been good at word
games, drunk or sober. And then the doctor walks Sara back
to the other room where the cop is waiting for her, half-
asleep on a brown metal chair.

The effort of collecting her mind has chased away the
last of the wine dervishes; Sara feels flat but relieved; it is
time to go home, to take the always compliant Parsival under
the wings of her rose duvet, to lie with him in the shadow of
Morpheus, to sing Angel to sleep even though she probably
won't be there. "Hey," she says to the cop, "what's your
name?" He looks at her for a moment, as if he doesn't know
who she is. Or perhaps as if she's not someone worth
answering.

"Penney," he says finally, sleep soaking in his vowels.
"Corporal Penney."

"Well, Mr. Corporal Henny Penney," Sara says in a teasing voice; she is going to tell him that the show's over, the
monkey died, the fat woman sang, but before she can get the

words out, he jumps out of the chair and grabs her. And
then he pushes her up against the wall; he is panting lightly;
his breath smells like onions. Sara says to him, "No, no it's all
right, you were just having a bad dream," but he snaps her
around and wrenches her arms behind her back; steel nips
the skin of her wrists; two bitter bangles join her hands
together. Sara turns her head and looks at the young foreign
doctor through the glass; the girl seems to be staring at the
struggling creatures on the other side, although her expression is indifferent, preoccupied. But when Sara mouths the
word *help*, the girl reacts: she shrugs her shoulders and
extends her arms, the palms of her hands facing up; she is a
Pilate, she is going to give Sara up to the soldiers even
though Sara is innocent and has proven it by answering all
her stupid, puerile questions, what is the date today and
repeat these three words after me, now say them again. The
cop looks through the glass at the girl with one eyebrow
raised. The girl shakes her head.

When they get to the police station, Sara asks where the
phone is even though she can see it sitting on the desk.
"Where is the telephone?" Sara says, as though she is
addressing a Cuban busboy in one of the hotels she used to
go to with her parents: there had been rows of them on the
Florida beaches, huge false white teeth lining the lips of the
ocean; they had eaten steak and lobster every night. Once,
her father had bought her an emerald ring in the hotel jew-
ellry shop, to match her eyes he said, but Sara's eyes aren't
green, they're hazel. There are no hazel jewels, though; hazel
is not precious or even semi-precious, it is just a colour that
can't make up its mind, a vacillating shade, a mongrel, a
mulatto.

Henny Penney tells Sara she can't use the phone, but he is lying; Sara knows her rights. "I'm entitled to a phone call," she says, pruning the words the way her mother would have, snipping at loose ends that have become snagged in her anxiety. Although Sara doesn't know whom she would phone. Angel would be at the blue-haired boy's and Sara doesn't want to call any of her friends. Not even John, who takes Sara for drives in the country on his motorcycle sometimes, and knows who she used to be. But Sara can't ask John to come here; it is not a place or a situation that exists within the boundaries of their friendship. Sara might as well be on the moon as in this place, except that it is easier to breathe here. A little.

All Sara's relationships are tenuous now; her depression has gnawed at the ties that bind, the gold chains she thought would always hold, the guy ropes of her sanity. But they have corroded; perhaps they hadn't been gold after all. "All that glisters is not gold," Sara says to Henny Penney. She means to sound like Portia, righteous and pure, but his face tells her that she has failed; perhaps he thinks it should be *glitters*, perhaps he thinks she is stupid or has a speech impediment. Sara has a frantic desire to tell him the difference, but she holds on to it so that it can't make any more trouble for her than she is already in.

"You aren't entitled to a phone call," says Henny Penney. "You haven't been arrested." He tells Sara to take off the cross she is wearing around her neck; it is small and black, made from the horn of a Jamaican cow. Sara and Mark went to Jamaica on a holiday once; he even asked her to marry him under the marimba moon, wed him in bare feet in the wooden church across from their hotel, but Sara had only laughed and made him waltz the length of the beach as a punishment. "Marry, sir? 'Not till God make men of some other

metal than earth,'" Sara had said, rolling Beatrice's words at
him along the spongy air. But Mark's earth had been a place
of safety for Sara, even though she knew the baseness of its
metal, could sense the dross even when love's clock pealed
out the witching hour; when she lay prone along Mark's
length she was like a child sprawled on the June grass, feeling the earth holding her against its magnetic heart so tight
she knew she could never fall off.

Sara places her hands under her hair and undoes the
clasp of the silver chain; the cross falls silently into the cop's
cupped hands. He puts it in a plastic bag and gives it to the
desk sergeant, a small man with a nose several sizes too big
for the rest of his face. "Then why am I here," says Sara,
"why can't I go home?"

"Because you are being detained under the Mental
Health Act. The doctor believed you to be a danger to yourself, and there weren't any beds free." Henny Penney's
expression is smug: he looks like a little boy who has just
caught a beetle in a bottle.

"So crazy people have no rights," says Sara. "I don't
believe you, you're a goddamn . . ."

Shut up, the cop tells her. Just shut up or. . .but he
doesn't finish his sentence. He turns away from her and
says something to the desk sergeant in a low voice, and
then laughs, a sound like steam escaping from a vent. One
hand on the wall clock above the desk points to twelve, the
other to five. All of a sudden Sara can't remember if it is
five o'clock in the morning or five o'clock at night.

A woman in a brown uniform comes around a corner
with three men trailing behind her; they are looking straight
ahead, not talking; they have emptied their faces before they
came into the room, and Sara wonders why. The woman

walks up to Sara, moves into the space that is Sara's by cultural right. "Up against the wall," she says to Sara in a voice that is cankered from wrongful use; Sara can't imagine her singing to a child, whispering to a lover. The woman is short and her body is shaped like a man's except that there are two bulges under her suit jacket, oversized badges announcing her gender in case anyone questions it; her grey hair looks like she cut it herself, not even using a bowl. "Up against the wall," the woman says again, and then she shoves Sara, jamming her right breast with the heel of one hand. Sara's head starts to swim; her stomach turns over and threatens to send a bottle of wine all over the woman's grim shoes.

"Send the men out," Sara says, "send the men out or I won't do it." Sara's voice is high and diluted, the voice of a frightened child; she expects the woman to laugh in her face. But the woman turns around and nods her head at the three cops who have arranged themselves on either side of the wall where Sara is to be splayed, ready for peeling, a live skin show; they slouch there with half-lidded eyes, tongues sliding out of their mouths from time to time to wet lips dry from salty thoughts. At the sound of the woman's voice, though, the men straighten up and move off down the hall that leads to the cellblock; the desk sergeant and Henny Penney go with them. As Sara starts walking towards the wall, one of the men drops back and goes up a short stairwell adjacent to the desk. Sara looks up into it on her way to the place of humiliation; she can see the cop hovering near the bottom step, she can even see his face although it is half in shadow—it is a harlequin's face, its expression as taut as an erection.

Sara goes over to the wall anyway; she puts her damp hands against it and spreads her legs. They resist at first, but

Sara makes them separate; this is the only road home she tells them, even if it is the long way around and brambled with wounds. The hairs on the back of Sara's neck prickle when the woman comes up behind her; the desire to move away, to wriggle, to twist and turn against the oncoming assault is relentless under Sara's skin. But she stays still as the woman's hands crawl all over her body, going slow as cold molasses running uphill in January, slow as love writhing in its death throes—"My love is as a fever, longing still/For that which longer nurseth the disease." Time passes, eons; galaxies are born and die but the woman's hands continue to finger Sara, their crude, creeping lust made more insidious by the sly latex gloves. Sara licks the beads of sweat that have formed on her upper lip and asks Holy Mary to pity her; she knows she won't be able to endure much longer; "run, baby, run" is tossing its head in hers, but she won't listen, can't listen because if she breaks away they will descend on her like the Assyrians upon the armies of Israel. But all of a sudden Sara's skin is free: she raises her head and pulls at the air with her mouth; it seems a long time since she has breathed. And then the side of one of the woman's hands stabs Sara hard between the legs, crumpling the soft tissue beneath the thin denim of her summer jeans.

Sara wheels around and cries out, pain hurling itself towards the woman on a spear of anger; she wants to clench her fists, but her hands are weak with shame. The woman is smiling at Sara, smiling and sucking on small taupe teeth; she is looking at something behind Sara's head, where there is nothing but the shadow of Sara's anguish. You bitch, Sara wants to say, you fucking cunt. But Sara couldn't say anything even if she wasn't afraid of what they would do to her if she did, and she must be, because she can't speak; her throat seems to have closed over, possibly to prevent the bile in it from getting into her mouth. Or maybe because her heart is threatening to leave her chest, to rise up and burst out of her mouth and fall in great fat wet pieces all over the green institutional carpet. And what would Sara do without a heart, where would she put Angel and Parsifal if she lets her heart be broken in this unshriven place by the gargoyle woman and the dog men? Sara bows her head and drops her hands to her sides and waits; finally the woman says "Follow me," and Sara does; her feet shuffle along the carpet as if they belonged to an elderly Chinese woman, as though they are attached to the flesh of her constricted heart.

The gargoyle woman puts Sara in a cell; she tells Sara that she has to stay there until the psychiatrist comes to evaluate her. "When," Sara says, "when is he coming?" Her voice is shaky and when her legs hear its unsteady rhythm they start to quiver; Sara sits down hard on the foam mattress that is like Kleenex between her and the concrete floor.

"Around ten," the woman says as she is locking the door that is a collection of iron bars, a zebra door through which the light from a latticed bulb shines in on Sara; it hurts her eyes, but there is nowhere to go to get away from it. Or from the camera that is leering at her from up in one corner of the wall. And then the woman grins at Sara and says, "Or maybe not until eleven. Or even twelve." And she walks away, whistling "Lara's Theme."

Sara assumes the lotus position; the flesh between her legs throbs when it is forced to compact between her thighs. "Aum" Sara says. "Aummmm." This is only a momentary illusion on the space-time continuum, it is not real, Sara tells herself, and then she falls over and cries into the grey plastic pillow until the matron comes to get her at ten-thirty. Once she thinks she hears an old man say, "Shut up, shut up for the love of Christ, we're trying to get some sleep down here," but Sara can't shut up for the love of Christ because although the words are familiar, they have no meaning to her as a pattern; they are coming through the static all jumbled, and she couldn't say three of them in a row even if Henny Penney came in and put both of his guns to her head.

The morning matron is not the one from the night before; she is a young, plump girl with a blonde perm. "Why are you crying?" she askes Sara; her voice sounds the way a guinea pig might speak if it could. Sara looks at her and opens her mouth, but she doesn't know what she is going to say. "I really hate the décor" is what comes out. "Oh," says the girl. She peers around the cell as if she's never taken a good look at it before, and then she takes the keys off her belt.

The psychiatrist looks like the White Rabbit from *Alice in Wonderland* and Sara tells him this, even though she knows she shouldn't. They are in an upstairs room of the police station. Sara is sitting on one side of a desk and the doctor is sitting on the other side. The desk is in the middle of the room and both of its chairs are old and lame, so it is difficult to tell which of them is in the position of power, except that he is wearing a suit and a neatly trimmed set of whiskers; a briefcase sits at his feet like a good dog. She has on second-hand clothes and her hair is dirty and dishevelled; her red-rimmed eyes are nearly swollen shut.

"It's like the Round Table," Sara whispers, and the doctor looks at her with concern in his eyes. "Never mind," says Sara. "Let's just do the test." Her voice has perked up a bit; the gentle man across the table is flooding Sara with good energy, her flesh is grateful but her mind cannot absorb it; it

is locked up tight against the world and Sara wonders if she
will find the key before it is too late and she fails this one last
thing. But she clears each semantic hurdle with grace and
finesse, even though she cannot focus clearly: her brain must
be on automatic pilot. Which is perfectly acceptable for the
kinds of questions the doctor is asking Sara, questions that
have to do with space and time and motion, but only as these
things relate to external reality. The doctor never once tries
to enter the country of Sara's heart.

As Sara speaks, the doctor's expression becomes more
and more downcast. At the end, he reaches across the desk
and takes her hand. "I don't think you should have been in
here, my dear," he says to Sara, his white whiskers twitching,
his beautiful eyes as sorrowful as a mother's. "I think a great
mistake has been made."

Sara smiles at him and pats the top of the hand that is
holding hers. "I don't think anyone should be in here, ever,
not even the people who work here," Sara says to him.
"Because how could you be a decent human being when you
have to do what they do in this place?"

"You may have a point there, my dear," says the White
Rabbit, and then he says, "Well, you can go now."

Sara collects her cross from the desk sergeant and puts it
in her pocket. As she is turning away, going toward the
morning light that is reaching in to her between the bars on
the window of the door, he says, "Wait a minute," and then
he reaches behind the desk and brings out a small plastic gro-
cery bag and hands it to Sara. She looks in it; there is something wrapped in newspaper inside. "Your knife," the cop
says. "We took it in case you had to go to court."

"You don't happen to have a loaf of whole wheat and a
jar of peanut butter handy, do you?" says Sara. The desk ser-

geant laughs—a short, narrow laugh—and then he gets up and opens the door for her.

Sara walks out of the police station into a light flurry of snow; the temperature has dropped to below zero overnight. Her used jacket is no match for the wind that is hurrying away out of the northeast, heading south as fast as it can. When Sara is a block from the police station, a cab passes her; in the back seat is the White Rabbit. Sara has no money for a cab; she must walk the two miles home in her cloth slippers on the cold black pavement that frost has spangled like the roll-on glitter Angel sometimes puts on her face before she goes to a dance. Sara is walking in the road because they never clear the sidewalks in this city. Too expensive, the council says. There doesn't seem to be money for anything anymore, snow clearing or children's lunch programs, or even a new shelter for the swans in the park. Or hospital beds. Sara wonders where all the money has gone: she imagines it riding on the back of the wind, a flock of green birds going south, their voices high and desolate, crying for the plight of the poor homeless swans beneath them.

When she gets home, she takes the bread knife out from the day-old newspaper in which it is sheathed. She has never liked bread knives; such big teeth you have, to cut into all that white softness, such big teeth you have, breadknife, such big sharp ugly teeth to cut and cut and cut, and why do you need to be so big and sharp and ugly because bread is so small and yielding and easy even if it does have a crust. But such a thin and brittle crust. And then Sara takes the knife and goes up to her violated bedroom. She takes off her jeans and sweater and puts on an old T-shirt, a white one with "England" on it in red letters that had been Mark's, and then she sits trembling on the side of her bed and sings "The

Butcher's Boy" all the way through. After she gets into bed, she sings the last verse over again.

Oh dig my grave
Dark wide and deep;
Put marble stones
At my head and feet.
And in the middle, a turtle dove,
So the world will know
I died for love.

Angel calls the police when she gets home from her boyfriend's at noon, and the cops take her mother away again, but this time they let the paramedics pick her carefully up out of the bed where she is asleep under the red sheets with the white cat curled next to her, crimson flecks all along his belly; the Red Queen and the red-and-white cat, and the thing with the red teeth between them. And Angel's mother sleeps through the ambulance ride, even though the siren sings in a loud falsetto all the way to the hospital. When she does wake up, she is in a good place, with her own mother, who looks like an elderly Guinevere; she says to Sara, "What doth ail thee, childe; is thy lambe of thy heart lost to thee?" And she folds Sara up in her long mink robe, and they go to sleep together on a bed that has the heads of animals—a lion, an eagle, a bull and a serpent—on the tops of its tall mahogany bedposts.

And then Sara wakes up again, and she isn't in such a good place, but the nurses are kind to her and there is lots to eat, and Angel comes almost every day. Angel is different now, quieter and softer. Sometimes she even lays her head in her mother's lap. And Sara strokes her daughter's hair, with its blond roots emerging like the tips of daffodils through a black frost.

Sara and her friend John are in Ron's Cycle Shop; they have just had lunch together, soggy fish and brewis, at Terry's Classic Cafe, and now they are standing in a small dim room, side by side with their shoulders touching, like a comfortably married couple. When John and Sara were colleagues at the university, they fought at least once a week, small hard scraps as merry as a clog dance. But now John is careful about what he says to Sara; he cuts his speech from the cloth of inanity, day-old news and stories about his kids. And Sara answers him in kind.

The owner of Ron's Cycle Shop is around fifty and big as a bear; he has a long brown ponytail streaked with grey and a face that makes him look like the kind of biker who deals and probably pimps too. Sara is a little nervous because this man could snap John in half with one hand while he molested Sara with the other, but as soon as he opens his mouth Sara relaxes because he is only a bayman after all. The shop is not much bigger than Sara's bedroom, but there is so much beautiful junk in it, it should be a church. And it is a shrine of sorts—The Holy Harley Chapel of Broken Motorcycle Dreams. All these pieces of departed motorcycles, and the clocks. An American eagle clock, a Jack Daniels clock, a Harley Davidson clock, a clock shaped like the number one and coloured like the American flag—stars across the top of the one, stripes running down it.

John asks Ron if he has an oil cooler for a 1985 Honda 650, and Ron goes into a back room and comes out with two of them. John picks one, and after he pays for it he says, "Sorry about Derek, man, that never should have happened." Ron is the brother of the manic-depressive guy the cops shot two weeks ago.

Ron hangs his head over the counter for a moment. And then he straightens up and starts to speak: his voice has the timbre of his forefathers, tones bred to leap over snapping waves and make holes in stiff sheets of wind.

"John, my brother was a difficult man, a real pain in the ass, but I don't know if he deserved to be shot. He had a knife, and he said he was going to do away with himself, so my mother called the ambulance. But the cops showed up instead. Four big bastards with bullet proof vests and guns. And my brother ran towards them, with this knife Mom used for skinning rabbits. It was as old as the hills, but sharp enough. Anyway, this cop shot my brother—in the ass, twice in the head, in the chest. Christ, if you were shooting a goddamn moose, you wouldn't do that to it. There was a fence between the cops and my brother, and the ambulance driver saw the cop who killed him kick it over afterwards so it would look better in court if they could say there wasn't anything between them and my brother when he came at them. The bastard who shot him knew the minute he did it there was going to be an investigation. You know what they tried to say? That my brother was trying to commit "suicide by cop," you know, get the cops to do it for him because he couldn't do it himself. But he fucking well wasn't, he wanted to live as much as you and me, only he was in pain all the time. Sometimes when we were up in the woods trouting he was the finest kind, but nothing them doctors gave him worked for long."

John has been holding on to the counter the whole time Ron has been speaking; his face is rigid, his knuckles are the colour of raw scallops. Sara has been watching the Jack Daniels clock, but the hands haven't moved. Nothing is moving in the shop except the agitated river of Ron's voice.

"And then they killed him. I wonder who's the real psycho, my brother or that arsehole who had such a big hard-on when he pulled out his gun that he couldn't stop pumping lead into poor old Derek. And there won't be a goddamn thing done about it. Sometimes I think about choking the life out of that bastard but I just don't have it in me. Besides, maybe someday when that cop is an old man, he'll have a child or a grandchild who's not quite right in the head, and then he'll pay for what he did, oh man, will he pay."

Ron's wrinkles get deeper while he is telling John about his brother; by the time he finishes, he looks like one of those dogs everyone was buying a few years back, the ones whose faces look like drapery folds when they are puppies. His eyes have gotten darker too; they have almost lost the point of light in the middle of the pupil, which is what happens when people are not really there with you anymore, when they are sick or full of grief or afraid, or whatever has put them in the place that locks the light out.

When Sara leaves Ron's Cycle Shop she is shivering although it is a warm day and she is wearing a sweater. After they get in the car, John takes a blanket out of the back seat and passes it to her. Sara wraps the blanket tight around her and pulls the sleeves of her sweater down over her hands. The scars on her wrists are throbbing; she looks out the window of John's car, searching. Across the street from the cycle shop, a police car is parked outside the Salvation Army centre for homeless men. Sara looks up past the car, past the doorway and the windows where men are leaning out smoking, sending white rings spinning across the placid face of the morning. On the roof of the building a flock of pigeons has arranged itself along a ledge; above them a granite cross keeps the sky from falling.

The proper name for pigeon is rock dove, Sara thinks, and she starts to sing. "My dove is like a white, white rose. . ." John starts the car.

Peripheral Vision

The coffee shop is called Bunches O' Bagels. It has booths, and pretty young waitresses, and the coffee comes in oversized mugs that look like cartoon mugs. Their bowls are thick and blue and shiny, and so are their handles. Lily has read somewhere that the Etruscans made the handles of their cooking pots in the likeness of angels. She half expects her mug to sprout tiny legs and arms and go dancing across the faux-marble surface of the table at which she and William are sitting, but it doesn't.

Lily has just explained about ghosts to William, who doesn't believe in them because he once spent the night in a haunted house on a bet and nothing happened. Ghosts, she told him, are like true love; they come only when you are not watching for them. Like strange birds, she had added, trying to jiggle William's mind so that the look of mild contempt on his face would waver, even temporarily. But it hadn't, so she appended "like the Holy Ghost" mentally, just to please herself, knowing coffee would be over if she said it out loud.

William detests Sentiment. Sentiment included ghosts, angels, country music, God, poetry and the St. Francis of Assisi Service for the Blessing of the Animals at the Cathedral of St. John the Divine that Lily had been to yesterday. She told William how primly the dogs had sat in the pews beside their owners, like good Christians. A Scotch terrier three rows from the back had barked more than it should have, but what Lily noticed most was an absence of the sound of random coughs, the shuffling of pages like pigeons taking off, and the murmur of an inattentive congregation, a sound Lily always found mildly irritating, like being on a bad phone line. Even though she could usually hear God above the static. Lily's father once said to her that she had been born with eyes to see and ears to hear, and Lily, who had been about fourteen at the time, replied, well, isn't everyone? No, her father said, not at all.

The people at the animal service had sat as primly and quietly as their dogs, but they had been ready to burst with the novelty of it all. Not that anyone who hadn't grown up in the Anglican Church would have noticed the bursting part. The service had been so full of good humour that even the gargoyles had joined in on "All Things Bright and Beautiful," including the one with the tonsure and a mouth like a turtle's. And at the end, a rooster had crowed like mad for the Son, the Son of Man, and some people had laughed. Not in an embarrassed way, but approvingly.

What Sentiment did not include, according to William, was the microchip, Kafka and Camus. And E.B. White, except for *Charlotte's Web*. William liked *Stuart Little*, though, because although Stuart was a mouse, he reminded William of Frank Sinatra. Lily and William were having coffee in Bunches O' Bagels partly because they played a lot of Frank Sinatra, and Louis Armstrong. And you could have a shot of Chivas in your coffee if you wanted one, and William had wanted one. Good Scotch and jazz weren't sentimental, either. William said that jazz was music for the male menopause. He said this in a sophisticated way, implying, Lily guessed, something to the effect that although he knew he was over the hill, he was sporting brand-name hiking boots. William's feet were like an old Chinese woman's and the rest of him looked like a Renaissance burgher. The pupils of William's eyes were always pinpoints, Lily had noticed long ago.

After Lily told William about the St. Francis of Assisi Service, he had bitten into his cinnamon and raisin bagel as though it had done him an injury, and looked steadily at Lily as he chewed, with no particular expression on his face, although his pupils pinned her mind so that it could only flutter a little. But she didn't really care about not being able to think of something to say; that was a burden she had never carried. After William swallowed, he said, "But, Lil, you know that's just a lot of anthropomorphic crap. Those poor animals must have been scared out of their wits—the SPCA should be raiding things like that, not organising them. I mean, what kind of dumb fuck would bring a roos-ter to church?"

Lily thought of the dumb fuck who had come in the side door and placed a cage with a rooster in it by the altar, next to a pony and some cat carriers. The pony had been given lots of hay, and it had eaten steadily throughout the service. Once or twice during the sermon it had looked up with strands of hay hanging out of its mouth like spaghetti noo-dles, and nodded briskly at the priest as if to say, "Carry on, boy, you're doing a fine job of it this morning."

The rooster man had walked down the centre aisle and taken a seat by himself in the pew across from Lily's. He looked so much like her father that Lily had almost yelled out "Thanks, God!" before she remembered she wasn't at home or in a Pentecostal tabernacle. Lily's father had died six years before, but they kept in touch. Lily sneaked glances at the rooster man out of the corner of her eye in between the

singing and the praying, and he hadn't disappeared.
Sometimes they did. But the rooster man stayed, his profile
illuminated by the light from the rose window. Lily had seen
her father so, many times.

The last time Lily and her father were in church together, though, he was horizontal instead of vertical. But it had
been a lovely ceremony. Lily and some of her father's friends
had pushed the casket up the centre aisle as though her
father were a baby asleep in a pram, and then she had taken
a seat in the front pew, the only time she had ever sat there.
Her father's sisters and brothers had come in from Salmon
Cove, and Lily sat between her Aunt Ida and her Uncle Art,
who had held her hands. And at the end the war veterans
came, and played a bugle, and said that at the going down of
the sun and in the morning they would remember her father.
And Lily had hoped that he was having a good day, with
everyone remembering him, even and especially God.

To keep William from laying further waste to the St.
Francis Service like a Crusader in a Saracen shrine, Lily was
forced to reach into her memory for a certain image, pull it
out, and scatter it across the table for him to peck at.

"Well, one dog did have diarrhea as they were finishing
up. It was the Newfoundland dog who was leading the pro-
cession at the end; you know, when the priest and the choir
come down and walk around the church. They all sort of
had to go around the mess, with their little banners and
everything, pretending they didn't see it. The smell was
awful."

William had put on his sardonic smile, and rolled his
eyes, happy as a clam. And then they had gotten onto ghosts
somehow, and when this started to go awry, which was
inevitable, Lily asked William to tell her about the time the

famous jazz singer Cleo Laine came to town and hung out
with him for three days. And William had begun, as always,
with "I was working at the Arts and Culture Centre one
summer, when the phone rang."

Asking William for the Cleo Laine story was like asking
for "Finnegan's Wake" from the fiddle player at The Rose, or
your favourite bedtime story from your mother. You knew
the tune or the story so well you didn't have to pay attention;
you could just lie back on the sounds and think about anything at all, or nothing. Lily's mother never had a chance to
read bedtime stories to Lily because she died six months
after Lily was born. When Lily was old enough, though, she
read bedtime stories to both of them. Last night they'd had
"What the Rose Did to the Cypress" from *The Brown Fairy
Book.*

William has just gotten to the part where Cleo Laine
describes to him what it was like being on "The Muppet
Show." ("'Imagine,' Cleo said to me, 'Trying to sing with a
bearded man in your crotch, holding up a puppet.'") This is
early on in the story, so Lily thinks some more about the St.
Francis service.

Lily loves the great neo-Gothic mass of the Cathedral,
vast and stained as Time, standing grimly off to one side of
a cluster of brightly coloured, newly renovated Victorian
row houses like the Archbishop of Canterbury resisting the
entreaties of a crowd of painted women. Over the last ten
years people with money have been moving into the downtown, reclaiming the slums as though they were Dutch
marshes. Or claiming them, rather: with the exception of
some of the larger houses, which had been cut up into flats
many years ago, the downtown had only ever been the habi-
tat of the poor, and students and artists. And sailors, too,

from all the seven seas, but they had been shooed away by the government when the cod fishery failed. It was more common than not to blame others for your own sins, Lily thought. It was what some people had to do to survive, she guessed. The weak, mostly; the ignorant, the disenfranchised. And those at the other pole, too: the powerful and corrupt.

Lily and William had lived downtown in the old days. On Friday nights, coming home from the pubs, they climbed hills that were nearly vertical in places: sometimes Lily felt like Spiderman. But it was okay being a half-cut Spiderman, held up on both sides by friends, with everyone singing "Nancy Whiskey." One night Lily and the rest of the crowd and the wife of the manager of the largest hotel on the waterfront danced on the tables in the bar, belting out "Liverpool Lou" at the top of their lungs. That was in the old hotel, which had drinking fountains for carriage horses in front of it. But it had been torn down sometime in the previous decade, and there was a new one on the same site. It looked like all the new hotels Lily had ever seen, in Toronto and New Hampshire and Amsterdam and London. And the young people cursed and fought now as they walked up from the new-style bars, and they ripped the flowers out of the window boxes of the new-old houses, and out of the planters the council had put on the freshly cobbled streets. In the fall, when the flowers were gone, they pitched rocks at the stained glass windows of the doors and the ceramic number plates beside them, and at the glass in the wrought iron lamp posts that stood sentinel for the new residents of the downtown core.

Thinking about the animal service reminds Lily of the golf course foxes. On the new golf courses that border the old city, displaced foxes have been making a nuisance of themselves, running off with the ball that would have been an eagle, or at least a birdie. The foxes also stole sandwiches from golf bags; they liked baloney sandwiches best. There was always a golf course in the city, but the old one had been swallowed up by suburbs. It never had foxes, or baloney sandwiches. As far as Lily could tell, only five people had been allowed to belong to the old golf club, and they were all dead now.

Lately, there had been letters to the paper saying that the golf course foxes should be destroyed because they were ruining everyone's game. They weren't ruining Lily's boyfriend's game, though: you could never, ever ruin Kevin's game.

Lily first heard of the foxes when Kevin took up golf last year. That Kevin should have taken up golf at all was a strange thing to Lily, but he had gone to golf in his own way, as he went to everything, as he had come to her. He went to the links at dawn or twilight once every couple of weeks with one or two of his best friends, dressed in black and carrying a set of borrowed clubs, and didn't say much about it. Kevin spoke only when he had to say something. Or if you asked him something.

One October night, Kevin came home all cold and shining, and his eyes had looked like their cat Simon's eyes when he was in the dark under the porch. He told Lily that he and Sean Stone were on the eighteenth green when an animal came out of the brush and picked up his ball, which had been only a foot from the hole. He and Stoney had stayed very still, and the animal brought the ball and placed it at Kevin's feet, and they saw it was a fox. Stoney laughed, and the fox moved away. They followed it, and the fox led them to a clearing, a clearing full of magic mushrooms, shining under the hunter's moon like miniature golf balls. Stoney said, "Oh, man, can you believe this?" and took their baloney sandwiches out of the pouch of his windbreaker and threw them to Kevin. And while Stoney filled his pouch with psychedelic fungi, Kevin unwrapped the sandwiches and tossed them, bit by bit, to the fox, who caught each piece as neatly as a Lab.

The first time Lily ever saw Kevin was at a party at William's. The crowd had been sitting around the kitchen table listening to William tell his stories: the one about being caught necking with a sitcom star's sister in the women's bathroom at a Vancouver hotel by the star himself, the getting-kicked-out-of-boarding-school-for-the-possession-of-illegal-substances story, and, of course, the Cleo Laine. Lily had been on the periphery of the group, floating on the familiar sounds of her herd, and wondering how many fairies could dance on the head of a pin, and would they even want to, when suddenly she felt a tug, as though something was pulling at her lining. It must be the moon, Lily thought; she is probably full, full and happy, like me. But when she got up to go to the bathroom, she saw a boy leaning against the wall, not far from where she had been sitting, and she knew, somehow, that he had been standing there all evening, leaning against the wall and pulling her to him. And when she came out of the bathroom, a shadow detached itself from the shadow that was the door to William's attic, and it took her in its arms and kissed her, and the kiss was the most unshadowy thing that had ever happened to Lily in her life. Since then, Lily has lived, moved and had her being in Kevin.

Lily glides away from the Cathedral and the foxes and Kevin's kiss and kicks her way downstream to be in the moment with William; some part of her has detected that it's time. As William's face starts to take shape, Lily notices that the geranium on the window-sill beside their booth is streaming with colour, and bright green sparks are darting through the waves of crimson and magenta and lilac like minnows—plant sprites, Lily thinks. And then she is back, and the geranium is only a shadow of itself, back-lit by an anaemic autumn sun.

William is saying, "And then Cleo Laine kissed me full on the lips, and went up the steps of the plane. At the top, she turned around, adjusted her mink stole for a moment, with her head down, like this, and then she looked up and back down at me. And she smiled, with that incredible mouth of hers, the mouth that sang "Bill" from *Showboat* for me on opening night at the Arts and Culture Centre, that red satin mouth, and she blew me a kiss. And then she went in the plane. And I never saw her again. But I don't want to. It would spoil everything."

Lily smiles and gently applauds, and William makes her a mock bow, his elbow missing his coffee cup by that much. But Lily knows that so many bad things that should happen never do. Perhaps the cup had shifted slightly, recognising that William was about to have a spatial lapse.

"So how's Kevin doing?" William asks, although he doesn't really want to know. Lily says "Fine." She knows that William, who has been secretly in love with Lily for years, believes she is with Kevin because he has big feet. Kevin is a sign painter, but only because the NHL scouts weren't around when he was younger. Kevin has never said this, but Lily knows it to be true. She has watched him play hockey often enough to recognise that he has the zen of it, born of pure love's desire and intelligence.

William says you're an Alpha Wolf, Lily once told Kevin, who grinned but said nothing. After that, when she wanted to tease him, she called him an Awful Woof. When she wanted to hurt him, she said nothing, after the first time, when she discovered that she was no longer alone under her skin.

William is a firm believer in the Biological Imperative. "It's all DNA," William said to Lily once. "Everything. I am a chromosome." William hated summer because the DNA of the entire planet was too loud then, the world was just one buzzing mass of procreation. The buzzing of the earth's DNA was so loud in summer that William felt dwarfed; he liked the winter better because it was quieter and he could pretend that his DNA had the upper hand. "In the winter, I can hear myself think," William had said to Lily. "And I am lord and master of my world again." William lived in the right place, thought Lily; no wonder Protestantism had arisen in the north, where for long stretches people didn't have to listen to the god buried under the ice. Lily could always hear it though, murmuring gently in its sleep.

William's wife had left him and their three children six months ago. He married Sheila not long after an LSD trip during which he had seen The Void. The Void, William told Lily, was blacker than a starless night on the bogs and as seductive as Cleo Laine. He had badly wanted to give into it, he said, but he fought like a tiger, and it had taken him a full year to make the horror manageable.

Lily has tried to explain to William about The Void. She has told him that it is only like when the lights go off in the theatre after the credits have rolled, and there is a bit of darkness before the overhead lights come on. William said Lily's metaphor was okay for a metaphor, but it was too Platonic or Socratic or something for him, and anyway, it was bullshit. He told Lily she didn't understand because she had never done acid, never had her mind chemically, scientifically expanded until it ran smack up against the big black Truth. There is life, William had told her, and after that there is The Void. Nothing. Nada. Zilch. "When I am eighty-five," William said to Lily, "I will willingly surrender to The Void, but until then, I am going to have things my way."

The year after The Void nearly got him, William went to computer school and married Sheila, and the first baby came. After the third baby, William bought a small house outside the city, and he put Sheila and the babies in it, and his computer, and a seventeenth-century mahogany sideboard carved all over with tiny heads he had inherited from his Methodist grandfather. For twelve years, William sat upstairs in the room with the dormer window, designing navigational software; underneath him, the house rocked gently with babies and dogs and cats and puppies and kittens; now and then the muted roar of Sheila's voice, singing and swearing and laughing, came up through the gaps in the softwood floor. William became leader of the local cub pack and a member of the PTA.

And then one Saturday morning William came in from the woodpile with his arms full of birch for the wood stove, and Sheila told him, right in front of the kids, right in his own kitchen, that she was leaving him for a twenty-four-year-old Texan named Tom. They had met on the Internet, and the Angel of Sheila's Higher Self had told her that Tom was her twin soul. They had been separated when Atlantis sank into the sea, Sheila said, but he was flying in tonight and she was going to meet him at the airport. And she wouldn't be coming back. She was crying, and her sobs smelt like rum, and William put the wood down and sent the children upstairs. Later, Sheila showed him a picture of Tom, who had a shaved head and a ring in his nose. When William saw the picture, he was sure things would blow over. He and Sheila had a great life: how could some loser with a nose ring screw it up?

William is particularly death on angels today because he has just come from a meeting with Sheila and the Angel of her Higher Self, a very curious specimen of the Heavenly Host, Lily thinks. It always delivered its messages in a shriek in the middle of the sidewalk on the city's main thoroughfare, the only place Sheila would see William. As a result of this morning's meeting, William was without his car for the day. Sheila had needed it to get to her new lover, a bass player who, although not her twin soul—Tom and his nose ring had gone back to Texas after two days—was apparently a karmic link from Sheila's last life.

"Why didn't you just tell her where to get off?" Lily asked William when he told her about Sheila taking the car.

"Because she is a very sick woman, and I am not about to disturb her any further. You know what her childhood was, Lil. I used to think we'd gotten those demons under control, but now I'm inclined to think it's a genetic thing. Anyway, she's the mother of my children." The way William said it sounded to Lily like "The Mother of My Children" and she thought it probably sounded like that to William, too, or else he would still have his car.

Lily knew what Sheila's childhood had been because it had taken place one street over from Kevin's childhood, down in the core, and contained many of the same elements:

an alcoholic father, a shrew of a mother, and more babies than could be loved or even properly fed, all living in a house smaller than the shoe house in *The Illustrated Mother Goose*, and under the twin shadows of the shame of sin and the fear of hell.

Sheila had been wild, as wild as they came. She slept with everyone they knew, except Kevin, who had refused her. Finally, she got to William. The boys of the core had shaken their heads at William and Sheila. "What is he at with that streel, don't he know what she is?" one of them had said to Lily. But William was a Protestant, and his grandmother still had maids, and his family lived uptown in the gatehouse of the mansion his great-grandfather had owned. The Gordons raised Golden Labs; Sheila's father kept two beagles in a Chihuahua-sized cage. They were never the same two, either. One always got shot in the fall because it went mad out in the woods after being shut up all year.

But Sheila had looked tame to William beside The Void.

"So," William says. "Is Kevin still playing hockey three nights a week? Or is he spending his evenings at the archives, reading Keats to you while you work? 'And there I shut her wild, wild eyes, with kisses four.' Jesus, I wish they hadn't made us memorize that crap. They don't do that to the kids anymore, lucky bastards." William laughs, at the idea of Kevin reading poetry, Lily assumes. And because he needs to let a little bitterness out.

"Still playing hockey. And painting." Not signs, though; not at night, anyway. At night, Kevin has begun to paint pictures—delicate, detailed pictures—with his long, deft hands. Some of them are of the small red lords of the marches, the vulpine refugees of the borderlands, the golf course foxes with their wild, wild eyes, and their triangular faces that are like Kevin's own. But Lily would never tell this to William.

"So what are you reading these days, Lil?"

"I'm reading 'The Prussian Officer'." Lily is actually reading *The Golden Bough*, and doesn't know why she has lied to William.

"Uh, Tolstoy? No, Chekhov."

"No, Lawrence."

"Oh, Lawrence. I'm afraid I outgrew Lawrence a long time ago, Lil. He sounds really profound until your testosterone levels stabilize, and then you realize he was just a tedious consumptive with a working class chip on his shoulder. I'm surprised you're still interested in that old foolishness."

"Well, I'm also reading a collection of poetry by Camus." Lily, who rarely ever lies, is appalled at such a whopper. What is it for, and where is it going?

"I didn't know Camus wrote poetry." William's ears go up into Mr. Spock points, and Lily thinks she sees his pupils dilate perhaps a fraction of a millimetre.

"Oh, yes. Volumes of it. Published posthumously, of course. Most of them were written a couple of years before he died, after his conversion to Catholicism." Lily wonders for a moment if she has multiple-personality disorder, but then realises she probably wouldn't be considering it if she did.

"His conversion to Catholicism?" William's face assumes an expression Lily has never seen on it before: it is not from his usual repertoire. Her mouth gets ready for the next lie, and she hopes it will be a good one. After all, continuity is important.

"Oh, yes. You didn't know? Apparently Camus fell in love with a girl from Rouen and found God in her golden hair. He died in perfect peace, they say, with the village priest, the girl, and his old mother at his bedside. His last words, apparently, were '*Le Dieu n'est pas existentialiste. Il est l'Existence Lui-même, et la Vie Eternelle.*'" Why how fluently I can lie, Lily thinks, and I never knew. For a moment it scares her: she thinks she will go home and start lying to Kevin, which would be worse than the most terrible thing that ever could be thought of. But then she relaxes; it would be easier to get with child a mandrake root than lie to Kevin.

"I didn't know that, Lil. Was he really sick in the end, or something?" William grabs for a logic-and-tonic, but Lily moves it firmly out of his reach.

"Oh no, he was quite well until the day before. I think he ate poisoned eels or mushrooms or something; you know the French, they'll eat anything as long as it's smothered in sauce. Even the beaks of larks."

"Could I borrow the book?" William's pupils are now the size of collar buttons, and Lily is sure that at any moment he is going to see the plant sprites, and perhaps even her father, whom she can feel next to her.

"Oh, William, I'm sorry," Lily says, "but it belongs to a friend, and she only lent it to me on the condition that I give it right back."

"What's the title? I can probably pick up a copy at Chapters." William, who doesn't believe in ghosts, is as pale as any spectre. Lily feels ashamed, and something else, too, something unwholesome that was imp-sized, but growing.

"It's called *Time's Fool.*" Lily has no idea where these words have waltzed in from: she thinks it might be Shakespeare; there are images of cupids and ships and compasses in her head. Without taking her eyes from William's face, Lily sends their waitress an SOS. A minute later, a geranium-haired girl appears beside William and Lily's booth and places their bill in the centre of the table.

Outside Bunches O' Bagels, Lily gives her gloveless hand to William, who raises it to his lips, as always. But today he holds her hand in his for a moment after it has touched his mouth, and looks at it. "I love your fingernails," he says awkwardly, with his head bent, and then he raises it and looks straight into her eyes. And Lily watches William's love for her rise up from his heart and stain his cheeks and shine steadily at the back of his eyes, and his pupils are as wide and dark and deep as The Void.

For a moment, Lily thinks she sees an angel in their depths.

ACKNOWLEDGEMENTS

"In the Chambers of the Sea" and "Peripheral Vision" have appeared in *TickleAce*; the former received *TickleAce*'s inaugural Cabot Award for short fiction (2001). "In the Chambers of the Sea" has also appeared in two anthologies, *The Journey Prize Anthology* and *Land, Sea and Time*. "In the Chambers of the Sea," "Peripheral Vision" and "Ladies Wear" won Newfoundland and Labrador Arts Awards.

I would like to thank the many people who made this book possible (you know who you are, even if you don't want to admit to it), especially Paul Bowdring, Gordon Rodgers, Anne Hart, Robbie Thomas, Carmelita McGrath, Anita Best, Sandra Martland, Ramona Dearing, Ken Harvey, Lisa Moore, Stan Dragland, Claire Wilkshire, Jessie Harvey, Helen Porter, Derek Rendell, Ronan Kennedy and the staff at Killick (particularly the ever-patient and embarrassingly encouraging Dwayne LaFitte); also, Mary MacNab, Kerry Irish, the Yates, Harry Barker and my parents, for always being there, even when time and space and death got in the way; and—last but never least—Krissy and Tracy and Scotty and Doobie, for giving me a Holmes away from home when I really needed one.